SIDELINED FOR THE HOLIDAYS

AUDREY MCCLELLAND

To my friend Lisa, who suggested the name Blake when I was looking for name suggestions ... the perfect name for my leading man.

1

———

This wasn't her dream job, not by any stretch, but it allowed Charlotte Court to do what she loved most in life and that was to write. She had always known she wanted to be a journalist. She had started a newspaper in fifth grade, not that three pieces of paper stapled together qualified as a newspaper, but it was the start of a lifelong passion. Filled with happenings going on at school, Charlotte would interview her classmates, teachers, and other staff members, and then write up a series of articles. Each Thursday night her father would help her print twenty or thirty copies of whatever she had, and every Friday morning she would head to school to distribute them. She had done this every week that entire year of fifth grade. Her love for journalism had started early, and nothing had stopped her until now.

"Earth to Charlotte," a voice echoed behind her.

Charlotte turned with a sly smile on her face, thankful for the distraction. "Oh, please, Lindsay. This is the first time you've spoken my name all morning."

They had been best friends since their freshman year at

the University of Rhode Island when they'd both joined the staff at the college newspaper - and hit it off immediately.

"Is it?" Lindsay laughed, as she grabbed an empty desk chair and wheeled it over next to Charlotte. "I'm not used to seeing you staring at a blank computer screen. You're usually typing away with a smile on your face, annoying the rest of us. Writing comes so easily for you."

"You're horrible," Charlotte laughed. "Sorry to disappoint you this morning," Charlotte said, sticking her tongue out at her friend.

"Have you heard back about the job?" Lindsay whispered as she scooted her chair closer to Charlotte. The office was pretty empty, but she didn't want prying ears to overhear their conversation.

"They didn't go with me," Charlotte answered, trying not to let her true disappointment show. "I got an email from them last night."

"Oh, bummer," Lindsay said. "I'm sorry, Char."

"They said I was a strong candidate, but they had a couple of others with more experience."

"I know you are disappointed, Char, but it will happen," Lindsay answered, reaching out to touch Charlotte's hand. "You've got big things ahead of you. Besides, did you *really* want to move to Chicago?"

"Thanks, Lindsay, and yes, I could have dealt with Chicago," Charlotte laughed at her friend. "But thank you for trying to make me feel better about it."

"Stay positive. It just wasn't the right job for you," Lindsay smiled back.

Charlotte turned from her friend and stared back at the blank screen in front of her. She wasn't used to looking at a blank screen. Normally, she could bang out an article in record time, but being rejected from yet another big publication was crushing. "I hope so, Lindsay. I just thought I'd be reporting on bigger things by now. I mean, here I am trying to write about the town's strategy about which trees to light up this year for the holidays. Apparently, some readers need to know why some trees were left out."

"Strategy?" Lindsay laughed. "I didn't even know there was one!"

"Yeah, neither did I," Charlotte nodded with a laugh. "I interviewed three people about it. Real riveting news, huh?" Charlotte asked, sounding defeated.

"Well... " Lindsay joked, trying to make light of it, "maybe people feel bad for the trees," she laughed.

Charlotte answered with a smile, "I guess that's a small town for you." She paused and then added, "Don't get me wrong, I love it here. I just thought it would be different, that's all."

"Char," Lindsay said kindly, "I know you want to report on bigger things, but you've got to remember that this is a small-town newspaper. Our editorial is all about town news, town happenings, and town gossip. This paper, in many ways, holds the town together. I mean... come on; people here still like to hold a paper in their hands. How crazy is that?"

"I know, you're absolutely right," Charlotte answered, not wanting to sound ungrateful because she really *did* love the small-town feel of Barrington, Rhode Island. In the last six months, the place had carved out a special place in her heart. Not to mention, it was Lindsay who had recommended her for this job in the first place, and she was thankful for the opportunity. It allowed her to put together a bigger and better portfolio filled with pieces other than just college articles. "I don't mean to be a downer on this Monday morning. I just... I don't know. I would love to have something more challenging to report on."

"And you will," Lindsay answered. "Everyone has to start somewhere, right?"

"Yes," Charlotte said, always thankful for Lindsay and her eternal optimism. "I know I have to pay my dues. It was just a tough blow last night, but I'll get over it."

"You should have called me," Lindsay said. "I would have dragged you out for a drink."

"It was easier to drink wine in bed and binge on Hall-mark movies," Charlotte laughed. "Which, I'm sure you know, could be set in this very town. Every other movie on that channel is set somewhere in New England."

"Oh, please," Lindsay joked, "if only this town was *like* a Hallmark movie! Then my prince charming wouldn't be so hard to find."

"You and your quest for prince charming," Charlotte said, rolling her eyes. "You have to stop thinking about it, and just let it happen."

"Well," Lindsay answered looking at her with knowing eyes. "We all can't be lucky enough to find our prince charming in college."

Charlotte looked down for a second at the photo she had of Dylan on her desk, and then shrugged her shoulders. "I guess so. I mean, it hasn't been easy with Dylan being in New York. Sometimes it feels like he's across the country. He's been so busy with his new job, and I've been busy here."

"Hey... maybe New York City is where you'll ultimately end up," Lindsay smiled. "I know you love it there."

Charlotte smiled at the thought of living in New York City, which would be a dream come true. She would kill for the chance to report on the news from the center of the universe. But in order to get a job there, she needed to work hard now and build up her resume.

"Well, until I hear from the *New York Times*, I'll be writing about lights in trees," Charlotte joked. "So, if you need me, this is where I'll be for the next hour."

"Don't forget," Lindsay added as she got up from her chair, "you're still new to town, still meeting people, and getting to know the lay of the land. You might even fall in love with the town so much you don't want to leave," she winked.

"I know you would love that, huh?" Charlotte responded, taking a sip of coffee. "And as much as it is growing on me, and it is, I just feel at a crossroads right now. That's all."

"It's different from what you expected, I know," Lindsay winked. "Small towns are different. I always knew I wanted to end up back here because of the community. For me, the magic of this town is that it's not like big cities."

"You mean a place where the lights on the trees *is* important news?" Charlotte winked.

Lindsay laughed, "In some weird way... yes!"

"Linds, I *do* love it here, in Barrington, and it's clear to me why coming back home was so important to you. It's an incredible community and it's your home. And I do know that the articles I'm writing are actually very meaningful to the town. Am I right?"

"Yes, you are." Lindsay looked at her watch, "We have a staff meeting in one hour. Let's not be late, you know how my father gets."

Charlotte watched Lindsay walk away and she smiled to herself. She was lucky to have a best friend like her. After graduation, Charlotte couldn't find work as a journalist anywhere. She applied for every job she could find, but none of them panned out. She kept hearing the same thing over and over, "You need more experience." She couldn't figure out how to get more experience without getting it from somewhere first. She had written over two hundred articles for her college newspaper, what more did she need? Yet, they all said she needed more.

Lindsay, on the other hand, had always made it clear that after graduation she was going to join her father, at her town's newspaper, so she never had to worry about applying anywhere. Her father had been the owner and editor of their town's newspaper, the *Barrington View*, for over thirty years, so her path was set. Lindsay had worked for her father part-time during college, and she had helped him grow and build the newspaper's online presence tenfold. He had been so impressed with his daughter that he promised Lindsay he would groom her to be his editor-in-chief someday, and that was exactly what he was doing.

Lindsay knew Charlotte had not been successful in finding a job right out of college, and she finally convinced her to talk with her father. He had been looking to hire a reporter, and Lindsay thought it might be a good foot in the door to gain additional experience. He had hired Charlotte on the spot, knowing that she was more than qualified for the position. But he had also made it clear that her work would be focused on the town because that's what every article would be about.

She had tried her best over the last six months, but Charlotte knew deep down that she just wasn't a small-town girl. Her hometown was Pittsburgh, and she still felt a hole in her heart about not being back there. Barrington was a momentary stop for her, and she needed to write her way to somewhere else.

2

"**A**re you freaking kidding me? Arrested?" Greg shouted as he walked into Blake Manor's apartment, not caring one bit that Blake was rocking a massive hangover, or that he was just wearing boxer shorts. "And please tell me you're alone right now."

Blake shut the door and followed Greg down the hallway toward his kitchen. "Yes, Jesus, Greg, keep it down... my head is killing me," Blake grumbled.

Most women would kill to see Blake Manor half-naked in his kitchen. Even rocking a hangover, he still looked like a Greek god, but he was hurting this morning because his normal hangover concoction of three Advil and pear juice wasn't working. Normally it did the trick, but not today.

"I don't want to hear about it right now, Greg," Blake answered. "I'm not in the mood."

"You're never in the mood," Greg shot back. "But see all this?" Greg gestured around Blake's penthouse apartment. "See this view of Central Park? See this brand new kitchen? See everything you've got in here? You're going to lose it all if you don't shape the fuck up."

"Greg," Blake said, trying to stay calm, "I'm telling you right now, I don't want to deal with it. I already know what you're going to say."

"Oh, you do?" Greg shouted back. "Well then, did you see this morning's newspaper?"

Blake's heart stopped for a second.

"I'm assuming by that pause that you haven't," Greg added.

Greg could be overly dramatic, but Blake knew by the tone of his voice that whatever was in the paper couldn't be good.

Greg tossed a newspaper on the kitchen counter. "Take a look."

Looking at the paper, Blake saw three full-color photos of himself from last night, along with the headline: WHAT THE BLAKE?

"Clever headline," Blake shrugged.

"You find this amusing?" Greg asked, irritated. "Well, maybe you'll find it amusing to know that I have a meeting this afternoon with the Skyscrapers owners about a potential suspension."

Blake stopped dead in his tracks. "Suspension? On what grounds?"

"You want me to show you the list? You were arrested last night. You have a Personal Conduct Policy in your contract, Blake. Remember that? You've been on shaky ground for the last couple of years, but I have a feeling the shit is going to hit the fan. Now I've got to try and save your ass from going under."

"All because of a bar fight?" Blake asked, feeling confused. "I didn't even start it."

"You're *always* the innocent one. You were THERE,"

Greg shouted. "That's all it takes. It's your face in the photos. You're the one people recognize."

"Well, for what it's worth, I told the owner I'd pay for all of the damages from the fight."

"You don't get it, do you? This has been mounting for months. This bar fight and arrest was the last straw for the team. You're all over the front pages and in the news here. Not to mention the constant partying. I've told you to tone it down, and you haven't, and this is what happens when you don't listen to your agent."

Blake picked up the paper and flung it across the room. He knew Greg was right, but he didn't want to admit it. He had been telling him to slow it down since the beginning of the season, and he hadn't. He loved this life, and he didn't want to tone it down.

"You did this to yourself," Greg said angrily. "You've turned into one of the best football players this team has seen in a long time, but guess what? You let it go to your head. I just hope I can save your ass from a suspension because I don't know how long you'll be out."

"All because I like to party?" Blake asked. "It's ridiculous. I still get the job done on the field. My personal life doesn't affect how I play, and the only thing the team owners want from me is to win games."

Greg knew he wasn't getting through to Blake. He looked like shit after a night of partying, followed by a night in jail. He had bailed Blake out last night when he'd called, but he didn't stick around to make sure he got home. He was sick of the bullshit with Blake. What killed Greg most was knowing that Blake hadn't been like this when he first signed on as his agent. Blake had been a reserved twenty-something kid who'd been drafted right out of college in the sixth round.

What had appealed to Greg about Blake was his sheer desire to get out there and prove himself. Normally a sixth-round pick is known as Mr. Irrelevant, and Blake wanted to prove them wrong. And, for the last four years, he had done just that. But, as often happens, the fame game went to his head.

"That's what you think but, whether you like it or not, you represent the New York Skyscrapers on and off the field. And I don't even want to get into the sponsorship deals you've missed out on over the last couple of years. Something's got to give, and I feel like we're there."

"So what?" Blake asked, sensing something he didn't like. "Are you saying you want out of this partnership?"

"Of being your agent?" Greg asked.

"Yeah," Blake nodded. "I feel like that's where you're going with this."

Greg exhaled loudly and rubbed his hands through his hair. "I know the potential you have, Blake. And I know you know the potential you have. When you're on that field, you're laser-focused, and you're a dream come true. When you're off the field you're becoming my worst nightmare. I'm not going anywhere, but you've got to fucking pull yourself together."

Blake stood with his arms crossed over his chest, not sure what to say, so he just stared back at Greg and nodded his head.

"My parents are going to kill me on this one," he breathed, allowing the seriousness of last night to sink in.

"Fucking good," Greg shot back with a smile. "They should. They're good people, and this is the last thing they deserve from you."

"Do you need me at the meeting today?" Blake asked, hoping Greg would say no.

Greg shook his head, "No... I'm going to try to work my

magic as best as I can, but I have a feeling there's something coming down on you. I'm just being straight with you. They need to make an example of you. You have breached their conduct policy several times. I mean, what the hell happened last night?"

Blake closed his eyes, wishing that last night hadn't happened, but knew he had to deal with it. "We were out partying after last night's win and things got out of hand. I started buying rounds of drinks for people at the bar and then, before I knew it, people were leaping behind the bar grabbing bottles of stuff left and right. Then bottles started breaking and glasses were being thrown. It turned crazy quickly. My buddies started fighting with guys there and before I knew it, the cops were there and the bar was pretty banged up. We all got cuffed and brought to the station. Listen, I felt bad for the owner. I did. I told him I'd pay for everything. I'm telling you, it wasn't my fault. I didn't start any of the fights, and I even tried to stay out of it."

Greg looked seriously at Blake, "And that's it?"

"Yes, even the cops knew I wasn't involved in the fight, but I still got arrested."

"What about the photos?"

"I don't know, there must have been people clicking away on their phones. Obviously, I didn't *ask* for them to be taken," Blake said, trying to make a joke.

"I'm telling you," Greg said, "you think everyone's your friend, but they're not. They're selling these photos, and likely videos, to the highest bidder. You have to keep your circle tight, and you've got to tone it down with the partying and the ladies."

"The ladies aren't my fault," Blake smiled.

"Well," Greg suggested, "pick one so you're not constantly being seen with someone new. It just looks bad."

"Spoken like a married man," Blake shot back while walking over to the sink to pour himself a glass of water.

"I might be married, but that has nothing to do with it. You have a certain reputation to maintain, and you're not doing it."

"Listen, Greg, I know my image is important, but it's not against the law to be out with beautiful women or to party. My God, I was so shy in high school, girls didn't give me a second look. I was the quiet jock in the corner. Let's just say I'm making up for lost time."

"Make it up some other way," Greg added.

Blake laughed a little at Greg's comment as he added some protein powder to his water. "I'll try my best. OK? I can't help it if women are drawn to me."

"They're drawn to your paycheck and fame."

"Ouch," Blake responded, making a winced face.

"You know what I mean. If I can't be straight with you, who will? But, listen to me... in the meantime, lay low all day. I only want you leaving this place to head to practice and that's it. My meeting with management is at 1 pm, and I have a feeling I'm going to be working my ass off for my money today."

Blake took a sip of his water and looked over at Greg. He knew he'd do whatever it took to keep him playing, and he was thankful he didn't feel worried about the outcome. Greg was a magician and had worked his magic for him numerous times. He also knew Greg tended to be overly dramatic about everything, and he was sure that was going on right now.

3

S taff meetings were important for journalists because every day brought new stories and a journalist's job was to report on them, even in small towns. The one thing Charlotte had discovered about living in a small town like Barrington was that everything was newsworthy--a new stop sign, a new ice cream flavor, a new hire at the market. It was news if the school painted its playground. If restaurants were hiring or a branch fell off a tree and blocked traffic, it was news. Everything was news and everyone wanted the paper to cover it. The number of calls, emails, and texts the staff got from townspeople asking for coverage was crazy but, over the last six months, Charlotte had become used to it.

Lindsay's father, Frank, did an incredible job fielding requests and knew exactly when it was time to tell people to back off. Charlotte couldn't believe that Lindsay wanted to walk in her father's footsteps because it seemed like a lot of pressure.

"Everyone ready for our morning meeting?" Frank shouted as he entered the conference room. He was a big man, around 6'4" and easily over 300 pounds. His stature alone made you stop and listen to what he had to say, but his voice was equally as big and as booming. "You know I hate starting late," he said.

The *Barrington View* had four reporters, three salespeople, a social media manager, and two photographers on staff. It was considered a big staff for a small-town local newspaper. A printed version of the paper came out once a week, on Monday morning, and the online version was updated daily with any new happenings. Frank held staff meetings every Monday morning to check-in and get an idea of what the week ahead looked like, giving out weekly assignments. Each reporter on staff was normally assigned two to three stories to report on, plus anything else that popped up during the week.

"It's December, people! With the holidays just a few weeks away, we're going to be busy." Frank smiled as he sat down at the head of the conference table. "I've got Charlotte working on a piece right now about why certain trees were chosen over others for the holiday lights this year. That done yet?" Frank asked, looking over at Charlotte.

"Just wrapped it up and sent it your way," Charlotte answered.

"I heard you thought it was riveting," Frank winked at Charlotte.

Charlotte looked over at Lindsay, who was sitting right next to her father. She rolled her eyes at her. "Thanks, Linds!"

The room erupted with laughter, as everyone looked back and forth at the two best friends as they made funny faces at each other.

"It's not that I didn't find it interesting, Frank," Charlotte began to explain. "It's just funny to me that it's important for people to know which *exact* trees will have lights."

Frank laughed. "You don't have to explain it to me, Charlotte. I've always thought it was crazy. But, yes, apparently, it's a very big deal when the town chooses the exact trees that will hold the lights for the annual holiday lighting. I don't know why people care about the unlit trees, but they do. If you ask me, any tree looks pretty damn good lit up. Thanks for taking this one."

Charlotte smiled back at Frank and nodded. Frank may look intimidating, but she knew he was a big teddy bear, a heck of a ball-buster, and had a heart of gold. She looked down at her notebook and opened it up to the page where she had jotted down story ideas for the week. She knew Frank loved it when his staff contributed ideas, so she always made sure to show up with fresh ideas.

"OK... let's keep moving it along. I've got five local businesses that want to be interviewed and featured about their upcoming holiday sales and events. I've got the high school in the middle of their winter sports season, so there's track and field, hockey, basketball, swimming, and wrestling to cover. And I've got vandalism going on at the middle school that needs to be covered. Ohhh, yes... and there are some holiday fundraisers around town that I need someone to follow up on. I have the list in my office."

Charlotte jotted down everything Frank said, knowing she wouldn't be assigned any of the sports stories because she hated sports, and knew nothing about them. She had been the girl in high school who spent all of her time at the school newspaper office, editing, writing, and laying things out. That was her home in high school, not the fields or the gymnasium. She never went to any sports matches, meets,

or games; she just made sure that they were covered in the
school newspaper.

"All right, who has good ideas for some feature stories
over the next couple of weeks? And we need filler online,
too."

Charlotte was never one to sit quietly at staff meetings,
and even though many of her ideas weren't meant for small-
town publication, she still loved to toss them out. "Frank,
what about trying to get a feature with the Governor and
seeing if he will share his thoughts and ideas about small-
town politics?"

Frank sat back in his chair and smiled over at Charlotte.
He knew she wasn't meant for small-town journalism, she
wanted something bigger, something more, but he loved her
tenacity and drive. She always came with ideas that were
grander and geared more for state or national news, but he
loved trying to make them work.

"And you think townspeople would be interested in
something like that?" Frank asked, anxious to hear her
answer because she always had one.

"Yeah, it's important to know what your Governor thinks
about your local politics, and how they're run. Each town
and city is different. It might inspire other areas in Rhode
Island to do the same with him."

"So you want to pitch him a quick Q&A-type piece about
Barrington?"

"Yes," Charlotte nodded, hoping he would agree. Having
a political piece with the Governor would help her portfolio.

Frank nodded with a spark in his eye. He loved Charlotte. She had become a family member of sorts ever since
meeting Lindsay at college. He knew she was destined for
big things someday, and he loved knowing that he would
have a hand in getting her there. He also thought she'd be a

great on-camera personality because she had the right look and was an incredible interviewer. She had the ability, when interviewing people, to have them completely let down their guard. This was a gift that not all journalists had. Charlotte listened when she interviewed people, and that was her secret. She listened and cared, and it reflected in all of her pieces, even the ones she didn't love being assigned to.

"I'll tell you what," Frank said, smiling at Charlotte. "If you can get the Governor to talk to you, you've got it. Make it work and tie it directly to Barrington. You know the drill."

Charlotte felt as if she had just won the lottery. She wanted her pieces to educate or entertain people, and she knew this was the kind of article that would certainly inform people about local politics.

"I've got one more for you, Frank," Charlotte said, while she looked around the room. She didn't want the rest of the staff to hate her for eating up additional time, but she also didn't want to let the moment pass.

"Whatcha got for me?" Frank asked, leaning back in his chair.

"What about doing a feature on each of the principals in our schools? Let the town get to know them on a deeper, more personal level?"

"Oh, I like that idea," Lindsay chimed in. "I don't think we've ever done anything like that before."

"I think it would be nice for the town to get to know them as people, not just as the heads of the schools. I would like to pull back the curtain and let them share why they chose this profession, and how they got here. If they're comfortable, they could even share about their family life."

"How many principals do we have in town?" Frank asked as he started jotting down the names of the schools.

"Six," Charlotte answered quickly.

"We can stagger the interviews out over the next couple of months because we're going to be pretty busy with the holiday, but I love the idea," Frank answered with an accepting nod. "Just make sure they all want to be featured."

"Will do," Charlotte smiled back, feeling a bit redeemed after the crappy news from last night. "I won't let you down, Frank." She would go back to those publications again, and show them what she could do, even in a small town. It was only just a matter of time.

4

The beginning of December was beautiful in New York City. Snow blanketed the streets and parks, leaving everything looking like a winter wonderland. The temperatures were always cold, but, for some reason in New York City, the energy just heated you up. There was also something special about the holiday season in New York City, and it was something that Blake had always loved about this time of year.

Blake hadn't yet heard back from Greg as he jumped into his town car to head to practice. He had found that driving himself posed difficulties when people started to recognize him at stop signs and red lights. A twenty-minute drive to the stadium would turn into something much longer, not to mention dealing with the fans following him the entire way there and back. Getting driven was the easiest mode of transportation for him, and it gave him time to mentally prepare for practice and game time.

He hadn't heard from his parents either, which was really pressing on his mind. The two people he didn't want to let down in life were Ben and Mary Manor. They had sacrificed so much raising him and his younger sister, Molly. His parents owned their own cleaning business and had put every dollar they had into their family. Living in Barrington wasn't always the easiest for them because it was an affluent town, but they knew the public school system would be the best for their kids. They scraped and worked hard to afford a modest home in town, and did their best to make sure their kids didn't want for much. Blake had always known that money was tight at home and, early on, when he realized football might be his career path, he also knew it could be a golden ticket for his family.

The second Blake signed his football contract with the New York Skyscrapers, he paid off the mortgage on his childhood home and offered to buy his parents a new house wherever they wanted. He didn't want them to worry about money another day in their life, and it felt really good to take that off their shoulders. It was his time to repay them for all the sacrifices they had made throughout the years. He'd been surprised when his parents said they did not want to leave the house that they had raised their kids in. They didn't want to be anywhere else; they wanted to stay put in the town and house they loved. They welcomed the help in paying off their home because they wouldn't feel the burden of debt any longer, but they didn't want to change their life. They wanted to live their regular life but without the constant worry of money. Blake helped them further by paying Molly's tuition at Boston College, where she was currently a junior.

As his driver wove in and out of the traffic, Blake sat back and tried to process everything from last night. He knew things had started to get out of hand when he heard bottles breaking behind the bar. He felt horrible for the owner as he watched him try to shut down the destruction, but there was nothing he could do. The bar-goers were drunk and completely immune to listening to some guy telling them to stop. The second he saw the cops show up, he knew it wasn't going to end well for him. Even though he hadn't been part of the bottle-breaking craziness, or the drunken hoopla behind the bar, he knew his name and face would be pulled into it.

Just as he was about to call one of his buddies from last night, the call he had been waiting for popped up on his caller id. He knew he couldn't avoid it, so he took a deep breath and went for it.

"Hey, Mom," Blake said as cheerful as he could.

"Blake," his mom responded with a worried tone. "What is going on? Your Dad and I have been getting calls and texts all day. Did you really get arrested?"

"It's not what it looks like, Mom," Blake answered, feeling his stomach start to churn. The last thing he wanted to do was worry his mom and dad. "Listen, I know it looks bad, but I've got it handled. I'm going to pay for all of the damages in the bar but believe me; the headlines you're seeing make it out to be a lot worse than it was. OK?"

"Is it true that you could get suspended?"

"Mom," Blake shot back. "Where did you hear that?"

"Your Dad told me," Mary Manor answered honestly. "Here, let me put it on speaker so he can hear you, too."

Blake didn't want his dad on the call. His mom he could deal with, but his dad? Not so much. Ben Manor didn't have time for this kind of bullshit, and Blake knew this call wasn't going to be pleasant.

"What the hell is going on, Blake?" Ben shouted down the phone. "Are you a freaking fool? Getting in bar fights? Getting arrested? Come on, you're better than that," Ben continued, very worked up.

"You sound like Greg," Blake responded in a flat tone, not wanting to push back against his father. He knew it was time to call it quits, and he wasn't about to challenge his own father on his foolishness.

"Good," Ben Manor yelled back. "You look like a damn fool in the news. I hope to God you pay for that man to get his bar back up and running."

"I wasn't part of that, Dad," Blake answered.

"Doesn't matter! You were there and by association, you were involved. You're there to play football, not be a horse's ass!"

"I know, Dad," Blake said, feeling like a teenager. "I don't know what else you want me to say. I fucked up."

"You fucked up big time. You've got your mom worried sick about you. You're the laughing stock of the football world right now. All eyes are on you and this craziness. By the looks of the photos, you seem to be in the center of the fighting."

"It's the press, Dad. They can make a photo look any way they want, especially if they want to bury someone."

"So they're burying you? You were an innocent bystander? I'm telling you, I'm sick and tired of listening to you try to talk yourself out of these things."

Blake exhaled loudly enough for his dad to hear.

"Don't get annoyed with me, Blake. You're the one whose reputation and conduct are on the line. I'm hoping you don't get suspended."

"Yeah, did you talk to Greg? Where did you hear about me getting suspended?" Blake asked, feeling worried.

"It's in your contract. There's some sort of conduct clause," Ben said seriously. "This is about the sixth public incident in the last few months that involves fighting and the cops. Not to mention, the destruction of property. You've already been given a warning from the Skyscrapers. What else do you expect them to do? Just allow you to keep partying like this without some sort of repercussion? It doesn't work that way."

"I know, Dad," was all Blake could say. He hated being reprimanded by his father. "Is Mom still there?" Even though he was twenty-five years old, his Mom still had a knack for making shitty things seem OK.

"She's here, yes. She doesn't sound like it, but she's just as upset as I am, Blake. Let me ask, what does Greg think about all of this?" Ben wondered out loud to his son. "He must be doing a ton of damage control right now."

Blake didn't want to tell his dad that Greg was meeting with the Skyscrapers management team because he knew it would unleash another layer of disappointment. It was clear that this was the wake-up call Blake needed to get his shit together. He loved partying and loved the ladies, but it was time to dial it back, at least during the season. He didn't want to destroy what he had worked so hard for, and it definitely seemed like he was heading in that direction.

"I'm supposed to touch base with him again this afternoon after practice," Blake shared, knowing he wasn't exactly lying, but just leaving out some key details at the moment.

No sooner did the words come out of his mouth than he heard another call coming through. He looked down to see that it was Greg.

"Dad," Blake said quickly. "It's Greg calling, I've got to go. I'll call you and Mom later tonight."

Blake held his breath, said a quick prayer, and switched over to answer Greg. "Please tell me you worked your magic," were the first words out of Blake's mouth.

"Depends on how you look at it," Greg responded seriously. "You're suspended through Christmas."

"That's like three games," Blake shouted, allowing the severity of the situation to sink in. "You've got to be kidding me! What do you mean it 'depends how you look at it?'"

"Well, they actually wanted you out for the rest of the season."

lake was trying his best not to explode in the town car, but he couldn't help it. How could something like this happen? It's not like the other players were boy scouts off the field. How come they were making an example out of him? His heart was pounding out of his chest and his head was throbbing.

"The season? They wanted me out for the rest of the season?" he shouted into the phone at Greg. "Over a fight in a bar, a stupid arrest, and some damage, which I've offered to pay for!"

"I told you they weren't happy with how things were going with you off the field," Greg responded, trying to stay calm. One thing he hated to do as an agent was damage control, especially when he knew his clients were acting like asses.

"I can't believe they were gunning for the rest of the season--that would have been insane," Blake yelled. "How did they settle on three games through Christmas? I mean, not that it's that much of a huge difference," he stated. "I'm still going to be out for three games."

"They're not happy with you, Blake. They're not happy at all. We actually went back and forth for a bit, and I wasn't sure how everything was going to land. The good thing is that they know you are worth gold to them on the field. They can't deny the fact that you move the ball and bring them wins, but they also can't have you representing them the way you have been off the field. It's that simple. It's bad PR for you, and for the team. Never mind the sponsorship deals I'm trying to manage."

"Seriously though, this is all because of the fight at the bar and the damage?" Blake asked.

"It's more than that, Blake. You're not seeing the bigger picture. Your partying reputation is out of control. They're constantly defending you to the media, or at least trying to. You got yourself into hot water last night with a major public disorder offense, and serious damage done to a much-loved local business that is one of the team's biggest supporters. The management team doesn't want to carry this kind of shit on their backs during the season. It's taking away too much attention from the team and the other players."

Blake sat, staring straight ahead. He didn't know what to say or how to react. He couldn't believe that the one thing he loved to do most in the world was being taken away from him for the next few weeks. Football was his life, and now he was supposed to sit out the next three games while the rest of his team played.

"And so, that's it? I can't try to fight this suspension?" Blake asked with hope in his voice.

"No," Greg said definitively. "There's nothing you can say that's going to change their minds. Just be glad this is all they're going to do. When I first got to the meeting, I was not prepared when they said they wanted you out for the rest of the season. Do you know what kind of damage that would have done to you? The Skyscrapers are on fire right now. You could easily be in the championships."

"I don't know what to do," Blake said, shaking his head. "And now I've got to go to practice and pretend everything is OK with the guys. How the hell am I going to do that?"

"Blake," Greg said in a flat and serious tone. "There's no practice for you. You're suspended as of right now. That means you're not allowed back until after Christmas."

"You've got to be kidding me," Blake yelled back, feeling so angry that tears were springing to his eyes. How could they suspend him from practice, too? If they didn't want him playing, that was one thing. But how was he supposed to keep himself in shape if he couldn't practice with his team?

"I'm not kidding you," Greg answered. "This is serious. You've really pissed off the top brass this time."

Blake sat back in his seat and shook his head. He dropped the phone into his lap and adjusted it to his speakerphone. He knew that his partying had been a bit extreme, but he never thought in a million years that it would result in something like this. All the work he had put in over the summer didn't mean anything right now. He had trained his ass off. He had worked his body to be in top condition. He knew that his endurance, speed, and strength were at their peak. To be told he couldn't be on the field with his teammates felt like he was having his oxygen cut off.

"I can't believe this," was all that Blake could say.

"I know, Blake," Greg remarked. "It sucks, but you've got to take this time right now to correct the wrongs. Stop the partying. Stop the craziness. When I first started working with you, you never went out. You'd be in every night studying football tapes from other teams. You hardly touched alcohol. You were never out with a girl, never mind a roomful of them. You've got to get back to basics."

Blake rubbed his eyes with his hands and looked out the window. He was almost at the stadium. He hadn't even had the chance to tell his driver to turn around and head back to his apartment.

"You know what the kicker is," Blake responded quietly. "Half the guys on my team party just as much, but none of this is happening to them."

"Yeah," Greg answered. "But these guys aren't on the front page of the newspapers and being written up on every gossip website. You've got the looks and the talent; you're the perfect target. Unfortunately, you're learning the hard way, Blake."

"So what? I'm supposed to lay low for the next month or so? We're talking about four weeks."

"Yeah," Greg said. "And you've still got to keep yourself in shape. The stadium, for you, isn't an option. We can find you a trainer who can come to you, or we can have them send you workouts, whatever you want. We will make this work, so don't worry about it."

"I guess so," Blake said, as the massiveness of the situation started to sink in. "Shit... this is going to suck."

"Want my advice, not only as your agent but as your friend?" Greg asked.

"What's that?" Blake responded, not quite sure what to expect.

"Get yourself out of the city. Eliminate the distractions for the time being. Go upstate or rent a house somewhere warm for the next month. You've got a few weeks to step away from it all. In the meantime, we need to get you some good PR. Enough of this partying shit. Find a place you love, go there, and I'll figure out a way to get you some good press."

"Good press?" Blake scoffed at Greg.

"Yeah, you heard me. Good press. That's what you need right now. Donate money toward a worthy cause, volunteer at a local school, or start dating a small-town librarian. I don't know, we'll find a way to make it work. Just do something that's going to erase this party boy image from the press. That's what you need to do over the next month."

Blake sat back in his seat and took a deep breath. "You know what, Greg, I actually know the perfect spot."

"Oh, yeah," Greg said, sounding hopeful. "Where's that?"

"I'm going home."

6

Charlotte sat across from Frank in his office, watching him scan her article. He had a large antique desk that almost filled his entire office. The only other pieces of furniture that fit in the space were his green leather chair and a small wooden chair for a visitor. Frank had had this office since he started at the *View*, and this was his royal throne, his home away from home. He had papers scattered all over his desk but, as Charlotte had come to realize within the first few weeks of working here, it was organized chaos. Frank knew where every piece of paper was, and to him, it was a well-oiled machine.

Frank had a funny way of proofreading, which entailed reading portions aloud. Charlotte could never tell if those were the sections he liked the most or the parts he thought needed the most work. Frank had requested a 2000-word article for the feature, but Charlotte had given him close to 3000, hoping he wouldn't notice. She knew he would chop away at it, but secretly hoped he would just find extra space to print it.

"I've got to hand it to you," Frank said, while he was still nose down reading the draft, making notes with his red pen. "I don't know how you scored this feature with the Governor so quickly, but you did it. I don't think even I could have pulled off this kind of quick turnaround."

Charlotte smiled to herself, knowing that it hadn't been easy, but where there's a will, there's a way. "Thanks, Frank."

"You going to tell me your secret?" Frank asked with a chuckle, still reading and wielding his red pen. It was customary not to send Frank an email of your article. He was old school and wanted it printed out so that he could hold it in his hands.

"Good journalists never reveal their secrets," Charlotte laughed. "Isn't that something they teach all of us in Journalism 101?"

"Touché," Frank laughed back. "Still, I'm impressed. You asked me about this feature three days ago, and I expected it would take you a few weeks to even get someone on the phone in the Governor's office, much less get the full article written."

"Let's just say I know a guy," Charlotte smiled.

"Now you sound like a true Rhode Islander," Frank shot back, and he looked up to wink at her.

Charlotte nodded back with a smile. She knew doing interviews with political leaders would be great for her portfolio, so the second Frank gave her the green light at their Monday meeting, she was like a dog with a bone.

She happened to have some pretty solid connections at the Rhode Island State House, so she called all of them on Monday afternoon to see who could help. She told them she needed only five minutes with the Governor, any time of the day, and, by the grace of God, on Tuesday afternoon one of her contacts called her. She told Charlotte to show up at a particular sandwich shop, at a particular time, in Providence, and she would make sure Charlotte got five minutes. Charlotte had made sure to be there with her notebook, pen, and list of questions. She didn't want to waste one second. The moment the Governor arrived, her contact introduced her and he was immediately impressed, not only with her young age but with her determination. Those five minutes turned into thirty. Charlotte left the meeting with enough content to write two articles, so she was pushing it by adding more content than Frank wanted, but she thought it was worth the try.

"All right," Frank said, looking up and placing the article down in front of him. "This is good, really good. It's nice to see the Governor talk about our particular town, and know so much about it. The people are going to love this."

Charlotte couldn't help a smile spreading across her face as Frank spoke. She was hoping he would be impressed with it.

"You do know you have to chop it down," Frank said with a devious smile. "You think I wouldn't notice the extra 1000 words?" He teased.

Charlotte's smile was replaced with a dramatic frown, "1000 words need to be cut? Are you sure you can't fit it all? That will take away from so much in the article."

"I can't fit 3000 words, Charlotte. I would like to, but I can't."

"What do you think I should cut?" Charlotte curiously asked.

"I made a few notes here and there in the margin. There's a bit of fluff in there you could get rid of, too."

"Fluff?" Charlotte laughed. "What do you mean by that?"

"We don't need to know about his background and personal info like that. He's been elected. Most people know about him. I would just stick to the key points he shared about Barrington and that's it."

Charlotte nodded, knowing that taking out some of the notes would change the feel of the feature, but she didn't want to risk not getting it printed. She needed to find a way to cut out about a third of the article, and she would find a way to do it.

"I'll figure it out," Charlotte nodded as she took the article from Frank.

"I know you will," Frank answered with a smile. "I hope you know that you're one hell of a reporter. I know this is just a stop for you on your career path--we all know that-- but we're glad to have you, and I hope you will keep giving it your all while you are here."

"That means a lot, coming from you," Charlotte said. "You know I love being with Lindsay and, believe it or not, as much as I'm craving big city stories, small-town life is growing on me, too."

"Small-town life has been my only life, so I'm glad to hear that," he laughed. "Whether you end up in a big city, or stay in small-town New England, writing is writing, and you're good at it."

"You know what it is, Frank... " Charlotte said softly. "I've just always wanted to tell people's stories. I love being able to listen to someone and then turn their story into something people want to read about. That's the magic for me. That's why pieces like this," she said, holding up her article about the Governor, "matter, and are important to me. I'm able to tell a story about what the Governor knows about Barrington, and what he's doing for the town, too."

"You've got a gift when it comes to interviewing people," Frank added. "Just keep interviewing people like this," he said, pointing at the article in her hands.

"I owe that to my mother and father," Charlotte smiled, feeling her heart pull. "They would let me interview them for hours when I was a kid. They knew my love for writing articles, so they would always pretend to be different people, and I would jot down notes as they went on and on with these lavish stories. My father would always tell me to listen to what the person was saying because you first have to hear stories with your heart. I've never forgotten that."

"They'd be proud of you, Charlotte," Frank smiled, knowing this was something Charlotte didn't normally talk about.

Charlotte looked down at the article in her hand, trying her best to wish away the tears. She knew if she concentrated on something else, her body would fight them off. It's what she had been doing for the last couple of years.

"So, if you happen to have any ideas for future features, keep me in mind. I already have three of the principals lined up for interviews for that other feature, too," Charlotte added as she got up to gather her things. "I'm trying my best, Frank, to widen my portfolio. I can't thank you enough for the opportunities you're giving me here. I will never forget it."

"Actually, Charlotte," Frank said with some slight hesitation in his voice as he rubbed his eyes. "I might have something for you."

"What's that?" Charlotte asked quickly.

"I had an idea pitched to me this morning, and I was going to assign one of the sports guys to it, but you just might be the perfect person for it with your interviewing skills and storytelling."

"Me? What's it about?"

"Blake Manor," Frank said with a smile on his face, waiting for Charlotte's eyes to open wide in excitement.

Instead, Frank was met with confusion. "Blake, who?" Charlotte asked, not sure why Frank seemed so excited about the name.

"Blake Manor. You've never heard of Blake Manor?" Frank asked confused.

Charlotte stared at Frank and tried her best to jog her memory. The name sounded vaguely familiar, but she couldn't place it for the life of her. "I can tell by how you're looking at me that I should know him," Charlotte said apologetically. "Is he a local business owner? Politician?"

"No," Frank chuckled and shrugged his shoulders. "I know you're not a sports fan, and I know you're not from Barrington, so maybe it's not so out of the realm of possibility you don't know him. He's just been all over the news lately, so I figured you'd know him. He's a professional football player, plays for the New York Skyscrapers, and he's going to be in Barrington for the next few weeks."

"Oh, why's that?" Charlotte responded.

"He got himself into some trouble and has been suspended from playing football for the next three games. His parents still live here, so he's decided to come home and stay with them as he waits it out. I was pitched by his agent to do a feel-good feature on him while he's back in town. Seems like they need some good press. STAT. I guess he's going to be doing some volunteering at the schools and helping out wherever he's needed."

"OK..." Charlotte shrugged, still not sure why Frank would want to give this story to her. "Is he the kind of guy who will have everyone in town on high alert?"

Frank chuckled, "You really have no clue who he is, huh?"

"Not one," Charlotte answered with her eyes wide open.

"You know I stay away from anything athletic, and that's for a good reason. I hate sports."

"Noted," Frank laughed back. "But you might want to reconsider your hatred for sports because this story will be good for your portfolio."

"Why's that?" She asked, intrigued.

"He's one of the best football players in the league and he's out because he's been suspended. Every sports journalist would kill for a story with this kid right now, but his agent isn't too trusting of the media right now."

"So he came to you? Why's that?"

"I've known Blake since he was a kid," Frank shared. "His parents are friends of mine, so I'm not a total stranger, but I'm also no fool. This could be great press for the paper. I mean, we're essentially going to be getting a scoop that every sports publication wants. Blake's worried about talking to anyone because he's been burned so much by the media, but he knows there's a trust factor with me. Apparently, his father is the one who told his agent to call me."

"I'm following you, but are you saying you want me to write this article?"

"If you want me to put it to you straight, I think a story like this could help you just as much as it could help him. It would put you on the map to have a one-on-one feature with Blake Manor."

Charlotte stood looking at Frank with a smile, "Then put me in, Coach. Isn't that what they say?"

7

Blake had forgotten how beautiful the drive to Rhode Island was from New York City. He hadn't done the drive on his own in ages. Normally, he'd fly private or have a driver bring him up here while he relaxed during the three-hour road trip. It had become too difficult for him to fly commercial or take Amtrak with people stopping and asking him for photos, or for his autograph. As much as he loved his fans, he sometimes missed his earlier days of anonymity.

The last three days had hit him hard. Football was his life. It was his reason for getting up every day, so being told he couldn't play was pure torture. Per Greg's suggestion, he had written personal letters to the team owners, management, and coaching staff, apologizing for his behavior. He wasn't expecting the suspension to be lifted, but he was hoping that the simple act would help mend fractures. He had walked around his apartment like a zombie for three days, packing up and trying to make some sort of solid plan for his training while back in Rhode Island.

The ring of his cell phone startled him as he sped along Route 95 passing through New Haven, CT, which put him about halfway home. He was hoping for a quiet ride. He didn't feel like dealing with work shit right now, but when he saw who was calling, he immediately answered the call.

"I was wondering when I was going to hear from you," Blake said with a devious grin.

"I figured I'd let the dust settle before I checked in," a seductive female voice answered on the other end. "Besides... you have my number, too."

Piper Saunders worked on-air at the *New York Beat* covering sports. She also had her own personal sports blog where she dished on sports and athletes. She covered football and baseball in New York City. With her tall 5'10" frame, gorgeous, tanned skin, and long chestnut brown hair, she couldn't be missed. She wore clothing that hugged every square inch of her body and, judging from her million followers on social media, she certainly had found her niche. She created thirty-second videos throughout the games for the *Beat*, as well as sharing them on her personal social media accounts. She knew she had something that worked for her, and she wasn't going to let any opportunity pass if it meant increasing her media presence.

Blake let out a small laugh, "Yeah, I know. What can I say, I've been in a daze the last few days, Piper," Blake answered honestly. "I was ordered by Greg to lay low."

"Well, you know you can always lay low with me," Piper snickered. "We've always had a good time laying low together."

"Don't tempt me to come back," Blake laughed back, feeling his body perk up.

"Where are you headed?" Piper asked, interested.

Blake knew that Piper was part of the press, but he also

knew they had a little something going that had never been defined. He didn't all-out trust Piper when it came to information about his team and his life. He was always hesitant, but he also knew that his whereabouts would hit the press sooner or later. It had already been reported everywhere that he was suspended, so it was just a matter of time before people knew where he was. At the moment, only a small group of people knew he was coming back home.

Taking a deep breath, knowing that Piper could leak the news in seconds, he said, "Rhode Island... for the time being, I'm heading back to see the folks."

"I thought that was where you'd go," Piper responded knowingly. "How long are you planning on staying?"

Blake knew he would be there for the next few weeks, but didn't want anyone knowing the actual extent of his stay, "Not sure yet, maybe a week or two."

"You know," Piper responded. "I've never been to Rhode Island. Maybe I could visit for a day or two while you're there, and you could give me a tour," she suggested.

"A tour of you sounds good," Blake teased. "But if you come to Rhode Island, you would be staying in my childhood bedroom with me," he laughed.

"Ohhhh... actually, that sounds kind of hot," Piper joked back. "I can only imagine how many girls saw that bedroom in high school."

Blake let out a deep laugh, knowing the real truth behind that statement. In high school, he had been so focused on football and getting himself a scholarship to take the burden off his parents, that he didn't do anything but go to school and play football. Girls were certainly not on his radar. Not to mention that he was so awkward around girls that they didn't even give him the time of day. It never occurred to him to ask anyone out. They stayed away from him, and he stayed away from them. Cut and dried.

"I don't know about that," Blake responded, not wanting to give too much away. "I wasn't exactly a ladies' man in high school."

"Why do I find that hard to believe?" Piper responded.

"Hey, believe what you want. I didn't have girls like you knocking down my door in high school, that's for sure."

"Well, I can certainly knock that door down now if you want me to," Piper joked, although Blake knew she wasn't really joking at all. He had a feeling if he suggested she be in Barrington tonight, she would do it. He liked that about her. She was sexy as hell, and if there was a regular woman to be seen with, Piper Saunders was the one. Every athlete in the city wanted her, but she had chosen him, even with his reputation...or maybe because of it.

"I'll keep that in mind. In the meantime, I've got to get home and get organized. My mom won't hear of me staying in a hotel, so this should be an interesting visit. I haven't been back home for an extended stay in a while, so I don't know what to expect."

"Whereabouts in Rhode Island?" Piper asked. "I don't think I've ever asked you about that. I know New Jersey and New York inside and out, but Rhode Island... I only know about Providence."

"Off the record right now?" Blake asked seriously. "I know you love a good scoop."

"Of course," Piper smiled. "You know me, I wouldn't do that to you. Besides, you think people will stay quiet forever?"

"True, but it's easier if people just think I'm in Rhode Island. I'm not broadcasting my hometown, not that it's hard to find it if you look it up. But I'm from Barrington, a super small town. It's the polar opposite of New York City. Families raise their kids and most never leave, which is exactly what my parents did, even after I offered to move them anywhere in the world."

"Sounds like the town I'm from in New Jersey. I'm the outcast of the family for moving away to the big bad city to chase my journalism dream."

"I always knew I'd leave Barrington for football," answered Blake, "but if there's a place to raise a kid, it's kind of the dream place to do it."

"Listen," Piper said, sounding more serious. "I'm not just saying this, but I'd love to visit. I feel like things between the two of us were starting to heat up and get a little more regular and... hot." Piper had a way of making everything sound sexy.

"Things with you are always hot," Blake joked back, thinking of all the times they had spent together. Blake always had a great time with Piper. She was always up for an adventure, always happy to see him, always in a great mood, and she drove him crazy in bed. He had a feeling she wanted to be exclusive, but he wasn't ready to cut off ties with other ladies, not yet. Piper had been the most regular girl he had been with in a long time. As far as he knew, she wanted to be more serious, but she was also smart enough not to push him. He wasn't ready to settle down with anyone, and she seemed to get that. Football was his one and only true love.

"You know what I mean," Piper teased back. "And don't forget... I'm around hot, sexy athletes every single day."

"Yeah, yeah, yeah," Blake teased back. "But let's face it, none of them hold a candle to me."

"They're pretty close but, lucky for you, my eyes seem to be on you right now," Piper replied seductively.

"So it's luck, huh? Doesn't have anything to do with my good looks and dashing personality?" Blake joked. He knew that Piper could pretty much have her pick when it came to guys.

"It's got to do with a lot of things, but I do miss you..." Piper said with a serious sense to her tone.

"I know," Blake answered, and although he didn't miss her in the sense that she wanted, he did miss her company. They had become closer over the last month or so, and she had spent numerous nights at his place. "Let me get settled and then I'll let you know when a visit would be good. I have a feeling I'm going to be craving a Piper visit sooner than you think," he shared, feeling his body start to heat up just thinking about her.

"Good," Piper smiled. "Crave all you want, I'm here for it, and ready for you to indulge. I've got to run, too... work is calling."

"Thanks for checking in, Piper. I'll call you soon," Blake added with a smile. He appreciated the fact that she cared enough to call to see how he was doing. Not many of his football buddies had done that yet. It seemed like everyone wanted to stay an arm's distance away for now.

"Ciao!" And with that Piper ended the call. It always made Blake smile when she used the Italian word. She did it with everyone, not just him-- her signature closing.

Piper seemed pretty cool about not being with him exclusively, and he liked that, too. At twenty-five, the farthest thing from Blake's mind was marriage, but he knew slowing it down with the ladies would be a good idea. He thought about Piper and how he had this smoking hot, Sofia Vergara lookalike, hot for him. He knew he was crazy for not locking her up. But it felt so good to have women of all ages swooning at his every move. He had always loved the fact that his heart had never been attached to any one woman because that would mean he risked losing all the others. But he knew he needed to clean up his reputation. Greg had made it clear that he needed to change, and quickly. The more he thought about Piper, the more he realized she might be the answer to that dilemma.

8

"Doing research I see," Lindsay said as she walked into Charlotte's living room and saw papers scattered all over her coffee table and floor, all of them filled with information about Blake Manor. Normally, Charlotte's living room was clean and tidy, without one speck of dust in sight, essentially the opposite of how Lindsay lived. It looked as if someone had taken reams of paper and just tossed them up into the air. Almost every inch of her living room carpet was covered with papers and some were even scattered all over her big, white, cozy couch. "Where am I supposed to sit?" Lindsay laughed.

Charlotte walked into her living room holding two glasses of wine. "Oh my God, Linds. I meant to clean up all these papers when I got home from work. The day just got away from me. Then I got chatting with my neighbor about some issue she wants me to write about for the paper, and that's when you got here. I completely forget about this mess."

"I think I'm just more surprised to see your place like this than anything," Lindsay laughed.

"This doesn't qualify as a mess," Charlotte shot back with a smile. "This is work. And if you give me a few minutes, I'll have everything cleaned up."

"Oh, Char... come on, it's me. You don't need to clean it up. Let me help you," Lindsay offered.

Charlotte placed the two wine glasses on her square glass coffee table. "I got it, Linds, but thank you. There's a method to my madness. I just need a quick second to file everything back into the folders I created."

"You don't trust me to touch anything, do you?" Lindsay laughed. "I swear, I don't know how we make it work. We're the best of friends, but we couldn't be more different. I do my best work in chaos. You work your best in crazy organization."

"As I've always said," Charlotte added, looking over at Lindsay as she placed paper after paper into a folder. "We balance each other out."

"I know," Lindsay smiled. "And don't get me started how different we are when it comes to men."

"I can sum it up in one quick statement... if there's a bad boy to be found, you'll find him," Charlotte said.

Lindsay stuck out her tongue at Charlotte and laughed.

"What can I say, I've got a thing for the bad boy or, better yet, the guys not looking for anything serious. I feel like that sums me up perfectly."

"And the ones with zero direction," Charlotte laughed. "It's like you walk around with a magnet just waiting to find them."

"They're just so much fun," Lindsay joked, grabbing one of the glasses of wine on the coffee table.

"Fun, yes... but not reliable," Charlotte said, holding her glass up to toast with Lindsay.

"None of them are like Dylan. Just say it! Although not

many men, at twenty-two, are like Dylan," Lindsay laughed as she took a sip. "He's just as organized about work as you are. We need to lighten him up a little," Lindsay joked. "But I will admit that you two do make a solid couple."

Charlotte rolled her eyes and smiled at her friend. She knew Lindsay wasn't the biggest Dylan fan, but that was only because he represented nothing that she looked for in a guy. Yes, maybe he wasn't as adventurous and wild as Lindsay liked, but he was everything Charlotte needed in her life. He was hard-working, predictable, reliable, smart, and driven. Was there crazy fireworks between them? Not like in the movies, but from the second she met him in college, she knew she felt something for him. They happened to meet at the library, studying on a Friday night while the rest of the school was at the football game. They hit it off and the rest was history. She had loved the fact that he wasn't from Rhode Island. It seemed everyone at the University of Rhode Island was from Rhode Island, and it was nice to meet someone who had zero ties to the state, just like her.

"I just hope our job paths align so we can be together sooner than later," Charlotte shrugged. "This distance thing is tough, but thankfully we're not putting too much pressure on each other. Although, it would be nice for him to come to visit me. I've been to see him four times since he moved to New York City. I told him I'm not going again until he makes the effort to come up here."

"I don't blame you," Lindsay agreed. "Don't make it too easy for him."

"And I feel like I have, right?" Charlotte asked, looking at Lindsay for reassurance.

"Yes, you have," Lindsay nodded. "You've made it way

too easy for him. Once you finally get yourself work in New York City, it will get easier, I'm sure."

"I hope so," Charlotte smiled.

"This article will give you a jumpstart, Char, and get you noticed by bigger publications," Lindsay added. "Just watch!"

"I hope so, Linds," Charlotte added and then looked around at the papers everywhere, "I must look like a Blake Manor stalker. I'm trying to read everything I can about him before we meet in a couple of days. Your dad has a meeting set up with him and his agent. Thankfully your dad will be there too. Meantime, I'm doing my homework."

Lindsay looked at some of the papers, "Actually, it's pretty interesting to see all these old photos and articles about Blake from his high school days. My God," she said, looking closely at one of the photos. "I forgot how different he looks now."

"Different?" Charlotte asked as she paused to grab a sip of wine.

"Yeah," Lindsay smiled as she picked up an old photo of Blake and flashed it at Charlotte. "He seemed so much smaller back in high school, not so much in height, but in his physique. He's really built now, but in these photos, he looks so small."

"Well, in all fairness, he was a teenager then," Charlotte responded with a smile as she grabbed the photo from Lindsay to take a closer look.

"I still can't believe you didn't know who he was until a couple of days ago," Lindsay laughed. "Who the hell doesn't know Blake Manor?"

"Oh, please, not everyone follows sports. Besides, I didn't grow up in Rhode Island," Charlotte added. "I mean, I vaguely recognized his name, but I pretty much ignore anything to do with sports. You know that."

"I know," Lindsay said shaking her head. "It's just surprising to me because he seems to make the news a lot, and it's not always in the sports section."

"Which is the point of this feature on him for the *View*. Do you know what he was like in high school?"

"I didn't go to high school with him, I was a couple of years behind him. He was a senior when I was in 8th grade. I remember him being the high school's standout football player. My dad would always talk about him. Not many guys from here go on to play at a big Division I school, and he did. He really seemed to excel in college. He went from being great to untouchable... and then, obviously, he was drafted by the Skyscrapers."

"I just hope the fact that I know nothing about football doesn't impact this story. The only thing I know is that you use a brown oval-shaped ball to play," she laughed. "Oh God... your dad has put way too much trust in me on this one. He thinks it would be a great article to add to my portfolio, and I love him for that."

"These articles have the ability to give you some great exposure. From what I'm hearing, everyone wants an interview with Blake Manor," Lindsay added.

"But what's the story?" Charlotte asked, sipping her wine. "I've been trying to come up with ideas for the last couple of days. I mean, it seems like he's untouchable on the field and an asshole off the field. I'll have to cover both sides, I can't lie and distort the truth."

"Apparently Blake's agent and Blake's father thought reaching out to the *Barrington View*--the paper that basically helped build Blake up in the first place--would be the best option for him. Selfishly, it will be incredible for our circulation and online traffic. But there's more to it. I mean, my father has known Ben and Mary Manor since they moved here over twenty years ago. His parents are amazing people. I don't know if you know their background, but they essentially cleaned houses to put Blake and his sister through school."

"Well, that's a good angle," Charlotte nodded. "He doesn't talk much about his family, at least not in the stuff I've seen."

"Yeah," Lindsay added, "Blake has always been super private about his family. I do know he offered to move them closer to him, or at least out of Barrington when he got drafted, but they didn't want to leave. They love it here."

Charlotte smiled, "That's the first redeeming thing I've heard about Blake Manor."

"I'm sure there's more, which is probably the direction Blake and his team want this feature to go in," Lindsay offered.

"I know. I think it's just more interesting to see what fame and money can do to someone," Charlotte added as she picked up a recent photo of him.

Lindsay watched her best friend study the photo, "There's one thing you can't deny about him."

"What's that?" Charlotte asked looking up from the photo.

"He's hot as hell."

9

B lake sat in his childhood living room, trying not to sweat through his suit as he watched his mother place a cheese and cracker tray, along with a gigantic plate of fruit, on the old coffee table in front of him. The living room hadn't been updated since he'd lived in Barrington, and it killed him that his parents wouldn't let him take care of any major renovations. As they continued to tell him, "We're good."

Being back home was like taking a trip back in time, the exception being the TV. His dad had splurged on a new 60" TV when Blake got drafted, so he could watch all the games without squinting at the television. That's how small the previous one had been. He also purchased the expensive football network to see Blake's games, since Rhode Island didn't air New York games. As much as Blake wished his parents would let him buy new things for them, seeing everything remain the same brought Blake some peace, too. The world was changing quickly, and it was nice seeing a few things stay the same.

"You went with the light gray suit," Mary Manor nodded at her son with a smile. "I like it with the blue shirt underneath. Makes your eyes pop."

Blake smiled, "You always say that when I wear blue."

"Well, I'm your mother," she smiled back. "I know best. You got your eyes from your father, one of the many reasons I fell in love with him."

"I don't know if I want to hear about the other reasons," Blake laughed as he watched his mother rearrange the trays on the coffee table for the fifth time.

"You know you don't have to do this, right?" Blake asked, motioning to the food.

"Always good to offer something to your guests, remember that..." Mary winked. "Besides, it will be nice to see Frank. I haven't seen him in a while. I'm glad you're giving him the story and not one of those big fancy publications."

Blake rolled his eyes at his mother and began to laugh, "Fancy publications? What do you mean by that?"

"All those big sports and news magazines, including the big newspapers in the city. I'm glad you opted to reach out to Frank and none of the others."

"I don't know if I'd say I opted for it, more like Greg did with Dad's help."

"Regardless," Mary said, walking back toward the kitchen, "what better place than to be featured than your hometown newspaper? I'll be listening from the kitchen," she joked, "so make sure you talk nice and loud so I can hear everything."

Right before Mary was about to walk back to the kitchen, she stopped and looked over at Blake. "Hey, did your sister reach out to you yet?"

Blake looked at his mother with a knowing look because she knew she had, "Why's that?"

"Just wondering," she said, looking at him as she waited for her answer.

"If you mean the lashing I got via text for messing up again, then yes... I heard from Molly," she said with a nod.

"Good," Mary smiled with a nod and left the room.

Blake shook his head and reached for the phone in his pocket. He had been waiting for his sister to give it to him and he admitted it, he'd deserved it. He hated thinking that his sister was ashamed of him, and had to deal with anyone taunting her at college about his stupidity.

Greg was due any minute, along with Frank. He wasn't sure what he was feeling about the idea of trying to get some good press. He wished he could just be at home, stay under the radar for a couple of weeks, and then head back to the city, where he belonged. People would forget about everything, it was just a matter of time. He had enjoyed growing up in Barrington, but as soon as he had experienced life outside of his small town, he'd loved it. New York City had always seemed unattainable when he was a kid. His parents never had the money to visit, so there were certain places that just seemed make-believe to him. He would read about New York City, and see pictures online and in books, but the thought of living there never occurred to him, until it happened.

The world opened up for him in New York City. He loved the fast, busy lifestyle--the 24-hour city that never slept. He loved the diversity and communities and seeing New Yorkers come together to cheer for their hometown teams, even though they were from different parts of the country and the world. His job gave him access to new places, and to new people. Everything seemed possible in New York City-- anything you wanted, at any time. New York City was the polar opposite of Barrington, and he had grown to love it.

"Greg here yet?" His father yelled as he pounded down the stairs.

"Not yet, Dad," Blake answered, as his father walked into the living room. "She made you dress up, too?" Blake chuckled as he looked at his father.

"Who, your Mom?" Ben Manor teased with a wink. "All I know is that when there's a suit laid out on the bed, you put it on. I don't ask, I just do."

"I thought this meeting would be fairly casual. I figured Frank was just coming over to brainstorm some ideas with us and Greg." Blake said, kind of surprised at the formality.

"Yeah," Ben nodded, "that's exactly what's happening. I just thought it would be a good idea to show we were taking things seriously. Don't forget that the team is watching every move you make during this suspension."

"I know, believe me," Blake answered, looking down at his phone while he scanned the stats of some of his opponents. "I still can't freaking believe I'm suspended. It's crushing me, seriously crushing me."

"You know what, Blake? I'm going to tell you something...again. You don't want to hear it, but I'm your father and I'll tell you whatever I want."

"What's that?" Blake asked, still looking down at his phone.

"Will you look up at me, please," his dad asked in an annoyed fatherly tone.

Blake put his phone on the coffee table and looked at his father. Even at twenty-five years old, he didn't want to piss off his dad. He locked eyes with his father so he knew he was listening to him.

"I want you to remember the crushing feeling you have right now. This is a lesson you need to learn. If you want your career to keep going, and be as successful as you're hoping it can be, then you have to act like an adult and stop the shit. You know how many guys would give their right arm to be in your position? I could name about ten right off the top of my head. You've been handed a golden ticket, and you're blowing it away. The time to stop acting like a spoiled brat is now. We didn't raise you this way. Get your head on straight. Your mom and I have worked too hard for you and your sister to watch you piss away the kind of opportunities that we never had. You and Molly are our dreams come true. Do you get that? The fame has gone to your head like a drug. For the love of God, just stop dicking around?"

Blake didn't look away; he just kept staring at his father, feeling more and more like hell. He hadn't stopped to think that this wasn't just about him. This had impacted and affected his parents, too. It had to suck reading about your son's shenanigans in the news, especially this last go-round. The photos of him that had been circulating on the Internet were horrible; the fighting, the alcohol, the girls, the damage to the bar, and then the arrest... it was all captured for everyone to see.

"I know, Dad, and I apologize," was all Blake could manage to say. For the first time since everything had happened, he truly felt like he was going to cry. He hated making his parents feel disappointed and embarrassed, and he knew he had done that to both of them. He knew things had spiraled a bit for him, but he hadn't realized just how bad it had truly gotten.

"Good, I just hope I got through to you this time." Ben

gave him a steely-eyed look and then walked over to grab a piece of fruit from one of the trays.

"Mom's going to kill you if she sees a piece missing from the fruit tray before Frank and Greg get here," Blake joked.

"I'll deny it to the day I die," Ben winked, then patted his son on his back. "Everything's going to be OK, son. Greg's advice on getting you some good press is a great idea, and *The Barrington View* is the best place for it. Frank's a good guy who won't let us down."

"I know you like Frank, but this interview will also boost the *View's* visibility," Blake said, looking over at his father. "Don't think Frank's not thinking about what it can do for him, too."

"Frank's no fool," Ben responded. "Of course he knows this will be good for the paper, but he wasn't trying to pitch you, me, or Greg for the story. Greg reached out to him. Frank has always been fair and good to you, not to mention, he's a family friend. If there's anyone I trust to help you right now, it's him and any potential ideas he might have."

Mary Manor poked her head into the living room and smiled as she saw her two guys sitting on the couch together. "Hey guys, two cars just pulled into the driveway. Looks like Greg and Frank are both here."

"You ready?" Ben asked, getting up to walk to the door. "Just remember, you have the final say in all of this."

Blake exhaled loudly and looked over at his father. "Do I?"

"Everyone's just looking out for you," Ben answered. "Remember that."

Ben and Blake walked to the front door and opened it to greet their guests. It was a beautiful December morning, but the weather still had a late October feel to it. As Frank closed his car door, his passenger door opened, and out came a cute, petite blonde woman dressed in a light blue suit and holding a tote bag.

"Who is that with Frank?" Blake asked, confused as he looked over at his father.

Ben squinted his eyes to get a better look, "I don't know. I've never seen her before."

10

Charlotte felt sick to her stomach, which was usually a good sign. Every time she had a big interview with someone, she would get butterflies and start feeling queasy. The good news was that when this happened, she normally did her best work. She wasn't an athlete by any stretch, but she felt that this was her body's way of telling her she was ready to give it her all, just like an athlete would be before a competition.

"You ready?" Frank asked her with a smile as he shut his car door and headed toward the Manor home.

"Yes, let's do this," she smiled back at Frank, trying to sound as professional as possible.

Charlotte looked toward the house and saw two figures standing in the doorway, one she assumed to be Mr. Manor and the other, Blake himself. Lindsay had told her that Blake was "hot as hell," but those three words didn't do him justice. He was mesmerizingly good-looking, even from a distance. Instantly, she felt her stomach do a few flips and knew she had to look away and do something to distract herself. All the photos and videos she had seen hadn't prepared her for the real thing. He was striking. She knew he was 6"4' and around 240 pounds, but his tousled dark brown hair, olive skin, muscular build, and chiseled face startled her. It was pretty clear why he was constantly surrounded by women off the gridiron.

As Frank approached the front door of the Manor home, Charlotte was right behind him and she could feel Blake's eyes on her. She didn't have to look up to confirm it, she just knew. It was a gut instinct that she had, and it didn't feel welcoming. Before Frank could even get a word out of his mouth to say hello or introduce her, Blake rudely asked, "Who is she? I wasn't told anyone else was coming."

Charlotte immediately turned and locked eyes with Blake, wanting to lash back with an even ruder reply, but she kept her cool and stared back at him with a deadpan expression, waiting for Frank to answer. She was used to dealing with all kinds of personalities and attitudes as a journalist, so although his question surprised her, she wasn't going to show that it had.

"This is Charlotte Court," Frank answered, motioning toward Charlotte. "She's one of my best interviewers at the *Barrington View*... actually, the best we've ever had."

"Thanks, Frank," Charlotte responded and looked up at Ben and Blake with a welcoming smile.

"Is she shadowing you?" Blake asked with an irritated tone to his voice. He then turned to Greg, who was next to Frank, "Can you make sure she signs an NDA?"

"I already took care of that, Blake," Frank interrupted, not giving Greg a chance to respond, obviously annoyed by this exchange. "Everything about this meeting has already been sent to Greg."

Blake looked over at Greg, who nodded his head, confirming that NDAs had been signed. Charlotte had never signed an NDA before now, and this had been a first for her. Normally, in her experience, if the person would not answer certain questions, she knew to stay away from the topic. Blake's agent was worried about her hearing things that were private in terms of his finances, contracts, and other things of a personal nature. She would never disclose private information like that, but she also knew her word meant nothing to them.

"Here," Ben chimed, trying to cover for his son's rude behavior. "Come on in. We can sit in the living room, there's plenty of room in there for everyone." Ben reached out his hand to Charlotte and smiled. "It's nice to meet you, Charlotte, I'm Ben Manor."

Charlotte smiled back and nodded her head. Ben was about Blake's height, which made her feel like a peanut at a mere 5'4". He resembled his father with his dark hair and olive skin. She hadn't noticed Blake's blue eyes in the photos she had seen, and as she looked into Ben's eyes it was clear that Blake had inherited the color from his father.

Once they were in the living room, Greg took control of the meeting. "Everyone, please sit. I don't want this to take too long, but I knew it was important for us all to meet and get on the same page," Greg began.

Charlotte walked to the couch and sat down. She opened her tote and grabbed her notebook and pen. As she sat up, she quickly locked eyes with Blake again. His face was motionless. She couldn't tell if he was pissed to have everyone there or not. She was normally great at reading people, but he just seemed like a blank page.

"Thanks, Greg," Frank jumped in. "And first," he said looking at Blake, "I appreciate you trusting us with this. From talking with everyone, it's clear you have choices in terms of who you want to speak to. I appreciated the call from Greg, and it's one we take very seriously."

"Thank you, Frank," Blake answered, nodding his head with a smile.

"This seems like the perfect fit," Greg chimed in, "especially under the circumstances. As I've told you, we are looking to get Blake's name in the news, but in a different capacity than he's been used to lately."

"That's putting it mildly," Blake smiled as he sat back in his seat and crossed his arms.

"Well," Frank added, "I think it's safe to say the press you've been getting isn't the kind of press you want. Fair enough?"

Blake looked over at Frank and nodded. "Yes, fair enough."

"The thing is, Frank," Ben Manor jumped in, "while he's home for the next few weeks, it would be good for him to show a different side to the press than what he usually gives them... and I mean the off the field kind of press," he said, looking over at Blake with a knowing eye.

"That I get," Frank answered. "And that's what we'll do, isn't that right, Charlotte?" Frank asked, looking toward Charlotte.

"Absolutely," Charlotte answered with a nod. "I've actually brainstormed a few ideas that I think might work well."

Charlotte opened her notebook and folded it over so she could easily read her notes. She didn't want to approach Blake with the same old sit-down interview format. She had spent the previous evening prepping, and coming up with ideas, and she thought she had something that would work for Blake. She wasn't sure he would go for what she wanted to propose, but she hoped he would see her bigger vision.

"Wait," Blake interjected. "You're doing the interviewing? Not Frank?"

Charlotte looked over at Frank, realizing that had he not told Blake about her involvement. No wonder Blake had given her the stink eye the moment she got out of the car and asked about the NDA. She didn't condone his attitude, but now it all made sense to her.

"Charlotte's taking the lead on this article, Blake," Frank said matter-of-factly. "She's the best I've got and, believe me, I wouldn't put just anyone on this story. I know how important this is for you."

"So you're not writing it?" Blake confirmed with Frank, completely dismissing Charlotte.

"I haven't written articles in years, Blake. I'm the editor who makes it all happen and makes it all look good. Believe me, you're in good hands," he said, looking at Charlotte with a smile.

Blake's temple tensed and he looked over at Charlotte, "Have you done any articles like this before? I'm not trying to be an asshole, but my reputation is on the line here. I can't afford to have anyone mess it up."

Charlotte was tempted to comment about how he had done enough for his reputation already, but she held her tongue. She wasn't going to let this spoiled brat shake her confidence. She needed this story more than he did. This could be her ticket to something bigger. She wasn't going to let this chance pass her by, so she cleared her throat, smiled, and took a deep breath. "I assure you that your reputation was top of mind as I was brainstorming ideas," she said confidently, and then she took a moment to look at Ben and Greg. She could tell she had their attention and she wasn't going to lose it. "Let me say this, I have watched every TV interview you have done, and I have read every interview that you've given. I think it's fair to say that you don't do many personal interviews," she stated, looking directly at Blake, waiting for him to answer.

Blake stared back at Charlotte and shook his head, "No... I've always tried to keep interviews about the game."

"Well, you've done a good job with that," Charlotte answered. "I was surprised when I could find only a few featured articles on you. And so, I don't think sitting down to interview you one-on-one is a good idea. You're not used to it, and you certainly don't seem to enjoy them. I also don't think it's advisable to plant one article about something positive that you're doing for the town, just for the sake of good press. People would assume you're just doing it for the positive attention, and not for the greater good. I think you need to do something a little different, something eye-catching, something people aren't *expecting* you to do."

Blake looked over at Greg, and then at his father. Charlotte could tell by his body language that he was a bit confused. Blake had been expecting a sit-down interview format. But she most definitely had his attention.

Greg sensed Blake's confusion and looked over at Charlotte, "What exactly are you proposing then?" he asked her.

Blake perked up, uncrossed his arms, and leaned forward. "Let's hear it."

One thing she had learned early on as a journalist was that the best way to gain someone's trust and attention was to give them what they wanted. She knew by the small number of one-on-one interviews Blake had done that he didn't like doing them. She needed another way of getting him to open up but in a less intrusive kind of way. He was an athlete, he liked to move around, he liked to do things. He wasn't the kind of guy who wanted to sit in an office talking about himself.

"It's the holiday season," Charlotte began. "Even though this will be my first Christmas in Barrington, I do know that this town goes all out for the season. I think you should consider taking this time to do some holiday good deeds for the town. Each week you could do something that we'd feature in the *Barrington View*, including photos and the impact it has on something or someone in the community. We tell why it was important to you to do whatever it is that you did that week, but we make it about the town, too, not just about you."

"You're proposing that the articles don't exactly focus on me then?" Blake asked.

"Yes, in a way... I mean, you want good press, and there's nothing like the holidays and good deeds to bring people together. We could showcase the great things you're doing, but not make it all about you. The good deeds would speak for themselves."

"Good deeds?" Blake asked. "Around town?"

"Yes," Charlotte nodded. "Together, we'd come up with a list of things that you could do for the people of the town. Maybe you surprise the teachers with a holiday lunch or organize a fundraiser for families in need. We can come up with a list that is meaningful to you, and then each week we run the article to show what you did, and why. The article would be published in the printed newspaper and online, and we'd make it available on social media, too. In addition, this would be good content for your social feeds."

Blake sat back in his seat, digesting everything Charlotte was saying. He had expected Frank to come to his house to discuss interview questions and talk about some additional good press that could be printed in the paper, but this idea came out of left field. He hadn't expected something creative like this, not to mention something that would run continuously for the few weeks he was home.

"What do you think, Blake?" Frank asked with a smile on his face, glancing from Charlotte to Blake. Charlotte had shared her idea with Frank beforehand, and he'd thought she had knocked it out of the park. He personally loved this angle and knew that it would be a big hit for the town. He also knew that everyone in town would be hoping that they would be lucky enough to be part of one of Blake's good deeds.

"I don't know about Blake," Ben Manor interrupted, "but I think it's genius. This would be an incredible way to give back to the town, but also to have repeated good press of a meaningful nature. The town would love something like this during the holidays."

Charlotte sat quietly, beaming inside, but trying her best to hold it in. She needed to play it cool; she didn't want to appear over eager. Blake didn't need to know how badly she needed him to agree to this idea. It would give her multiple interviews with him during the holiday season, which would certainly beef up her portfolio. She was annoyed that Blake was taking his time to respond. It was obvious he was thinking about it, but she couldn't get over his cockiness. He should be thankful that he had a team of people in front of him carefully orchestrating and thinking about his well-being. He was the one who got himself into this mess, and he should be thanking his lucky stars for people like Greg and his father.

"Blake?" Ben asked, looking at his son, waiting for him to respond. "What do you think?" Ben looked a little embarrassed as he waited for Blake to say something, anything.

Blake looked directly at Frank, "And you would get the final edit of the pieces, right?"

Frank nodded, "Nothing gets printed in my paper until I have read it and approved it."

Charlotte looked down at her notebook, wanting to fling it across the room at Blake. Did he think she would try to sabotage him? Or did he think this was her first rodeo when it came to writing a feature piece?

"I think this is the best route to take, Blake," Greg chimed in. "I told you that you need good press, and it can't get better than this. Do you know how many eyeballs will see these articles?"

"And it won't look odd that I suddenly decided to do these good deeds after being suspended?" Blake asked.

"People are going to be watching your next move, so you might as well make it a good one," Charlotte added quickly. "People will always talk. I'm sure you know that."

"Fine, I'm in," Blake breathed with a relieved tone. "I just want to make sure that I personally pick the things that I do for the town."

"Absolutely," Charlotte nodded with a smile, feeling like she had just won the lottery. This story was now in her hands, and she wouldn't mess it up. Her ticket to her future was in the palm of her hand. She couldn't wait to send her updated portfolio to the publication in New York that hadn't hired her.

"Great," Frank smiled, looking between Blake and Charlotte, "Why don't the two of you exchange contact information, or make a plan to meet up, so we can get moving immediately?" Then, speaking to everyone, he said, "Unfortunately, I've got to get going because of a deadline, but I appreciate the three of you making time for us today."

"Thanks, Frank," Blake said with a smile, reaching out to shake Frank's hand. He looked over at Charlotte who had packed up her things and was ready to leave. "Why don't we meet up tomorrow morning back here at the house, and we can start working on a list of ideas?"

"Sounds like a plan," Charlotte answered. "How's 9 am?"

"Works for me," Blake responded with a nod as he grabbed his phone to lock in the time.

Frank walked to the door with Greg and Ben, who were trying to eavesdrop on the conversation between Blake and Charlotte, but not having much luck. Greg looked over at Frank and whispered so only he and Ben could hear, "I'll give it to you guys, this is a great idea."

"I told you she was good," Frank responded with a knowing tone.

"I was impressed that she arrived knowing so much about him," Greg added. "Anyone who takes the time to watch and read all of his interviews deserves some props."

"She's thorough; even at her age, she's one of the best."

"Well, it shows," Ben smiled, looking over at Charlotte as she grabbed her tote bag and headed toward Frank.

"I mean, considering she didn't know who the hell he was when I gave her this assignment, makes me realize just how special she really is," Frank interjected as he opened the door to head outside.

Blake happened to catch what Frank had just said and looked up from his phone. Frank and Charlotte had disappeared out the front door, but Greg and his father stood there watching them leave. "Wait a second, did he just say she didn't know who I was?"

"He did," Ben Manor answered in disbelief, "and that just makes this a little more interesting."

11

Blake walked up the creaky steps to his childhood bedroom, wishing he were back in New York City, in his own space. As much as he loved being with his parents, he needed alone time. His bedroom had been his sanctuary as a kid and teenager. It was where he had dreamed big and wished upon every star in the sky to become better and better at football. A lot of his buddies in town didn't have the same set of pressures that he had growing up. He needed to make something of himself, not only as a ticket to get out of Barrington but to help his family. He hated seeing his parents work around the clock; constantly dealing with financial worries. It killed him that he wasn't able to do more as a teenager to relieve any of their stress, but if he had taken on a job, it would have taken him away from football. His father wouldn't hear of it, He knew Blake had something special, and he wanted that talent to shine.

Laying on his bed, thinking about the meeting, he couldn't get Charlotte Court out of his head. The second she left, he did a quick Google search on her. There were hardly any photos of her, just loads of articles she had written for the newspaper at the University of Rhode Island. He had felt blindsided at first when she'd shown up with Frank. He thought Frank was trying to pull a fast one on him. He was so used to people taking advantage of him for their own personal gains that he constantly had an extra guard up.

But there was something about Charlotte, He couldn't put his finger on it, and he couldn't deny the fact that he had been impressed with what he'd read about her online. She had been the editor of her college newspaper and had won numerous journalism awards at URI. She had written dozens of articles for the *Barrington View* and, from what he read, all were recent and well-written. She had written articles that centered around education reform and political issues for larger online publications. She seemed to interview a lot of local politicians and business owners. From what it looked like, she was more geared for a career at the *New York Times* or the *Boston Globe* than a small-town newspaper.

She even looked like she belonged in a big city; she came to the meeting in business attire, along with a leather tote filled with notebooks, folders, and papers. She had a serious air about her, almost stuffy. Her blonde hair was in a perfect twist, she wore hardly any makeup, and her pearl earrings and necklace made her appear a lot older than she was. She had graduated from college in May, making her about twenty-one or twenty-two, which surprised him. He thought she was older, just based on her appearance and demeanor. He wondered if she was the kind of girl who would ever let her hair down. There were so many go-getters in New York, so it was interesting to have one right here in town. She definitely impressed him, because she had nailed him to a "T."

"You mind if I come in?" Mary Manor asked from Blake's doorway, interrupting her son's thoughts.

"Hey, Mom," Blake smiled. "My door is always open."

"Don't say that," she laughed. "I know you don't mean that when you're at your place."

"Touché," Blake laughed in response. "How about this? My bedroom door at home is always open for you!"

"Much better," Mary said with a wink.

Mary sat down on the edge of the bed. "It's nice having you here. I can't tell you how many times I walk by your room and wish you were here," she said.

"It's weird being back, under the circumstances," Blake said with a shrug. "Not weird in a bad way, Mom... I don't want you to think that, it's just not where I thought I'd be right now during the season."

"I know," Mary nodded. "It's not where we thought you would be either, but sometimes life has a way of doing things that we don't expect."

"I guess so," Blake answered as he placed his cell phone on the nightstand.

"Look, I know your dad has already spoken to you, but I have something to say, as well." Looking him in the eyes she continued, "As your mom, I've always felt we had a special bond, and we've always been open and honest about things. I want you to know that I love you and I know, deep down, you are a wonderful person, a wonderful son, but you have disappointed me, and your dad, and your sister. Your behavior has been awful—we raised you better than that. It affects the family, and we have all had to cover for you. It has not been easy. You're twenty-five, Blake, an adult, and I, for one, expect more from you. I'm not going to speak of this again, but I want you to think about what I have said."

"Mom, I can't tell you how sorry I am. I haven't meant

to embarrass you guys. I was thinking about myself, but this suspension has made me realize I've acted like a damn fool. I promise you, I will do better." Blake hugged his mom in a long embrace. He was not going to make empty promises to the people most important to him. He needed to change.

Hoping to lighten the mood, Blake looked around his room and said, "Mom, I can't believe you haven't gotten rid of any of this stuff."

"Hey," Mary joked, "I could sell this stuff on eBay as a side hustle."

Blake burst out laughing. If there was one person he loved, it was his mother. She had always been honest with him and she had a great sense of humor. She always knew when to keep things light and fun.

"So, how did the meeting go?" Mary asked. Ben had said he thought it went well, and that there was a good plan in place for their son.

"Weren't you listening in the kitchen?" Blake teased.

"Oh, I tried," Mary said with a nod. "It's not that easy when people mumble!"

"Well, considering the woman who is writing the article didn't know who I was, let's just say I'm hoping for the best."

"Dad told me," Mary smiled. "You know, honey, contrary to popular belief, not everyone follows football."

"But you're not a journalist," Blake responded quickly. "I don't know, maybe it's better she didn't know who I was."

"Why's that?" Mary asked.

"Because people get weird around me, and sometimes they don't want to tell me the truth about things. She had no problem jumping right in and telling me exactly what she felt would be the best action to take with the feature. Normally people just back down."

"So she wasn't intimidated by *Blake Manor*. Is that what you're saying?" Mary winked.

"Makes me sound like an ass," Blake shrugged, "but yes."

"From what I know about her, she has a pretty extensive background in journalism. I love reading her articles in the *View*. She's new to town, but she brings a fresh breath of air to the paper."

"Oh, yeah?" Blake asked curiously.

"Contrary to popular belief, I don't live under a rock, Blake. It's a small town, people talk. I mean, I know it's not your fancy-schmancy New York City," Mary laughed, "but we have new things happening here, too."

"Fancy-schmancy New York City," Blake laughed.

"But, in all seriousness," Mary said, reaching out to touch her son's arm, "did you feel good about the meeting and the direction of the article?"

Blake nodded, "I do. I actually think everything Charlotte said was smart and made a lot of sense. She mentioned that she did a ton of research on me, and I've got to be honest... it showed. She picked up on the fact that I don't do many interviews. I didn't have to tell her that I hate doing them and that I don't trust anyone in the media. I know it kills Greg that I refuse so many of them, but it's just how I am. I'm literally only doing this for damage control. Being suspended has been like a death sentence to me."

"You know," Mary said, treading lightly. "I've wondered. Why the change in you over the last couple of years? You went from not going out at all, to being out almost every night. What happened? I mean, I remember your father telling you a couple of times when you first joined the team that you should go out and meet people, feel part of the team. You've done a complete 180."

Blake looked at his mom and wished he knew the exact

answer. He wasn't sure what the big switch was for him, but he knew it had happened somewhere along the way. "I don't know. I just know that it feels good to go out and have everyone give you the five-star treatment. I love it. I feel unstoppable, and on top of the world. It's the only way I can describe it."

Mary looked at her son and nodded her head, thankful for his candidness. "You know, you can channel that feeling in different ways." She didn't raise him to be disrespectful, rude, or spoiled, so it had been difficult to see so much about him like that in the news.

"I know, Mom," Blake responded. "I just haven't done it, and I promise, I plan to do it."

"So tell me, what exactly does Charlotte Court want you to do?" Mary asked, knowing that Blake was smart enough to know she'd had enough of his antics and behavior.

"She wants me to do good deeds for the town during the holiday season," Blake replied.

"Sounds interesting. What does she have in mind?" Mary asked.

"I think the plan is to do something every week, so that will make three or four articles altogether, depending on how long I'm here."

Mary smiled at Blake, "I like that idea, and I'm sure the town will be excited about it, too. Do you know what kinds of things you'll want to do? Do they have to be holiday-themed?"

Blake shook his head, "No... it doesn't seem like it. She's coming by tomorrow, and we're going to meet and discuss all of those details."

"For what it's worth, I think this will be really good for you. Not only for the press, but for you personally. It's been a while since you've been back home to enjoy the beauty and togetherness of this community. Nobody here has ever given up on you. We're your biggest fans!"

Blake nodded his head at his mother and smiled. "I know there's a piece of you that wishes I lived here in town with a wife and kids."

Mary laughed. "Hey, a mom can dream, right?"

"So you'd rather not have a professional football player as a son?" He asked with a laugh.

"Well... I didn't say *that*!" Mary laughed again. "You're a good boy, Blake. You always have been. I just wish the world knew the Blake Manor I know."

"Mom, my reputation isn't *that* bad."

"Yes, Blake, it is!" she said, shaking her head. "But I know that's not who you are. I just hope that you know that too. You've gone overboard with the fun for the last couple of years. I always worried it would catch up with you and cause something like this to happen."

"The suspension?" Blake asked, looking seriously at his mom.

"To be honest with you, yes. Either a suspension for a few games, or potentially traded to another team, or worse... kicked off the team."

"They can't do that, Mom. I'd have to do a hell of a lot worse."

"I'd say a three-game suspension is pretty bad, Blake. This is your *job*; it's not something to be taken lightly. I know things happened quickly for you, and it's tough to be fresh out of college and thrown into the spotlight... and suddenly have money. I just want you to know that I believe in you, and I only want the best for you. You just need to get back on track, or you risk losing everything you've worked for... everything *we've* worked for."

Blake knew she was right, and he didn't know what to

say. This was her way of setting him straight, and he knew that. He gave his mom another big hug. As he embraced her, he could tell she was crying.

"Are you crying, Mom?" Blake asked, pulling away to look into her eyes, and he had his answer. "Mom, don't cry. Everything will work out, I promise," knowing this situation was so much bigger than just him, and he needed to remember that.

"I just love you so much," Mary whispered. "You have a gift that millions of kids wish they had. I just don't want you to blow it."

The last person he ever wanted to disappoint was his mother. She had always been his biggest fan. There was something special about their relationship, they had always had an amazing bond. He knew she was there for anything, and that kind of comfort was priceless.

"Mom," Blake said softly. "I'm not going to blow it, OK? I promise you. Please don't worry."

"That's my job. I can't help it," Mary smiled, wiping away the tears.

"And I'm telling you that you don't have to worry, Mom," Blake said, rubbing her back. "I promise I'll fix all this shit in my life, in the press, and get back on my team."

"Use this opportunity with Charlotte," Mary said, wiping the tears away.

Blake looked at his mother and nodded. "I will... although, I have to say, she doesn't seem like the warmest person in the world, so I think the next few weeks are going to crawl by slowly."

"What do you mean she doesn't seem warm?" Mary asked.

"My gut reaction to her? She seems uptight and boring,

along with the fact that she seems to have something to prove."

"You got that all from one meeting?" Mary asked confused.

"Mom... if there's one thing I know, it's women."

12

"He's a total spoiled brat!" Charlotte shouted as she struggled to keep up with Lindsay as they rounded the final turn of the Barrington High School track.

"Come on," Lindsay shouted back as she panted. "He couldn't have been that bad."

"Oh, yeah?" Charlotte asked, trying to catch up. The only thing she could see was the back of Lindsay's red ponytail bouncing up and down, but she knew she could hear her. "He's where he is because he got suspended for his unacceptable bad behavior. If that doesn't have spoiled brat written all over it, I don't know what does."

"Well, my dad said the meeting went well," Lindsay said, letting Charlotte catch up for a second.

Charlotte adjusted her headband as she ran and grabbed her shirt to wipe her forehead. "Did he tell you that he hardly acknowledged me until your father gave me the floor? And even then, he didn't really say much until I finished my pitch."

"No, Dad didn't mention that," Lindsay answered. "But...

the most important part," she laughed as she ran along, "is that you've been noticeably quiet about how freaking hot he is."

Charlotte felt her body heat up for a split second as she thought about Blake but was able to push it away when she thought about his attitude. "He's not bad on the eyes."

"Not bad on the eyes, my ass!" Lindsay said loudly. "I know he's not your type at all, but he's one hell of a specimen. You've got to give me that."

"You're freaking crazy!" Charlotte laughed, as she tried to keep her pace up and not slow down.

"His body alone is built like a Greek god, but then add in those blue eyes, perfectly chiseled features, and brown hair that you just want to rake your fingers through..."

"Jeez, Linds... you need some water?" Charlotte joked.

"Just admit it," Lindsay laughed, looking over her shoulder at Charlotte.

"Yes, he's good-looking, in that athletic kind of way," Charlotte responded. "I mean... my God, it's his job to stay fit, so I'm not going to give him extra points for that. But yes, there's a reason women fall prey to his antics, and it's obvious that his looks play a huge part in that. He's a catch if you're attracted to guys like that, which I'm not."

"Well," Lindsay laughed again, slowing down so she could see Charlotte next to her. "He's obviously not *your* type."

"What's that supposed to mean?" Charlotte shot back.

"Look at Dylan. He's the polar opposite of someone like Blake. He's small..."

"He's not small, he's short," Charlotte interrupted.

"OK," Lindsay said with an eye roll. "He's short. He's blonde. He's not into sports. He's serious. He's more... I don't know..." Lindsay didn't want to say it, but she knew it was the only way to really describe Dylan.

"He's what?" Charlotte asked, knowing that Lindsay had something on the tip of her tongue.

"He's a good looking nerdy guy. There, I said it," Lindsay joked and stuck her tongue out.

"That's not a bad thing. I've always been attracted to the bookworm type over the jock. I've been like this my entire life," Charlotte answered.

"Yes, but can nerds be sexy in bed?" Lindsay asked.

Lindsay kept running, keeping a steady pace with Charlotte. She loved evening runs more than anything—they were so good for her body, mind, and soul. Running was her escape from stress, and she had strong-armed Charlotte into it a couple of months ago. She knew Charlotte needed something in her life to help burn off energy and stress. Running had always been the answer for her. It was nice to see Charlotte not only give it a try but stick with it.

"Oh my God..." Charlotte snorted. "Yes, of course, they can!"

"I'll take your word for it," Lindsay said.

"You should join me over the next few weeks with Blake. I have a feeling I'm going to need all the backup and help I can get. I just know he's going to be a cocky ass with me."

"Listen, I'm not trying to defend him, Char," Lindsay responded, "but remember, he doesn't even like the media. You said it yourself--he rarely does interviews. Not to mention, this entire thing is all about damage control."

"Which is why he should be a little bit more appreciative about what we're all trying to do for him," Charlotte shot back. "God... I spent so much time researching him, and football, and I freaking hate football!"

Lindsay let out a laugh, "Shows true dedication to your

craft my friend!"

Charlotte reached out and nudged Lindsay, "All I can say is that this had better freaking help my portfolio!"

It was a beautiful evening in December. The air even smelled cold, but they could not feel it yet. Except for the girl's high school soccer team that was practicing, the track was empty of runners. The one thing that Charlotte loved about Barrington was that the high school overlooked Narragansett Bay. Seeing the beauty of the water from the track calmed her soul. Pittsburgh wasn't a coastal area, so she never got to experience so much water, and see how much it influenced the community. The best way she could describe Barrington was that you felt like you lived in a Hallmark movie.

"So tell me, what's the plan now?" Lindsay asked as she picked up her pace a bit, trying to bring it in strong on the last lap.

Sensing Lindsay's shift in gear, Charlotte followed suit. "I'm coming up with a list of good deeds for him, just to make it easier. He said he wanted to pick them, but I have a feeling he's going to come up with nothing. I gave him some broad ideas this morning, but nothing concrete or detailed."

"Did he like any of them?" Lindsay asked.

"Oh, I don't know," Charlotte interjected. "He was in a mood today, so I didn't get too much from him. I want him to tell me what he wants to do but, as I said, I'll probably be prying it out of him. Thank God he's not suspended for more than three games. I don't know what the hell I would do if it was any longer!"

"Well, I'm anxious to see it all come to life. Dad was gushing about it, and you know he doesn't gush."

Charlotte smiled to herself as she pushed on to keep up with Lindsay. She loved knowing that Frank liked the angle of the article. She knew it was a gamble asking Blake to do more than one interview, but she knew if she masked the interviews with some good deeds, it wouldn't even come across as an interview.

"I hope it comes out the way I want it," Charlotte breathed. "For what it's worth, I think the town will love it."

As Lindsay and Charlotte rounded the last 1/4 mile of their last lap, they were both panting heavily, unable to speak. The second they crossed the line at the finish, they both slowed down to a walk, their hands above their heads, breathing in the crisp cold air.

Charlotte walked to a grassy area near the track and plopped down to stretch her legs. She watched as Lindsay slowly walked over and did the same thing. Charlotte learned the hard way what happened if she didn't stretch after a run; she wouldn't be able to walk the next day. As she watched Lindsay stretch, she also saw her take in a deep breath and exhale with a huge smile.

"Feeling good?" Charlotte asked, wondering why Lindsay was sitting there with a smile on her face.

"Yeah," Lindsay nodded. "There's nothing like this town. I feel so at home and at peace here. I can't explain it."

"You really do love this town, don't you?" Charlotte asked.

"I do," Lindsay nodded. "I feel proud to live here and make a difference, in some small way, with the *View*."

"Charlotte responded, "Even though my body and soul crave New York City, this place has grown on me big time," she smiled.

"We might be a small town, but we do have some pretty amazing people that have come from here, Blake Manor being one of them."

"Yes," Charlotte agreed with a shrug. "Amazing? I don't

know about that, the jury's still out. But talented on the football field? Yes."

"Lindsay laughed. "The good thing is that he's on board with the direction of the feature."

"Yeah, but I've still got to spend time with him," Charlotte said, rolling her eyes.

Charlotte stood up and walked toward where she had left her bag and water bottle. As much as she had come to the track with Lindsay, originally kicking and screaming, she had learned to love it. The extra benefit was that she noticed her body becoming extra toned with all the running. She had a body that stopped traffic, to begin with, not that she put it on display very often, but she loved seeing muscles start to pop up on her body.

She grabbed her phone and noticed she had a few missed calls and texts, one text being from Blake.

She turned to Lindsay and held up her phone, "Speaking of the devil, guess whose text I missed?"

"The man of the hour?" Lindsay smiled, walking over to grab her stuff, too.

"Even his texts are rude," Charlotte said looking down at the phone.

"Why? What does it say?"

"*9 am doesn't work for me anymore. 11 am is the only time I can make happen.*"

"You call that rude?" Lindsay asked, waiting to see if there was something else.

"Yes," Charlotte nodded. "He expects me to drop everything tomorrow for him at 11 am, but we had originally planned for 9 am. He's the one who agreed to the time."

"I don't know, Char," Lindsay said shaking her head, "I think millions of women would kill for a text like that from Blake Manor."

13

_____

Charlotte pulled up to the Manor residence at exactly 11 am on the nose. She had gone back and forth on what to wear, which was silly, she knew. She didn't care what Blake Manor thought of her, or her clothing, but she found herself looking in her mirror a few too many times. She wanted to make sure she looked professional, yet stylish, too. She decided on wearing her dark wash skinny jeans, navy blue double-breasted blazer with gold buttons over a white tank, and beige pointed-toe flats. Her hair was up in a top knot bun with a few strands down to frame her face. She always wore her hair up when she worked, to keep it out of her face because normally she was writing furiously as she interviewed people. She knew she didn't have the fashion style of Lindsay, who always seemed to make outfits look stylish and effortless, but she felt that she looked good.

The Manor home was an understated light blue colonial on a quiet street in Barrington. At the previous meeting, Charlotte hadn't had a chance to get a good look at it because she had been so nervous, but today was different.

She noticed that the house seemed a bit dated, which surprised her, because, with the size of Blake's contract, he could have torn the house down and rebuilt it.

As Charlotte walked up to the front door, she looked around and admired the view. It was a picture-perfect home for a family, much different from how she grew up. There were beautiful flowers planted along the front of the house, and pretty stepping stones leading to the backyard. One could tell a family lived here, and it gave her heart a tug because this was something she had dreamt of having as a kid.

As Charlotte was about to ring the doorbell, the front door opened abruptly, and there stood Mary Manor with a huge grin on her face. "You must be Charlotte!"

"Yes," Charlotte smiled. "And you must be Mrs. Manor. It's nice to meet you."

"Please call me Mary. Mrs. Manor makes me sound too old!" she laughed.

"Mary it is," Charlotte smiled. The first thing she noticed about Mary Manor was her smile. It was so welcoming and it lit up her face. She was on the taller side with short brown hair that fell to her shoulders. She was wearing a pair of brown corduroy pants with a denim shirt, a perfect winter outfit. She also smelled good, a mixture of vanilla and lavender.

"Come on in," Mary said, opening the door. "Blake's still working out, but he should be back soon."

"Soon?" Charlotte asked, trying not to give away her irritation.

"Yes, dear," Mary answered. "He went to the high school this morning to work out in the gym. His old high school football coaches are still at the school, so they opened up the gym for him to use while he's home.

They're going to help keep him in shape for the Skyscrapers."

Charlotte smiled at Mary, but in actuality wanted to scream. She had rearranged her entire morning to be here at 11 am. Did Blake think that he was her only priority? She had other weekly tasks waiting for her at the *View*. This is what annoyed her about celebrities and jocks like Blake-- they just assumed everyone else would bow down to their wants and needs.

"Do you happen to know how long he'll be? I only have until 12 pm to meet with him today. Unfortunately, I'm under deadline for another story, and I have some meetings to get to today."

"He should be here any minute. I called him about 10 minutes ago because he had mentioned that he had a meeting set up with you, and I didn't want this to happen. Blake seems to run on his own schedule sometimes, and it drives me crazy! He's been like this his entire life," Mary said, shaking her head. "I'm so sorry. Why don't you come in and sit down."

"Oh, it's not your fault," Charlotte responded as she walked over to their living room couch and took a seat next to Mary. She could tell Mary felt bad that Blake was late, and she didn't want to make her feel any worse. It wasn't Mary's fault that her son was disrespectful about other people's time. "While I have you," Charlotte said with a smile, "do you mind if I ask you a few questions about Blake? You know, before he gets home."

"What kinds of questions?" Mary asked with a hesitant smile.

"Just about Blake," Charlotte answered as she took out her notebook and pen. "It might be good for me to get your thoughts on things, too."

"Oh, I don't know," Mary said nervously. "I would hate to do this without my husband here. I'm so bad at things like this."

"At what?" Charlotte asked.

"Just at being interviewed," she laughed nervously.

"I promise," Charlotte said with honest eyes. "I'm not going to ask you anything too personal, and if you don't want to answer any question, you can just let me know. I actually hadn't planned anything like this, so we can just roll with it and see how it works out. Sound OK?"

Mary was still hesitant. She had learned a long time ago that whatever she said to the press could always be misconstrued or twisted. Blake had told her numerous times not to say anything to anyone about him, especially the media. She knew he meant more of the bigger publications, not so much the town paper, but she was still worried she would say the wrong thing.

"Oh goodness, Charlotte. I'm not sure," Mary said with concerned eyes.

Charlotte didn't want to push. She knew she could push someone like Blake if she needed to, which she might actually enjoy at this point, but she didn't want to push Mary. She seemed so sweet, and she didn't want to violate her trust.

"How about this," Charlotte said with a smile as she put her notebook and pen back into her tote bag. "Tell me how Blake got into playing football."

Mary immediately smiled and her eyes lit up. "Blake didn't start playing football until he was in seventh grade. In this town most kids play soccer, which is what we put Blake in when he was in elementary school," she laughed. "I could tell immediately that Blake wasn't made for the soccer field. He was always a little bit bigger than the other boys his age in height and stature. We didn't have the heart to tell him that his playing was so bad," she laughed out loud, remembering back.

"Aw," Charlotte added, seeing the love in Mary's eyes for her son.

"He kept at soccer until seventh grade when he had just turned thirteen. He complained the entire way home after a game, begging us to let him quit. We, of course, were fine with him quitting, but we didn't want him to quit and do nothing. We told him if he quit, he needed to start a new sport or another activity."

"And so he chose football?" Charlotte asked, nodding her head.

"Actually," Mary smiled, "he decided that he was going to start running. So, he asked my husband to take him to the high school every afternoon to run laps with him. That's when he discovered football. Or, actually... I should say, football discovered him."

"How so?" Charlotte asked, now intrigued by this story. She always thought someone like Blake must have been playing ever since being five or six.

"One day, the football coaches were working out with some of their players, and they saw Blake running laps and were impressed by his size. He'd always had the body of a linebacker, even in middle school."

"Wow," Charlotte said impressed. "So he was recruited in middle school to play for the high school team," she asked.

"In some ways, yes," Mary nodded. "The coaches saw a young boy running, but when they talked to Ben and heard his soccer backstory, they were impressed with his tenacity and determination not to give up. The second Blake heard they thought he'd make a good football player, was all he needed to hear, and he switched gears immediately."

"That's pretty incredible," Charlotte said, nodding her head. "Actually, I don't know anything about football, or sports in general. My parents were never into sports, so it wasn't something I grew up with, but hearing stories like this, and knowing where Blake went with it... it's pretty remarkable."

"I think it's a good story," Mary smiled. "From the time they handed him a football, that was it. It was what he was meant to do. He was strong enough to tackle just about anybody. He could throw a ball further than anyone on the team, even in seventh grade! And he began to really learn about the game. He became obsessed with it, which was good in a way because we all had to learn the game, too!"

"That's funny," Charlotte smiled, liking Mary more and more by the minute. Just by being with her, Charlotte could tell Mary was a kind woman with a warm heart. She reminded Charlotte in many ways of her own mother, and it made her heart beat a little faster just to feel that small connection with this woman.

Charlotte was jolted from her thoughts by a slam of the door, "I know I'm late!" was all she heard from the front of the house.

"Guess who's home?" Mary winked. "We're in here, Blake!"

Blake came barreling around the corner still sweaty and dressed in his workout clothes. Charlotte could feel her heart come to a startling halt at the sight of his glistening sweaty body. His dark hair was soaking wet, and so were his clothes. You could see the outline of his chiseled chest, his tee-shirt plastered to his body.

"Oh my God," Mary said, shaking her head. "You're a

mess!"

Blake took his shirt off and wiped the sweat from his hair and head. Charlotte wasn't sure if he was trying to prank her or not, because it looked like a soft porno film was being shot in his family living room as he started to undress.

"Blake! I don't want sweat dripping all over my living room carpet! Are you kidding me?" Mary shouted. "Go upstairs and change. You stink, too!"

"Can you give me five minutes to shower?" Blake asked looking directly at Charlotte.

"She needs to leave by noon, so hurry up!" Mary chimed in, looking at her son with an irritated mom look. "I can't believe you're this late. It's after 11:30!"

Charlotte collected herself from seeing Blake Manor half-naked in front of her, and just nodded her head. She didn't want him to know that his naked chest had distracted her. A professional journalist didn't get distracted from her story, she reminded herself.

"Please don't hold this against him," Mary said, looking at Charlotte with concerned eyes. "He really needs this article right now."

Charlotte saw, for the first time, the worry in Mary's eyes. The impact of Blake's behavior hadn't just impacted Blake; it was also affecting his mother. She knew that she didn't know what it was like to be a mother, or even what it felt like to have a mother worry about you, but a mother's love was always a mother's love. She could sense the unknown in Mary's eyes, and even in her voice.

"I won't, Mary," Charlotte said, reaching out her hand to touch Mary's. Mary Manor was a wonderful woman, it was obvious, but she couldn't become attached to this story, not one bit. She wasn't a Blake fan, and she knew she wouldn't become one, but his mom was a different story.

14

As Blake left the living room to go shower, Mary had to call her daughter, which left Charlotte sitting in the living room by herself. She couldn't help but be a bit nosey, so she took the opportunity to walk around and check out the photos on the shelves and hanging on the walls. Growing up, her mom and dad never had family photos on display. All of their living room shelves, tables, and nooks, and crannies were filled with books. That's what happened when you grew up as the daughter of two academics.

Charlotte loved her upbringing, but it wasn't until she started to visit friends' houses in middle school and high school that she noticed how different her family life had been. She found herself wishing that her mom and dad had added more personal touches throughout their home, just like here in the Manor home.

She walked over to the mantle and smiled as she looked at photo after photo of the Manor family. There was a photo of Ben and Mary on their wedding day, a photo of Mary holding a baby boy, and one of her holding a baby girl.

There were framed school photos of Blake and his sister, and family photos of them throughout the years. She smiled, thinking that if she had children of her own, these were the things she'd want to do. She had long forgotten how much she yearned for these simple kinds of traditions.

"And... I'm back! In just under ten minutes," bellowed a voice behind her. "Not bad if I do say so myself."

Charlotte turned around to find Blake dressed in a white tee-shirt and jeans that had a relaxed, distressed fit. He looked like a Calvin Klein model standing there, but that was something she would never admit to Lindsay.

Trying to be as professional as she could, and not allow herself to be bothered by his appearance, she replied, "I only have about twenty minutes, so let's try to get through what we can."

"You can't stay a little longer?" Blake asked. "I don't know how much we're going to get done in twenty minutes."

"Well," Charlotte said, finding herself getting agitated, "I was here at 11 am, ready to work."

"I can't help it if people want to grab an autograph, or take a photo with me," Blake responded with a smile.

"You could if you told them you had a meeting at 11," Charlotte lobbed back at him with a smirk.

Blake wasn't used to anyone but his parents, sister, or Greg giving him direct pushback on stuff. He could tell she was annoyed at his tardiness, but he wasn't about to disappoint some of the high school students who had waited for him to be done with his workout to say hello and introduce themselves.

"I guess we'll just try to get done what we can in the next twenty minutes then," Blake said dryly, trying to make eye contact with Charlotte as she took out her notebook and pen.

"Sounds like a plan," Charlotte answered back, still not looking up at Blake. She gathered her things and opened to a page that was filled with a bunch of notes. "I know that you understand the direction of the articles, and where we want to go with them, but for now we need to come up with some good deed ideas that you can do around town."

"I want to do something for the high school, I know that," Blake jumped in.

"OK... what do you want to do?" Charlotte asked, looking up at Blake for the first time since she sat down.

"What do you mean?" Blake asked, sounding confused.

"Well, what do you want to do for the high school? Do you have an idea for a good deed that you could do there?"

"Well," Blake said, feeling a little stupid that he hadn't actually thought of a specific idea. "I, ugh... I'm not sure. I just know that the high school really shaped me, and I would love to give something back to them."

Charlotte sat there, realizing she was going to have to help Blake figure out some solid ideas.

"Do they need anything at the high school?"

"Yeah, turf," Blake laughed, "but I can't make that happen."

"Turf—you mean like grass?" Charlotte asked, jotting it down in her notes. "Why couldn't something like that happen?"

"You don't know what turf is?" Blake laughed. "Come on, you're putting me on."

Charlotte shook her head, "No, Blake, I'm not putting you on. I can assure you I know as much about football as you probably know about the symphony."

"Ouch!" Blake shouted. "I don't know if that was necessary."

"I'm just saying, don't assume everyone knows everything there is to know about football. There are people in this world who care about things other than the game of football."

"Hey," Blake said, looking at Charlotte, annoyed. "I'm not trying to be a dick here. And, for the record, just like you did some research on me, I did a little Google research on you, and I already know you don't know much about football. OK?"

"You Googled me?" Charlotte laughed.

"Yeah," Blake answered. "Listen... Greg and my dad might trust you, and Frank, but you've got my reputation in your hands, and I don't want just anyone writing about me. I've got a lot riding on this."

Charlotte looked at Blake and nodded her head, thinking back to Mary and her plea. "I know you do, and I'm trying my best to make it work. There's going to be a little bit of a learning curve for me because I don't know much about football, but I do know about journalism. I'm up for the challenge."

Blake looked at Charlotte as she lowered her head and started jotting something else in her notebook. He didn't know what he'd done to piss her off so much or annoy her, but it seemed clear that she wasn't his biggest fan. Not by a long shot. He didn't want her hating him. After all, he was going to be spending a lot of time with her over the next few weeks. He just wished she wasn't so buttoned up. He was used to women falling prey to his powers and kowtowing to everything he said. She was different. He could already tell she was nothing like any woman he'd been with.

"Listen, turf is made of synthetic fibers that are designed to look like natural grass. Professional football fields are turf fields. It's easier than maintaining natural grass, and everything that goes along with it. The problem is that turf is super expensive, and there's no way it can be done in a week."

Charlotte looked up at Blake and locked eyes with him. "Thank you," she said with a smile.

Blake noticed her blue eyes as she looked at him. He recognized the color because it was the same color blue as his. Not deep blue, not light blue, perfectly in the middle. Charlotte was an attractive woman in a natural way. She didn't wear makeup, or dress in a sexy way; she was more of a classic beauty with perfectly proportioned features.

"OK, so that answers my question about why it can't be done. Is there anything else that you think the high school might like or need? Maybe something for the sports teams since you're one of their most famous athletic alumni?"

"Most famous?" Blake laughed. "Who else would there be?" He watched Charlotte struggle for a second to answer the question. He was a ballbuster, he knew it, and he didn't want to be a total dick, but he couldn't help it on this one. He knew she had lobbed that little piece at him as a jab.

"OK, fine..." Charlotte said, putting up her hands in the air and laughing, knowing she had been caught. "In any case, is there anything you think the sports teams could use?"

Blake sat back in his seat and put his hands behind his head. He had walked through the entire high school this morning with his old football coaches. He had graduated seven years ago, so it wasn't like he had been gone for a long time, but long enough not to know what they needed. He thought back to his school tour, and he couldn't help but think about the fitness center, and how it could use a bit of a refresh. He had used much of the equipment this morning to work out, and much of the equipment had been there since he was a student. He noticed that the weight room could use more free weights, for one thing.

"You know," Blake said, feeling a bit inspired. "The fitness center could use a few things. Maybe that's the first thing I do."

"Oh," Charlotte said, perking up and caught off guard by Blake's good idea. "That's a good one. Was the fitness center a place you used a lot as an athlete?"

Blake smiled and thought back to his early days of weightlifting. "Yeah, I spent hours in there as a teenager." The fitness center had been his home away from home. His coaches had even given him his own key. He would lift with his teammates, but when they all went off to a party, or head out on dates, he would stay back to lift more, or run on the treadmill, or do some cycling. He always felt safer tucked away in the gym at the high school, rather than at parties or on dates.

"Well, that sounds perfect for this first holiday good deed for the community," Charlotte agreed as she jotted away in her notebook. "The high school was where you lifted and worked out?"

"Yes," Blake nodded. "My parents didn't have the money for me to join a gym or anything like that. The high school gym was a free place for me to work out, and it was perfect."

Charlotte looked up at Blake and then at her notes. Lindsay had told her about Blake's back-story, and how his parents had worked so hard to give him and his sister everything. She wanted to get more out of Blake about his upbringing, but she didn't want to push, not yet. She needed him to trust her, and they weren't there yet. She jotted down a bunch of notes, including finding out more about Blake's modest beginnings.

Noticing that it was a bit after 12 pm, Charlotte sat up

quickly and began to pack up her things. "I've got to run. I'm going to be late for an interview, and I'm under deadline for it. Now that we know the first good deed, we can get rolling with it and begin outlining the next one. We've got to keep them moving."

"With one quick call to Greg, I can have him organize the new equipment and weights for the high school," Blake said. "I'll donate around $10,000 worth of stuff, and I know I can get a good discount, which will allow me to purchase a good amount of equipment."

Charlotte nodded, completely oblivious to this world of money and status. She would kill for $10,000 right now to pay off some of her student debt, and not feel like she needed to work herself into the ground. It killed her to realize that spending $10,000 was no big deal for him. She had just started working three nights a week at a local restaurant for the extra cash. She was desperately trying to put money aside for her eventual next big move, and this was the only way she could do it.

"Sounds good," Charlotte nodded as she packed up her final things. "I'm sure the school will love it." As Charlotte walked toward the door she tripped, but thankfully caught herself from falling flat on her face. "Oh my God, that was close!" She gushed, her cheeks were red, obviously embarrassed.

"You OK?" Blake asked, coming up behind her.

"Yes, yes... I'm fine," Charlotte quickly answered, hoping that she hadn't twisted her ankle. "Please tell your mother it was wonderful meeting her."

Blake knew she was in a rush to get to an interview, but he couldn't help feeling bad that he had held her up. "Hey, Charlotte, for what it's worth, I'm sorry I was late."

Charlotte turned toward Blake at the door and cocked

her head to the side with a smile, "Well, what do you know, Blake Manor knows how to apologize," she winked and with that, she slammed the door shut.

Blake laughed out loud and said to himself, "What do you know, she actually has a sense of humor."

15

Charlotte was furiously typing away on her laptop at work and didn't notice Frank walk by her desk. He admired Charlotte's work ethic and knew that she worked harder than two people put together. She had a fire in her belly that couldn't be manufactured. You either had that kind of grit and determination, or you didn't. There was no in-between.

"What has your head down typing today?" Frank asked curiously. She had already hit her deadline, so he wasn't sure what else she had up her sleeve. "Already feeling inspired with our celebrity in town?"

"Not yet," Charlotte smiled, "I'm working on something, but this has nothing to do with Blake Manor. This is my first feature with one of the school principals. I'm starting with Joe Hanover from Barrington High."

"Oh, yes, great guy," Frank said, nodding. "I think the parents in this town are going to love those highlights."

"Me, too," Charlotte smiled. "I've included some really interesting things, things you'd never expect from a principal."

"Oh, yeah," Frank said curiously, "like what?"

"For starters, he's an avid guitarist who plays every Saturday night at clubs around the state. How cool is that?"

"That's pretty nifty. I didn't know that. I never would have pegged him as a musician."

"He also has eight tattoos, and he said I could include that detail in the article," Charlotte said, pleased as can be.

Frank laughed. He didn't know how she did it, but Charlotte definitely had a way of getting people to open up and share details about their personal life. She had a soothing way about her that put people at ease. "So, tell me, how did it go this afternoon with Blake?" Frank asked.

Charlotte looked up and smiled at Frank, "He was forty minutes late, so that should give you a good indication."

"Shit," Frank said, as he leaned against Charlotte's desk. "Are you kidding me? Where the hell was he?"

"He was working out at the high school. Apparently, he was mobbed by fans when he was leaving and didn't want to turn down any autographs or photo ops."

"So did you get anything?" Frank asked, hoping for a positive answer. He didn't want this to be a total pain in the ass for Charlotte.

"I did," Charlotte nodded. "I didn't get much from him, but I got some great stuff from Mary."

"Mary?" Frank asked. "His mom?"

"Yes," Charlotte smiled. "She's lovely. She sat with me the entire time I waited for Blake to get home. She wasn't comfortable with me asking her direct questions, so I put my pen away and just let her talk."

"About what?" Frank asked.

"She told me how Blake got started with football. You know, he only started in seventh grade? I suspect most people probably think he's been playing his entire life. He started a bit late, and only got serious about it in high school."

"Interesting," Frank nodded with a smile. "It's good to have that kind of info on the back burner. Shows that he really is a true talent, and not someone who was created by camps and a lifetime of playing."

"He also decided on his first good deed, which I think is a great one to start with."

"What's that?" Frank asked curiously.

"He's going to donate $10,000 worth of equipment and weights to the fitness center at the high school. This will directly benefit the students, and it naturally makes sense for him."

"I like this one, the town will go crazy over it," Frank answered.

"I need to hash out the exact details, including when they're going to surprise the school with it, but this idea is set in stone. Blake is going to work out the details with his agent, and get moving on it immediately."

"Stay on him," Frank urged, "I want this to run in next week's paper. Can we fast-track it that quickly?"

"I can ask him," Charlotte began, "we don't need the school to have all of the new equipment and weights in place to run the story, do we?"

Frank scratched his head and shrugged his shoulders. "I'd like to get photos to run along with the piece, so if it's possible, yes. I'd like to make sure everything is in place for the kickoff of this feature."

Charlotte grabbed her "Blake notebook" and opened it up to her notes. She added a note to ask Blake how long it would take for everything to happen. Her notebooks were her saving grace. She constantly used two or three note-books, but since she knew that Blake was going to be taking up so much of her time, she bought one just for him. She already had about ten pages of notes and ideas.

"I'd stay on him, Charlotte. I have a feeling Blake's going to be a little scattered about this. It is important for him, but I also have a feeling he's dealing with a ton of other things, too. I got the impression the other day that some of his sponsorship deals have been impacted by his suspension."

She nodded her head and rolled her eyes. "I don't want to sound unsympathetic, but I have the impression he seems to think the world revolves around him. I hope I'm wrong, but he didn't even apologize for being late for our meeting until I was leaving."

"He's a good kid, Charlotte. You'll see."

Charlotte looked up at Frank, "I don't know, Frank. You know him better than I do."

"Give him a chance and don't be so quick to judge, at least not yet. You need to be impartial, right?"

"Yes, but you get the final edit," she laughed. "You know I can't write anything horrible."

"I'm not asking you to lie, but I am saying to give him a chance. Let your guard down, too. Your best writing comes when you're passionate about what you're writing about."

"Well, I can assure you I'm not passionate about Blake Manor or football," Charlotte interjected.

"You know what I mean," Frank chuckled. "I've seen you do your best work when there's a piece of yourself in the story. Find a way to connect with him."

Charlotte stared at Frank, not sure what to say. She had nothing in common with Blake Manor; there *was* no common ground. He was rich, she was not. He was a celebrity, she was not. He had a family who adored him, she was on her own. He commanded attention and praise, she preferred the background. He partied like it was his last day on earth, and she didn't party at all.

"You know that's not going to be easy for me?" she asked.

"I have faith in you," Frank nodded. "Why don't you have him meet you here tomorrow. I'll clear the conference area for a couple of hours, and you can work through your questions and notes with him."

"That's not a bad idea," Charlotte agreed. "Be good to have him on my *turf*. Which, by the way, I just learned about today. Turf is fancy grass!" she laughed. "Can you tell me this, Frank? The high school needs turf, but he seemed to think it would be difficult to do for the high school. Do you know why?"

"Oh, jeez. The price tag alone would be killer. I can't believe you didn't know what turf was," he laughed.

"Well, I do now!"

"My advice to you is to grab a book on football and learn a bit about the game. You're someone who loves to research, so learn as much as you can."

"I already did research on Blake," Charlotte said. "Why learn about the game? This isn't about the game of football, it's about Blake."

"You know about him, yes. But it might help to know a little bit about the actual game of football. What position he plays. How the game is played. Why he is so valuable as a player. I'm not telling you to become an expert; I'm just suggesting you learn a thing or two. Start finding common ground."

"Can common ground be that I know the name of the Pittsburgh football team?" Charlotte winked.

"That's a start," Frank laughed. "And do yourself a favor. Finish this piece and get the heck out of here. It's almost 8 pm."

Charlotte looked at her watch and shook her head. "Oh my God, I didn't know it was that late."

"I saw your lights were on," Frank shared as he lifted himself off Charlotte's desk. "Give yourself the gift of going home and unwinding. Seems like, after the day you've had, you deserve it. We're going to start getting inundated with holiday requests for the paper, so when you can catch up on rest, take my advice and do it."

Charlotte smiled and looked back at her laptop. She had a few more sentences to write, and then she would call it a day. She knew tomorrow night she'd be working at the Irish Pub, and she wouldn't have time to catch up then.

She grabbed her phone and searched for Blake's number. She would text him about their next meeting. She liked the idea of having him on her turf, and not his own. She smiled to herself as she typed, "*I have time tomorrow at 10 am. I suggest we meet me at the View offices off of Maple Avenue.*" She looked at it once more and bit her lip. She wanted the ball to be in her court, and make sure he knew that she called the shots, too. She normally wouldn't send a text like this, especially one that wasn't overly friendly. She liked to use emojis and exclamation points. This one had none of that. She closed her eyes, took a deep breath, and hit send.

Within a few seconds, she heard her phone ding and she looked down. "I can be available at 11 am. See you tomorrow."

She rolled her eyes and tossed her phone to the side. One thing was for sure; Blake Manor definitely knew how to make her blood boil and, for some reason, she kind of liked it.

16

———

Walking into Barrington High School still seemed surreal to Blake. It was like going back in time because not much had changed, but he had. The school looked the same inside. The same hallways, lockers, restrooms. The football field was the same. Even a majority of the teachers were the same. It wasn't that Blake hadn't liked high school; it had always been a means to an end. It was a necessary evil. He had never been a great student so, academically, he'd struggled. It was football that made high school memorable for him. There was nothing like hearing the chant of your name from the stands. There was nothing like having the popular kids give you five in the hallways and look out for you. Playing football in high school allowed him to believe he could be someone someday, and he never forgot it.

"There he is," a booming voice shouted behind him.

Blake didn't have to turn around in the school parking lot to know it was his old head football coach, John Gorman. He'd know that voice anywhere.

"You back for more?" Coach taunted.

Blake stopped, turned around, and laughed, "You think you can beat me down that quick?"

Coach Gorman was the one who had spotted Blake running laps when he was thirteen years old. He'd known by the sheer size and build of him that he needed to try football. He didn't have many big, athletic-looking kids on his team, so when he found out that Blake was still a year or more from heading into high school, he kept his eyes on him. He was the one who had encouraged Blake to get into Pop Warner football. He knew that if he was going to play in high school, he'd need to get used to being dressed in pads and know what it felt like to tackle the shit out of someone. He didn't want Blake showing up to practice in high school never having played a day of tackle football in his life. You could work on technique and skill work, but knowing what it felt like to run in full pads and go after another kid on the field couldn't be practiced enough.

"I don't know," Coach Gorman joked. "You seemed a little soft to me yesterday on some of the drills I was giving you."

Greg was currently trying to find Blake a trainer to work with him every day but, in the meantime, Coach Gorman was more than pleased to step in. He knew football training better than most professional football coaches.

"I will give you that," Blake said, touching his arms. "My body hasn't hurt like this in a long time."

"They not working all your muscles there?" Coach Gorman asked, surprised.

"It's more specialized-type training during the season," Blake answered. "I've got to keep my body moving, but I don't want to overdo it."

"It's a good thing you have a few weeks, then," Coach

answered. "I'll be helping you out, so when you're ready to go back, you'll be ready for anything coming."

Blake shrugged his shoulders in agreement. "You're the boss."

"Is your agent still trying to find someone to come here for the next few weeks to train with you?"

"Yeah," Blake nodded as they walked into the school and headed toward the fitness center. "It's been a little tough. He had one guy all lined up, but he had to back out due to a client conflict. So, he's still searching."

"I'm more than happy to step in as long as you need me," Coach said as he slapped Blake on the back. "My door is always open, I hope you know that."

"Thanks, Coach. That means a lot."

"Hey," Coach Gorman said, looking over at Blake. "I hope I'm not overstepping, but I feel like it's my duty to say something because you're one of the finest players I've coached, and you mean something to me."

Blake smiled, knowing where this was going.

"I'm not going to keep it at, but I do want to say this to you. There are kids that walk these hallways who want to be the next Blake Manor. Because of you, they think it's possible. Your personal life is your personal life, but take ownership over the fact that kids look up to you, whether you want them to or not. Just remember that, OK? I know it sucks being suspended but think of this as a reset, and a new beginning. This is when people will see what you're really made of. Got it?"

Blake looked at Coach Gorman and nodded his head, "Got it."

"Good, because I actually have some kids in the gym this morning, so be ready for a bit of fandom coming down on you."

"Oh, shit," Blake laughed. "How many are we talking? Am I going to be able to get a workout in?"

"I told them to leave you alone. These are guys who are conditioning right now for next Fall. You know I like kids to be committed all year," he smiled. "Word got out yesterday that you were here lifting and doing some training drills with me. You know teens and social media. One kid posts something online, or some stupid shit like that, and they all know."

"Tell me about it," Blake said, looking over at Coach with a knowing glance.

"Yeah, you live in a fishbowl. I don't know how you do it. I'm surprised you don't have people following your every move while you're back here in town."

As they walked toward the fitness center, Blake stopped in his tracks. There had to be about thirty guys standing at the doors waiting for him, and as soon as they spotted him, all he could hear were whispers. They were all dressed in workout clothes, anxiously waiting for Coach to unlock the doors. It reminded Blake of high school and working out with his team. He hadn't kept in super close touch with any of the guys from his high school football team due to being so laser-focused in college on football. He had tried here and there, but his buddies didn't understand the regimen and rigorous training he was doing. But seeing these guys made him wish he had a close buddy or two right now to hang out with. For all intents and purposes, even though the football world was watching him, he felt more alone than ever.

"Gentlemen," Coach Gorman nodded.

A sea of deep hello's erupted from the group of guys. Blake was only twenty-five years old and young by any standard, but these guys looked like kids to him. He was looking at each and every one of them; it was crazy to think that this was the age where football started to change everything for him.

"I'm sure you've all heard of Blake Manor," Coach announced, motioning to Blake. "He's home over the holidays and will be in here training with me from time to time. I don't want anyone bothering him. He's here to work, not play. Got it?"

The group of boys nodded their heads and looked over at Blake. He wasn't sure if he should say anything. They all seemed to be expecting him to do something, but he wasn't sure exactly what it was that he should say or do.

"Nice to meet you guys," Blake announced loudly.

"Before I open these doors," Coach shouted, looking around at the players, "anyone have any questions for Blake? Because once these doors open, it's go time. No talking. No pictures. No social media. Nothing. Got it? I'm not having that shit done on my time."

Blake saw a hand go up in the back, but he couldn't see the kid's face.

"Yeah, you got a question, Alex?" Coach asked.

"Yeah," a voice from the back answered. "I have a question for Blake."

"Sure, what is it?" Blake asked, wishing he could see what the kid looked like.

"How long did you play football before high school? Coach said you started on the late side."

Blake heard a few of the guys laugh after the question was asked, and it reminded him of his soccer days. The guys on his team used to love ribbing him whenever he asked a question.

"You guys mind moving, so I can see who I'm talking

with?" Blake asked, annoyed that none of them had the sense to do it.

"Shorty has a question," a booming voice came from the back, which caused all the guys to start laughing.

As the boys moved, Blake locked eyes with a young kid in the back. He was definitely on the short side but looked stocky and built. He might not be able to attack a 6'6" guy coming at him, but maybe he could run a football down the field in record time.

"You just start playing?" Blake asked, feeling bad for the kid.

"Yeah, I'm a freshman. I only started playing last year."

"Were you doing something else?" Blake asked, wondering if the kid had a similar story to his own.

"No," the kid said quietly. "I had to wait for high school."

"Were you ready for it?" Blake asked with a smile.

"Yes, sir," the kid said politely.

"You like it?" Blake asked. He could see the guys rolling their eyes at the kid, and it made Blake feel even more badly for the kid. He respected any kid who had the balls to speak up and ask a question. He knew that not everyone had that kind of guts.

"Yeah," the kid nodded with a smile. "I love it."

"That's what matters. If you love something you can put all of yourself into it."

"Is that what you did?" the kid asked, which made Blake smile because he could tell the kid was listening and really wanted to know.

"Coach found me when I was in seventh grade, and gave me a chance. He's the one you need to impress and work hard for every single day. He's got the tools to make you better and better. That's what he did for me. He encouraged me to try the local Pop Warner league for kids in town right before high school. If he sees something in you, he's not going to let you back down. He's going to keep pulling everything he can out of you."

"Were you good right away?" the kid asked, still causing some of the other guys to chuckle.

Blake looked over at Coach, "Maybe I should let Coach Gorman answer that one for you."

Coach Gorman laughed. "You want me to be honest, or bull shit you?"

"Honesty has always been your best trait," Blake joked, which caused the guys to laugh in unison.

"You didn't know left from right, or right from left, when you started, but you had a natural ability that you don't find too often. You also were open to listening and doing what you were told. You can't fake work ethic. You can't fake someone giving 120%. Every single time you stepped onto this field you gave all of yourself to the sport. That's what made you different, and that's what made you shine. Also, Blake didn't get caught up in the normal high school crap of partying, girlfriends, and wildness," Coach said looking at Blake with a wink.

Blake smiled back at Coach Gorman and looked back into the group for the kid, "Hey... what's your name?"

"Me?" the kid said, almost shocked that Blake was asking.

"Yeah," Blake nodded. "What's your name?"

"I'm Alex, sir," the kid answered.

"I'll tell you what, Alex, why don't you partner up with me today in the gym? We'll push each other. Sound good?"

Blake looked over at Coach Gorman who nodded at him with a discreet smile. The group of boys quickly became stone silent, and you could have heard a pin drop. Nobody expected Blake to do something like that, not for a random kid, and not for Alex.

Just as walking into a crowded club in New York City and having everyone scream your name gave Blake a sense of satisfaction, he felt the exact same way by helping this kid.

17

"I know I'm late," Blake said loudly as he walked into the conference room of the *Barrington View* offices, and saw Charlotte working away at her laptop. She had her notebook out in front of her, along with a pen and a bunch of clipped articles. Her hair was up again, this time in a ponytail, and she was wearing brown tortoiseshell glasses that he hadn't seen before. She was wearing a yellow crewneck sweater, which seemed to at least, brighten the room. As much as he was hoping it reflected her attitude today, he couldn't help but notice how pretty she looked just sitting there.

"Just wondering, do you own a phone?" Charlotte asked with a hint of irritation as she looked up. Blake was still dressed in his workout clothes, obviously showing that he had come directly from the gym.

"You know I do," Blake said, flashing a smile, as he held his phone up.

"So you do have the ability to text or call to say that you're going to be late?"

Blake smiled, enjoying this little banter from Charlotte

as he sat down in a chair one over from her. "OK... I get it. I've been late two days in a row. I know it's bad. Let me say sorry now to save any hostility on your end."

"Honestly, it's just rude, Blake," Charlotte said, looking him directly in the eyes. "I was only able to clear a few hours this afternoon for you, and now you're an hour late. I know you don't have plans going on, but I have a job to do and, contrary to what you might think, you're not the only story I'm working on."

Seeing that Charlotte appeared a bit more pissed than yesterday, he felt bad that he was late, but he got talking with the kid, Alex, whom he had worked out with. That kid probably got in trouble, as well, because they were only supposed to be in the fitness center for an hour, and Alex was with him for over three. Blake did find out Alex hadn't played any sports before high school because his parents didn't have the extra money to pay for them. They didn't want people in town finding out about it and giving him charity, so they just told him that he needed to wait until high school when sports and equipment would be free. It broke Blake's heart to hear this because the story was so familiar. He had spent extra time with Alex talking about football and sharing his own personal story. He normally didn't talk about his family's struggle with money, but he felt Alex needed to hear it. There was something about Alex that reminded him of himself; he felt a kinship with him.

"I'm sorry, Charlotte. I got caught up at the high school talking with a student."

"Before or after your workout," Charlotte shot back, motioning to his clothing.

"OK, I can tell you are pissed. What do I need to do to make up for it? Do you want coffee? Do you want a new laptop? You want a new car?" He thought maybe joking would calm her down.

But instead, Charlotte looked up at Blake and began to laugh. He had caught her off guard with the car comment, and it broke the ice a bit.

"I just ask that you be respectful of my time," Charlotte said, looking at him and playfully tossing a pen at him.

"OK, respectful of your time. That I can do," Blake smiled back at Charlotte.

"Do you always throw money at problems? Because, sure, I could use a new car. Mine is running on borrowed time, but I wouldn't dream of taking advantage of you that way." Then she looked at her notes. Clearly, the conversation was over.

Blake could tell he had slightly smoothed things over with her. He didn't want her pissed because that wouldn't be good for either one of them. She was actually smiling more today, and he liked getting a glimpse of what happiness look liked on her. And, he couldn't get over how pretty she looked today.

"So, where do we begin today?" Blake asked, ready to get going. After being at the high school this morning with the kids, he was extra excited about the surprise gifting of the equipment and weights.

"We need to see if we can fast-track your first-holiday good deed," Charlotte said, grabbing her notebook and flipping to a blank page. "And that's a direct order from Frank, not from me. He wants this story in next week's paper, which means we have about six days to make it happen. Is that *remotely* doable?"

Blake looked at her confused, "What do you mean doable?"

"Well, Frank would love photos to go along with each

article. I know it's asking the impossible, but is there any way you would be able to get moving on this? Even if we could get one piece of new equipment in there, we could grab some photos for the paper."

"It's happening on Friday," Blake said, looking directly at Charlotte. "Everything's set."

"How do you mean?" Charlotte asked.

"Greg made it happen. After you left yesterday, I called him and he got the ball rolling. He wants this good press more than I do! He called me last night to let me know that everything's a done deal, and everything will be delivered on Friday afternoon! I talked to Coach today on the QT, and he almost started crying. This donation means a whole lot to him, and to the school. They're going to rename the fitness center, the '*Blake Manor Fitness Center*' which I said was too much, but he wouldn't hear of it."

Charlotte sat speechlessly. She didn't know what to say. She had expected Blake to drag his feet a bit, but she had been wrong. He hadn't had to do the heavy lifting himself, but he had got the job done, and she was shocked.

"OK... " she said softly as she crossed a few things off the list. "So is it OK if I go with the article on Friday when this is gifted? Also, what did you end up being able to get?"

"I'll get you the full list, but there is lots of stuff. It's practically going to be a new gym. The cool thing is that there's lots of space, so much of the current equipment can stay. The best part is that the equipment they're going to get rid of will be auctioned off to make money for the high school Booster Club. So it's a win, win for everyone."

"Well, I'm impressed, Blake. It is amazing that everything happened so quickly. I guess now I need to get a move on and interview for this first story. We want this first story about you to be the kickoff, and really pull people in for the next one. There will be people knowing that you're doing this for damage control, and there's nothing we can do to stop that. But I want to tell the other side of things in this article, and I want you to share your thoughts about why this donation is so important."

Blake nodded his head and readjusted himself in his seat. Charlotte sensed he was shutting down a little. It wasn't difficult to read someone like Blake. He was outgoing until he wasn't, and breaking down that wall was what Charlotte needed to do.

"Can I ask you something off the record?" Charlotte asked.

"What?" Blake asked hesitantly with a smile.

"Why don't you like doing interviews? I haven't read one thing of substance about you in the papers, or online. Why is that?"

"As I told you, I like interviews to be about the game, not me."

"But people want to know the real you, especially when you have the kind of reputation you do."

"Oh, yeah," Blake chuckled, leaning back in his seat and folding his arms. "And what's that?"

"Oh, please," Charlotte laughed with a blush. "You know you have a reputation."

"Yeah, of course, I do," Blake smiled, finding it funny that her cheeks were getting red. "I'm asking you to tell me what you think it is."

"OK," Charlotte said, sitting back in her seat, too. "I'll bite. You're known as a party boy, a ladies' man, a player, a stupid jock, and someone who is a spoiled athletic brat."

Blake closed his eyes and made a sound as if he had just been shot. "OUCH! That hurts. That's how you think people see me?"

"Yes, I think that's how *some* people see you," Charlotte nodded. "You don't agree?"

"I don't think I'm a stupid jock, or a spoiled brat," Blake laughed with a shrug. "That's pushing it. And, let me say this, all the guys on my team party and entertain the ladies. I'm just the one who seems to make the headlines."

"But you flaunt it, they don't."

"Maybe," Blake agreed with a shrug. "Let me say this, too. My reputation has never affected my playing. I've always over-delivered, which is why this suspension really pisses me off."

"But you do understand why they had to suspend you?"

Blake looked at Charlotte and locked eyes with her for a few seconds. He knew she understood him, that much was certain. He knew if this was going to be a good article, he needed to stay truthful. Besides, he didn't want to hide. He had already embarrassed his family in ways he couldn't imagine. He was fully aware of the damage he had done, and he knew he had to clean it up for everyone, including himself. He had loved the freedom of partying and playing the character of Blake Manor that everyone loved to watch but, in reality, that wasn't the real him at all.

"Yes," Blake answered softly.

Charlotte didn't want Blake to be anything other than truthful, and she knew he was being honest with her now, just by allowing her access to him. "Why don't we do this. Why don't you interview me first?"

"What?" Blake laughed. "I don't know how to interview anyone."

"Oh come on, everyone knows how to interview someone. Why don't you ask me three questions, anything you want? Hopefully, this will break the ice a bit."

"Are you going to answer them?" Blake asked, feeling

like this was stupid, but appreciating what Charlotte was attempting to do. She knew he hated answering questions about himself, so she was letting him start with her.

"Yes," Charlotte nodded. "I don't remember the last time someone interviewed me, so this will be fun. Just remember not to ask 'yes' or 'no' questions. Ask me something that I have to talk about."

Blake closed his eyes and then slowly opened them. "OK, I've got the first question for you. What does your family think about you interviewing me?" He laughed nervously.

He noticed Charlotte's smile disappear quickly, and her eyes changed. The light had just gone out, and he watched her look down at her lap. "My... ugh... my parents don't know about this interview."

"Oh, God," Blake said smiling. "Am I that bad that you don't want to tell them?"

Charlotte looked up at Blake and gave him a small, forced smile. "No, it's not that at all. Although, I doubt my father would have known who you are," she smiled to herself and then looked back down. "My father wasn't into sports. He could tell you about every book that had been written, but he wouldn't know a football stat to save his life, or any athletic stat for that matter."

Blake just stared at Charlotte, knowing that the past tense she used meant something, and he wasn't expecting that.

"My parents were killed in a car accident during my sophomore year of college," Charlotte said quickly, and then looked into her tote for a tissue. Every time she said these words out loud, it hit her again-- a wave of pained anguish that she would never get over, and never get used to. Time hadn't healed her wounds. It had done the opposite; it had intensified them.

"Oh, Charlotte," Blake said, staring at her and noticing the tears building up in her eyes. "I'm so sorry. I...I had no idea. I would never have asked if I had known." He felt like shit and knew this had to be about the tenth strike against him.

Charlotte smiled and wiped away a stray tear. "Oh, I know, Blake," she said softly. "It's not something I talk about a lot. But I will say my father would have gotten a kick out of this article. He knows I'm a fish out of water when it comes to anything athletic. My parents were in the academic world, both professors at a small college in Pittsburgh. They were all about books, and they loved that I was all about writing," she smiled. "It was just the three of us, I didn't have any siblings. They would spend hours reading, and I would spend hours writing."

"So you always knew you wanted to be a journalist?" Blake asked.

"Yes, ever since I was a little girl. My parents loved that I wanted to go into the field." Charlotte smiled, feeling herself becoming more relaxed.

The accident had happened a little over three and a half years ago, and at times it still felt like yesterday. The worst part was that her parents were just innocently driving to work together, and they were tragically hit by some guy speeding and losing control of his car. His stupid mistake ended their lives. As difficult as it was, she knew her parents wouldn't want her to stop living. She had a small extended family, nobody she was super close with, so it was Lindsay and her family who took her in and made her feel part of something while remaining at URI. The only other thing that had brought her peace was writing. She threw herself into the newspaper at school, and it filled all her free time. The paper, Lindsay and her family, and eventually Dylan, got her through a very hard time. She had crafted out a perfect little life for herself, and she was proud of how far she had come in the last few years.

"Well, I'm sure they would be proud of you," Blake smiled. "I can't imagine how difficult it has been for you. You didn't have any desire to go back to Pittsburgh after college, huh?"

Charlotte shook her head. "As much as I love it, it's still too tough for me to go home. Rhode Island has grown on me, but my real goal is to get to New York City. That's the ultimate dream for me. I want to write for one of those big publications."

"Even though papers and magazines are folding every week?" Blake joked with a wink.

"Hey, there will always be room for news, offline and online. I'm fine with any way I can get myself a byline."

"OK... " Blake nodded, "that's a cool goal to have."

"I've just got to make it happen," Charlotte nodded with confidence, feeling warm inside when she looked up and locked eyes with Blake. "And I will stop at nothing!"

"That's the first thing you've said that sounds like something I would say," Blake chuckled, trying to lighten the mood as best as he could. "I've got one more question for you, a fun one," Blake said with a sly eye.

"I think you've asked your three questions, now it's my turn," Charlotte responded, as she collected herself.

"One more," Blake urged. "It's a question I love hearing people answer because everyone's answers are so different."

"OK..." Charlotte said, intrigued by Blake's excitement.

"What's one thing you hate?" he teased.

"One thing I hate?" Charlotte laughed. "How is this a fun question?"

"Because, seriously, everyone has a different answer. And everyone has one thing that bugs the hell of them."

"Hmm... " Charlotte thought. "One thing I hate," she repeated.

"Yeah," Blake nodded. "And not something boring, like... stale bread for example."

"You're making this harder," Charlotte said, shaking her head. "I mean I hate spiders, elevators, and heights."

"Those are basic things that most people hate. Come on, what's something you just hate that nobody knows about."

Charlotte laughed and closed her eyes for a second. "OK, I've got one."

Blake liked seeing her smile; it lit up her entire face.

"I hate men in turtlenecks," she said with a disgusted look on her face. "It just drives me crazy."

Blake let out a belly laugh and covered his face with his hands, "Now that's what I'm talking about. That's something I wouldn't expect someone to say."

As she laughed along with him she grabbed her pen and pulled her notebook a little closer. He had done it, he had some way, somehow, broken down their wall a little bit. She could feel it, and she was thankful. She wasn't comfortable opening up to people about her past, because it required her to relive it, which was something she tried to avoid at all costs. She appreciated Blake using a stupid question to break her out of her sad funk. He wasn't as stupid as she had pegged him to be, although she would ever admit that to him.

"OK, now it's my turn. I've got forty-five minutes until I need to leave to get across town for an interview. You ready?"

Blake sat back in his seat, not wanting to answer any

questions, but he owed it to a lot of people, including Charlotte, to keep his side of the bargain. Hearing her open up a bit about herself helped him get a better handle on her. It was always interesting to learn why some people hustle the way they do, and he was beginning to understand why Charlotte seemed to be constantly rushing around--she needed to be.

"All right, have at it," Blake remarked. "Just don't call me a stupid jock again."

"How about you tell me one thing that *you* hate," Charlotte started as her lead-off question. She smiled, knowing it was probably the smartest place to start with him.

18

"So, it went well?" Mary Manor asked as she walked into her dining room with a snack for her son. He had papers strewn all over the table and was trying to organize them into piles.

Mary loved having Blake home. It made her really feel like a mom again. With both of her kids out of the house-- one working, and one in college, she missed doting and caring for her kids.

"Yes, Mom, the meeting was good," Blake nodded, and then looked longingly at the snack she had prepared—her famous nachos. "And I'm telling you right now, you can not fatten me up. I'm on a strict diet and workout regimen while I'm here."

"Oh, come on. This isn't going to kill you," Mary said as she made him a plate filled with chips and cheese.

"I still don't understand why you've got all of your old newspaper clippings out. I thought you said Charlotte had read everything there was to be had about you," Mary said.

Blake shrugged his shoulders. "She did, but these are for me. I'm going to take these back to the city with me when I leave. I had them all lying loose in some boxes in my closet. I'm going through everything and putting them in order by date."

Mary just smiled and walked back into the kitchen. She kept stealing glances at Blake working away at the table. She used to love watching her two kids doing homework while she was in the kitchen making dinner. It always touched her heart when the kids would clean up the kitchen after dinner. They knew she had cleaned houses all day just to put food on their table.

Blake looked up and caught her watching him. "What?" he smiled.

"It's just good to have you home, Blake. It's been a while. I know your training schedule keeps you busy in the off-season, but it would be nice to have you home every now and then for an extended stay. What can I say; it's nice cooking for you again."

Blake watched his mother work in the kitchen. It had become more apparent to him on this visit that his parents were looking older. He always thought of them the way they had looked back when he was in high school, but the appearance of grey hair, and a few extra wrinkles, showed him that time didn't standstill.

"I wish you would let me update this kitchen, Mom," Blake said. He knew his mother loved to bake and cook, and she was using appliances that were over fifteen years old...at least. "Imagine having it opened up with an island and all new appliances. We could make it really nice, and nothing would make me happier."

"Blake, I don't need that stuff. I'm perfectly happy with what I've got," Mary answered.

"I hear what you are saying, Mom, but I think it is time for a refresh in here—and Molly agrees with me. This kitchen is so dark --we could brighten everything up and I bet it would look twice the size, too."

"What are you," Mary laughed, "a home improvement guy now? I like the dark cabinets, it hides the dirt better!" she joked.

"You deserve the best, Mom," Blake responded. "I bet if you ask Dad about updating everything he would be on board."

"What makes you say that?" She laughed. "He never uses this kitchen, this is my domain. His domain is right in there," she said, pointing toward the living room. "Why don't you convince him to redo the furniture in there? That I can get on board with. I wouldn't mind a new couch, chair, and coffee table." she smiled and winked over at Blake.

He didn't know how his parents managed to do it, but they had a love that really worked. They had been together for over thirty years, high school sweethearts who fell in love early and just got lucky. Growing up, he had always known that he wanted something like that for himself. But after college things changed.

It was surreal to him when he started seeing women show up at games with his name on their chest. He had heard of groupies, but it was one thing to hear about them, and another to experience it. As a young man, it was flattering to have women throw themselves at him, and it was tough, almost impossible, to ignore. His thoughts were interrupted when he saw his mother startle when the doorbell rang.

She called out to Ben to go see who it was because she was wrist-deep in the sink washing dishes. "You expecting someone, Blake?" she asked looking over at him.

Blake shook his head, he wasn't expecting anyone. There couldn't be anything else that Charlotte needed – they had covered a lot of ground in their forty-five-minute interview this afternoon, and he had actually enjoyed it, knowing that what he said wouldn't be misconstrued or twisted. He had been impressed with Charlotte's questions, her patience, her follow-up inquiries, and how she listened. At the end of his interview, he had fully realized just how bad his behavior had been over the last couple of years. He was a different person, and he didn't much like what he saw.

"Blake!" his father yelled from the front door. "Someone's here for you!"

Blake looked up at his mother and shrugged his shoulders. "I have no clue who this could be."

"Maybe it's one of the kids in the neighborhood coming over for an autograph," his mother smiled. "Be nice if it is!"

Blake got up and walked into the living room and almost died when his eyes locked with Piper's. "Piper? What are you doing here?"

"Surprise!" She beamed. "I knew I would surprise you! I got you, didn't I?"

Blake's eyes opened wide and he nodded his head as he went to give her a hug. He caught his father staring at him.

"You should have told me you were coming. How the heck did you manage to find out where I live?"

"Oh, God, Blake... " Piper scoffed. "I'm a journalist, it's my job is to uncover things. It wasn't difficult to find out where your parents live."

"And you made the trip all the way here just to see me?"

"Well, yes and no," she chuckled. "I have to be in Boston tomorrow night for work, so I thought this would be a nice stop on my road trip. Are you glad I came?" she smiled, moving in for another hug.

Feeling a little uncomfortable with his father standing there while Piper was coming in hot on his body, he started to shuffle her into the living room to try to put a little space between them, first saying, "Dad, this is Piper Saunders."

Ben smiled and extended his hand, "Of course, good to meet you, Piper. Nice to meet you in person. I'm used to seeing you on TV every weekend. We're big fans," Ben said politely, lying through his teeth for his son.

"Oh, you're a gem! You're just as handsome as Blake!" Piper went over and gave him a bear hug, which surprised Ben at the same time.

"I thought I heard a woman's voice," Mary interrupted from the corner of the living room. Her eyes were drawn to a beautiful brunette dressed in a white crop top with a navy blazer over it, along with skinny jeans and black knee-high boots.

"You must be Blake's mother!" Piper gushed and walked over to give her a hug. "I'm Piper Saunders, so wonderful to meet you."

The first thing that struck Mary was that Piper seemed to be introducing herself as if Blake had already told them all about her. She knew who Piper Saunders was from TV. She reported on all of the football games. But she had no idea she was connected to her son, at least not seriously.

"It's a pleasure to meet you," Mary said, pulling back from the hug. "Blake didn't tell us you were coming," she said, looking over at Blake who appeared just as surprised as she was.

"I surprised him," she squeaked in a high-pitched tone, her words gushing out in a rush. "And I totally got him. He was shocked! I need to be in Boston tomorrow, so I thought I'd come in and see Blake, and thought it would be cool to see where he grew up. This town is the cutest. I can't get over it."

"Did you drive here or take the train from New York?"

Blake asked, walking to the door to peer outside to see if Piper had a car with her. That was when he noticed the suitcases near the doorway. She was obviously planning on spending the night in Barrington, but he wasn't sure where.

"Oh, please. I could never drive that far by myself. I took the train to Providence and then took an Uber from the station. My driver gave me a tour all the way here."

Wanting to get her alone to see what her plans were for the night, Blake said the first thing that came to mind. "You hungry?" He was hoping she had booked a hotel somewhere in Providence. There was no way she could stay here at his parent's house; he was getting hot just thinking about a night with her again. As much as this surprise visit wasn't something he would have suggested, she might be the fun he needed right now.

"I'm starved," Piper nodded, smiling at Blake and then looking at his parents.

"Let's go out for a bite to eat," Blake said quickly. "It's early enough, and there shouldn't be any crowds to worry about," Blake answered. "My Range Rover is parked in the garage. Let's grab it and head out. We'll pick up your suitcases when we get back and bring them to your hotel," he added, wanting her to know staying here wasn't an option.

Piper smiled goodbye to Ben and Mary and followed Blake to the door connecting the house to the garage. He had parked in there to avoid people doing random drop-ins, or having a few teenagers think it would be funny to egg his car. People treated celebrities in all different kinds of ways.

"Are you really surprised?" Piper asked she hopped into his car. "I wasn't sure if I should tell you ahead or not."

"Yes, I'm very surprised," Blake answered, turning on the car.

"Good," Piper declared back. "I told you I missed you. I

need a little Blake time. I've been having withdrawals," she laughed, trying to cozy up on his arm as he backed out of the driveway.

"I've been busy here working out and settling in," Blake smiled. "It's a bit weird being here and not in the city. It's so much quieter. It's so quiet, it's even tough to fall asleep at night."

"Well... maybe tonight you'll have a tough time falling asleep for a completely different reason," she taunted.

"So you're spending the night in Providence?" Blake asked.

"I hadn't booked anything yet. I figured hotels here would be easy to come by. Besides, if you weren't around, I would have just headed to Boston. Now we can hole up in a hotel tonight and tomorrow until I need to head to Boston," she whispered, trailing her finger down his neck.

Blake felt shivers go down his spine, and his body was perking up in places it shouldn't be. He also knew that Piper didn't necessarily care where and when things happened. Normally he wouldn't mind, but the last thing he needed right now was to be identified over anything scandalous.

"Let's grab a bite first, I'll show you around town a bit, and then we'll find a hotel in Providence. Sound good?" Blake asked.

Piper smiled, "Sounds great." She was just satisfied to be here with Blake. Piper had always had a thing for Blake and his bad-boy antics. The fact that he was hot as hell didn't hurt either. She loved the fact that women everywhere wanted him but, even more, she loved her direct access to him. He might not be ready to settle down, but she could certainly enjoy the benefits while she waited for it to happen.

"There's an Irish Pub two towns over that's a fun place.

It's got great food and, even though it's usually busy, it's a local crowd, so they won't be intense. We might get asked to pose for a few photos, but nothing crazy."

"I'm not the one afraid of the press," Piper joked.

"True. If you had your way, you would have called ahead to make sure press was waiting for us." He joked back.

Piper smiled back, knowing that on some level, he was right. Being seen with Blake Manor was always good for a little press boost, even for her.

19

Charlotte was sweating buckets as she ran to the bar to grab a round of beers for a table of young professionals. She wasn't sure why Finnegan's was so busy on a Wednesday night, but it was. Normally, the crowd filtered in slowly throughout the night, but a sudden rush kept her on her toes. She shouldn't complain because more tables meant more tips.

"You got that, Charlotte?" James asked from behind the bar, pointing to the tray full of drinks she was holding.

"Yes, thanks, James!" Charlotte shouted. "Just trying to catch my breath for a second."

"I don't know what's going on tonight, but we've almost got a full house here," James said, motioning to the bar.

"And, only the two of us on the floor tonight isn't helping," Charlotte added. Two of the other waitresses had called in sick, adding to the craziness.

"Yeah, but we're two of the best!" James smiled at Charlotte with his thumbs up.

Charlotte left to deliver the drinks and grab a couple of

orders. The good thing about waitressing on a busy night was that it made the time fly by quickly. This job opened up at Finnegan's about a month ago, and she was lucky to have it. She could only work part-time a couple of evenings a week, and most restaurants were looking for full-time, but she got lucky here and they worked around her schedule. To sweeten the pot a little bit more for them, she told the owner that she would include a free ad for the pub in the *Barrington View* if any open ad space occurred during the week. Frank had been kind enough to tell her she could offer this because he knew how important the extra cash was to her.

"You have a new table, Charlotte," Amber, the teenage hostess, yelled to Charlotte who was in the kitchen checking on some of her orders. "They're in the corner near the fireplace."

Charlotte walked over to Amber, looking over to where she had sat them, but she couldn't see their faces. She wondered if Lindsay had come in with a friend for the evening. "How many people?" Charlotte asked, hoping it would be a small party. So far tonight, she seemed to be getting big groups, and she would love a bit of a break.

"Just two," Amber said. "I don't know who they are, but it seems like they must be famous or something. People were whispering and pointing as I sat them. They wanted a table in the corner, so I did the best I could with what we had available."

Not many celebrities came in; maybe it was one of the McKay sisters. She had heard that TV star Asher Dawson, and his wife Susan McKay, had come in this summer when they were visiting her family. Charlotte hadn't had any McKay sightings herself, but maybe her luck would change tonight. Her food order wasn't ready yet, so she decided to head out to the dining room and get a glimpse of the new customers.

As she walked towards her new table, she froze when her eyes locked with Blake's. He was facing her and seemed just as shocked to see her. Charlotte couldn't see the woman he was with, but it wasn't out of the realm of possibility for Blake to hang out with someone while he was in town. She suddenly felt embarrassed. She hated to wait on people she knew. She worried that she wouldn't be taken seriously as a journalist if people saw her working another job.

She put a fake smile on her face and walked over to their table. "Hi, Blake! Good to see you," she said, friendly as can be, trying to make it seem as if it was no big deal that she was here waiting on him.

"Hey, Charlotte," Blake responded surprised and confused at the same time. "I didn't know you worked at Finnegan's. This a regular gig for you?"

Charlotte nodded and smiled, trying to fight back a dose of humiliation, "Yes, just a few nights a week."

She turned to smile at the woman he was with and froze for a second, but this time it was because of the sheer beauty of this woman. She was gorgeous, unfairly so. Perfect hair. Perfect makeup. Perfect smile. Perfect outfit. She even smelled perfect. She was the exact kind of woman she pictured Blake with.

"This is Piper," Blake said, motioning to Piper.

"I'm Piper Saunders," she said, extending her hand and speaking in a way that made Charlotte think she should know who she was. "How do you and Blake know each other? Friends from high school?"

"Actually," Blake said, clearing his throat and speaking to Piper, "Charlotte's the reporter writing the article on me in the town paper."

"*You're* the one writing them?" Piper asked in a confused tone, looking up at Charlotte. "I thought you said she was a full-time journalist, you didn't tell me she was a waitress, too."

Charlotte looked down at her work clothes and chuckled nervously, "Oh... it's just part-time. Writing doesn't pay all the bills, at least not for me yet. It was one of the first lessons I learned when I started writing for a small-town newspaper. Waitressing is a way to make some extra money."

"Oh my God," Piper laughed. "God bless you. When I applied for waitressing jobs when I was in college, my parents knew how bad I would be, so they actually paid me not to waitress! Honest to God, Blake... that's a true story," Piper said, amused with herself.

"Well," Blake said, knowing Charlotte didn't have that luxury, "We all can't have parents like that."

"I know," Piper said as she swept her hair out of her face and looked up to get a better look at Charlotte. "So you work at the local paper? That's so wonderful. Good for you."

"Yes, I'm on the staff there as a reporter," Charlotte nodded, beginning to feel her face heat up. She must have looked lame standing there in a wrinkled denim shirt, a messy black apron around her waist, black jeans, and her hair tossed up a loose bun. She had worn a little makeup for work but was positive it had disappeared. "It's my full-time job. I just graduated from college six months ago."

He could sense that Charlotte felt uncomfortable with Piper, so he interjected. "Yeah, I was just telling Piper how you came up with the idea of the holiday good deeds, and how each one will be tied back to an interview with me."

"Oh, nice. Yeah, they should be good articles for you and

the town," Charlotte nodded. "The first one runs next week. We're all really excited about them."

"And for Blake," Piper interrupted and then flashed her smile at Blake, "That's the most important thing right now."

"Yes, and for Blake, too," Charlotte added and then grabbed her notebook from her apron, trying to distract herself.

"So you've only been at the local paper since you graduated?" Piper asked Charlotte.

"Yes, since May," Charlotte answered.

"Oh, so not that long," Piper added with a shrug and then looked over at Blake with concern. "I hope you know what a big deal it is to get a scoop like this. I'm surprised they gave it to someone so junior... but lucky you, Charlotte!"

"Well, she was the editor of her college newspaper before that, right Charlotte?" Blake added, looking over at her with a smile.

"Yes, I was," Charlotte smiled, thankful for the lifeboat Blake tossed at her. "It was the best way for me to get my foot in the door. I knew starting at a small paper would be the best way to work my way up. The printed version of the *View* still beats the online stats, which is unheard of," she said.

"It might be small, but it's like the *New York Times* of our town," Blake laughed and looked up at Charlotte. "Right?"

"Oh, that's super cute," Piper said obnoxiously.

"I know it's not a national publication, but you have to start somewhere. The team is great and, yes, I'm lucky enough to be working on Blake's article, and a few other things, too," Charlotte said.

"I'm sure," Piper smiled. "I'm actually a journalist, too. Well, I'm on-air and I write, too... so I'm a double threat. At least that's what some of my colleagues tell me," she laughed. "I do it all, right Blake? I'm assuming you are hoping to leave the small-town paper and go bigger at some point, yes?"

Charlotte could tell that Piper was talking down to her, but she didn't want to appear bothered by it. What Piper didn't know was that she had already been through hell and back. She could toss anything at her at this point and she would be OK, but you couldn't explain something like that to a woman like Piper. One other thing Charlotte knew for certain was that Piper wasn't a girl's girl, which was obvious. She knew that immediately.

"Yes, my dream is to end up in New York City," Charlotte nodded. "That's my goal."

"New York City is really hard to break into," Piper chimed in. "I'm just telling you because I know how cutthroat the industry can be. Being on-air certainly is cutthroat, but writing is just as tough. Everyone thinks they're the next big thing," Piper nodded looking at Charlotte. "But I guess you'll never know if you don't try, right?"

Blake sat there, watching this go down, and was wondering what the hell was going on. He had never seen Piper act this way but, then again, he had never really seen Piper around other women before.

"True," Charlotte remarked, "Well... for what it's worth, you certainly *look* like you'd be on air. Obviously, you're not covered in leftovers or spilled beer like me," Charlotte said, trying to make a joke, motioning to her clothing. "So, you must be doing something right. You cover sports? Is that how you two know each other?"

"Yes, sports is *all* I do. What can I say, I love being around these hunky men," and she reached over to caress Blake's hand. "But listen, we've taken up so much of your time and

I'm so hungry. Do you mind if we place our order now? I just want a plain salad with grilled chicken, and I'll have olive oil on the side. For my cocktail... hmm... Blake, babe, are you doing beer or an actual cocktail?"

"I'm just going to have a beer," Blake responded, trying to keep a straight face. In all the time they had been hooking up, Piper had never called him "babe" before.

"What about you, Blake?" Charlotte inquired, trying her hardest not to make eye contact with him. She couldn't believe Piper was the kind of woman he would involve himself with. She'd had a fairly good meeting with him yesterday and, as much as it was hard to admit, he was turning out to be completely different than she had anticipated. He had been kind, thoughtful, and even funny as he answered her questions, even talking a bit about his upbringing. She had found herself actually enjoying their time together and kind of upset when it was time to head to her next meeting.

"I'll make it easy and just get the fish and chips and a Bud Light," Blake answered.

"Sounds good, guys. I'll get your drinks started," Charlotte said and then walked off, feeling relieved to be away from the table. She had never been made to feel so small and unaccomplished. Her parents had raised her to be strong, brave, and a go-getter. Women like Piper Saunders loved to walk in their stilettos over other women because of their own low self-esteem issues. It was no wonder that athletes fell for women like her, all boobs and body. No substance at all.

~

"Piper, was that necessary?" Blake asked the second Charlotte walked away from their table. "You were really rude to Charlotte."

"Honestly, Blake. I'm shocked that you and anyone on your team would trust a rookie reporter with your feature. These are important articles for you. You do know that?"

"Of course I do," Blake answered.

"Then why would you let someone like her do the stories and not me?"

"Is that what this is about?" Blake responded. "You wanted the 'scoop'? Don't you think that would have come with a conflict of interest?"

Piper rolled her eyes at Blake and shook her head. "I'm a professional, I know how to stay neutral."

"Listen, Charlotte's a good reporter. She's trying really hard to make sure she gets what she needs from me. We're just at the beginning of the interviews. I'm sure they're going to be fine. Besides, her editor, who happens to be a family friend, gets a final look before anything goes to print."

Piper flashed a sly smile at Blake. She didn't want to upset him, but she wanted to look out for him, too. She didn't trust any woman around Blake, not as far as she could spit. She knew women would kill to be with someone like him because of his fame and money. His suspension was a blip on the radar right now, but she knew he would come back with a vengeance, and become the king of New York City football again.

"I'm sorry, OK," Piper whined with a smile. "I'm just looking out for you."

Blake lowered his head and frowned, "Well... you've got a funny way of showing it. Go easy on her. I gave her a tough time earlier this week trying to make her prove her worth. She's a hard worker, and she's taking this very seriously."

"She must be a big football fan then, huh?"

"Actually, she doesn't know much about the game, which is working to my advantage because she's not asking about the game."

"Well... don't forget, she might just be looking to hook up with you," Charlotte shrugged. "You know how women are."

"Charlotte?" Blake asked with a chuckle. "Oh, I doubt that. I'm pretty sure she hated my guts until yesterday when the ice began to melt a little bit. Believe me, you're wrong about that assumption."

"Oh, yeah," Piper shot back. "Is she blind?"

Blake sat back in his seat, shaking his head and laughing. Piper was a piece of work. He knew lots of women wanted to get in his pants, but if there was one thing he knew for sure in this world, Charlotte Court was not one of them.

20

Lindsay listened as Charlotte related the entire sequence of events that happened with Blake and Piper on Wednesday night. She couldn't get over the fact that Charlotte had waited two whole days before telling her everything.

"I still can't believe that you're just telling me now," Lindsay announced.

"I didn't see you yesterday," Charlotte responded.

"You should have at least whet my appetite with a text. You know I love gossip like this."

Charlotte laughed and tossed a carrot stick at Lindsay from across her kitchen counter. Every Friday night they got together and ordered takeout, but tonight they were going out. Charlotte had set up appetizers for them at her place before heading out for dinner at a popular place in Barrington, the Bluewater Grille. Lindsay knew that Charlotte had been working her butt off lately at the paper, and also at Finnegan's, and wanted to bring her best friend out for a little night on the town.

"So you haven't seen Blake since Wednesday?" Lindsay asked.

Charlotte shook her head as she grabbed a carrot stick and dipped it into the ranch dressing. "No," she shook her head. "I'm done with my first round of interviewing about the surprise donation at the high school. We had a photographer lined up to take photos at the delivery this afternoon."

"You didn't go?" Lindsay asked, surprised. That wasn't normally Charlotte's style. She loved being part of every component of her pieces.

"I couldn't make it today," Charlotte answered. "I wanted to, but I had an interview with another principal and then, immediately afterward, I had another interview with the women putting together the holiday craft show happening next weekend. Besides, I trust all our photographers, and I've already got the photos and they're perfect."

"Did Blake go?" Lindsay asked, wondering why Charlotte hadn't rescheduled things to make it work.

"Yeah," she nodded, not making eye contact with Charlotte. "He was there."

Lindsay looked at her friend and smiled. She didn't want to press it because she knew Charlotte already had strong feelings about being on this story. Blake seemed as if he was going to make her work for this article, but she was proud of her friend for putting aside her hatred of sports and making the best of it. Not to mention, she didn't want tonight to be about work, she wanted it to be fun with her bestie.

"Well," Lindsay said, "I still can't believe he's dating Piper Saunders. And, by the way, she was probably rude because she was annoyed that you didn't know who she was! She's always on TV."

"You know I don't follow sports," Charlotte shot back.

"Yeah, but she's someone who is always in the public eye, and I'm surprised you didn't know her."

"Well, no one could have missed her the other night at Finnegan's. She was wearing a cropped top that barely covered her boobs. Every guy in the bar stopped what they were doing when she got up to go to the bathroom, even the old cronies," Charlotte laughed. "You can tell she loves the attention."

"Yeah, she's definitely a sex pot, and she knows it."

"She's exactly the kind of woman I pictured Blake with," Charlotte offered.

"What's that? Sexy and gorgeous?" Lindsay smiled.

"Yes," Charlotte laughed back. "Guys like him always go for girls like that. It's all about their image. Although I have to say, his parents seem totally normal, which is nice to see. Mary Manor is a sweetheart."

"They really are a great family, or at least that's what my father has always said, and you know he's going to tell you the truth. He doesn't bullshit about anything."

Charlotte looked down at the veggies on the counter and said, "So, tell me this, do you think Piper Saunders is in her kitchen right now, on a Friday night, enjoying veggies with a girlfriend?"

"Hell, no! I think she's probably on her way to a club right now in a private car. Or, she's still here with Blake on their way to somewhere fabulous and exclusive."

Charlotte walked over to the mirror in her hallway and looked at her reflection. She was wearing an oversized grey crewneck sweatshirt with "Nantucket" across the chest, along with black leggings. She had every intention of trying to work out this evening before Lindsay came over, but time got away from her as she was finishing up the last articles she needed to get to Frank for review.

Lindsay peered around the corner and saw her best friend looking at herself in the mirror. "You might not be Piper Saunders, but you're a hell of a hot chick," she laughed.

"Oh, please. You know I have no ambition to look like Piper. I did a little research about her online and, believe me, she changed her look completely a few years ago to play with the big boys in the sports world. She used to be more classic and elegant looking, and now she's all sexy... and then there's me."

"You're so good at what you do, you don't need to rely on your looks. Although, you know, you could show off that smoking hot body a little more," Lindsay winked.

"Who, me?" Charlotte laughed.

"Yeah, you! You know you have an incredible body, but you hide it."

"I don't hide it," Charlotte corrected her. "I dress appropriately for what I do for a living. Imagine your father's face if I showed up in a cropped top and leggings for an interview at the school committee meeting."

"No, but every now and then..." Lindsay said, walking over to her friend as she was still looking in the mirror. "You should let your hair down once in a while," she said as she tugged at the hair elastic holding up Charlotte's hair. "I mean it, literally, Char. You *should* let your hair down sometimes. Look at that gorgeous mane of blonde hair!"

Charlotte looked at her hair in the mirror. She had always had long, thick hair that was naturally blonde. She had never needed to add highlights or color to it. Her mom's hair had been exactly the same. She knew she had great hair--she had been told that her entire life--but it had been a long time since she had taken the time to style or do anything with it.

"You know," Charlotte smiled, playing with her hair, "Dylan has always loved my hair down."

"You look hot with it down," Lindsay laughed. "Maybe if you sent photos of yourself with your hair down he'd come to visit more often," Lindsay winked.

Charlotte laughed to herself and looked back at her reflection. It had been a few weeks since she had seen Dylan. They talked whenever they could, but even their phone calls had dwindled a bit. She knew he was as busy, but it would be nice to see him more often, even for a quick weekend visit. She had FaceTimed him earlier in the day to say hello, but he didn't pick up. He texted her back saying that he was busy and he would call later.

"Listen," Lindsay announced with a spark in her eyes, "why don't we dress up for dinner tonight!"

"But we're just going to Bluewater," Charlotte answered.

"Yeah, but tonight let's do our hair and makeup, and look all cute! Come on," Lindsay urged.

"But I'm not looking for a guy," Charlotte laughed.

"But I am, and you never know when your soul mate will cross your path. Just remember that," Lindsay joked. "Not to mention, they have live music tonight, so there should be a decent crowd."

Charlotte rolled her eyes at her best friend and stuck out her tongue. "Fine! But only because I love you. Otherwise, I'd roll in with this look and feel completely OK about it."

"Yeah," Lindsay nodded. "Spoken like a woman who already has a guy. Come on," she said walking toward Charlotte's bedroom closet, "Let's go have some fun!"

Charlotte smiled and looked down at her phone, wishing Dylan had called back. Thankfully, she had Lindsay with her who always did a great job at creating fun. The last thing she felt like doing was changing out of her comfy clothes, but she owed it to Lindsay to have a little fun tonight. After all, maybe Lindsay would meet her soul mate.

BLUEWATER WAS PACKED solid-- it was over an hour's wait for a table. Lindsay and Charlotte were lucky enough to get the last two available stools at the bar. They had planned to get to Bluewater around 7 pm, but when Lindsay had the idea for makeovers, it had delayed them an extra hour.

Lindsay looked beautiful with her red hair cascading down her back. Charlotte had straightened it for her, and she looked like she had just come out of a salon. She had amped up her eye makeup with golden tones to set off her gorgeous green eyes, and added pink blush to brighten her cheeks. Since she hadn't brought any of her own dressy clothes to Charlotte's house, she borrowed a pair of skinny black jeans, a black crewneck sweater, and a pair of black heels that Charlotte had forgotten she owned. Lindsay looked dressed to kill, and she was ready to meet the man of her dreams tonight.

Charlotte took the time to do her hair and makeup, and she looked like a completely different person. Her hair was styled in big, loose, sexy waves. Her makeup was done to perfection-- a skill Lindsay didn't even know Charlotte possessed. She had created a sultry smoky eye on herself, bronzed her cheeks, and wore a red lip. It all worked beautifully with her navy blue bowtie blouse and tight, dark wash skinny jeans. Lindsay couldn't talk Charlotte into wearing a heel, so wore her black pointed-toe flats.

"Everyone is staring," Charlotte whispered as they sat down.

"It's because they're probably wondering who the hell

I'm with," Lindsay laughed. "You look like a different human being when you put some energy into yourself."

"I do put energy into myself," Charlotte laughed. "And you know I wear makeup."

"You put zero energy into yourself. And a tiny bit of bronzer and lip gloss does not count as makeup. You go for that Plain Jane look, and you know it," Lindsay shot back. "Even in college, I think I saw you dress up twice, and that was only for the Journalism Award banquets."

"I like to look professional, you know that. Besides, I hardly have any free time as it is, and doing this," she said pointing to her hair and makeup, "takes time."

"For what it's worth, you look insanely gorgeous tonight," Lindsay smiled. "Although, I still can't believe you brought that big ass work tote with you. But, other than that, you're picture perfect."

"This 'big ass work tote' is my life," Charlotte laughed. "Besides, you never know when a story will break."

"Well, let's enjoy the night before we turn into pump- kins!" Lindsay smiled and gave Charlotte's arm a loving squeeze while they perused the drink menu.

21

B lake knew that going out to dinner would mean no privacy, but his parents were super excited about the possibility. Bluewater was a favorite place for them and he knew, deep down, they were excited to show him off around town.

"At least they tucked us away in the corner so you won't be mobbed the entire time we're here," Mary smiled at her son.

Bluewater always looked so beautiful in the wintertime. They had set up igloos all along the outside patio for customers to enjoy. The interior of the restaurant was filled with nautical holiday decorations and pretty twinkling lights. It always made Mary feel warm and cozy to be inside Bluewater during the colder months. They made it so welcoming for everyone.

"You know that doesn't bother me," Blake smiled. "It actually hasn't been too bad tonight, which is surprising considering they're pretty full."

The Manor family had been seated at a small round table in the back that easily fit four chairs. Since Molly was still at school, it was just the three of them, but it still felt like a family meal to Mary. She couldn't wait to have Molly home for the holiday break, and then both of her kids would be home. Not having Blake home over the last eight or so years had been an adjustment for her. She was so happy for his success, but that meant he no longer lived at home.

Blake happened to be sitting in one of the chairs that faced out towards the restaurant, so he was able to see everything going on around him. He had worn a baseball hat to dinner, much to the chagrin of his mother, but he figured it would be a fairly decent disguise. Although he wasn't hounded in Barrington like he was in New York City, a few young boys had approached, asking for his autograph and a photo. A couple of his dad's buddies had come over to chat and BS about the football season, asking innocently when he would be heading back to New York. He could handle these kinds of disruptions. In New York, people would be coming to his table every two minutes asking for something or wanting something. It was a much different vibe here at home, and he had missed this hometown feel.

"So, do you have any ideas on what the next good deed will be?" Ben asked, looking over at his son.

"Actually, I think I do. I want to run it by Charlotte, but I think I want to set up a scholarship fund at the high school and turn it into an annual thing."

"Oh, Blake. I love that idea. What would the scholarship be for?" Mary asked.

"I'd love to give $3000 every holiday season to a student at the school who is doing great things in the community."

"That's a great one, son," Ben smiled. "What made you come up with that idea?"

"I met this kid, Alex, at the school, who reminded me of

how things used to be for us. His parents don't make a ton of money, so he wasn't able to play sports before high school, or do things that cost extra. He's finally able to play football because it's free. What really impressed me about this kid was that, on top of working out and keeping up with his grades, he started a free tutoring program for kids in middle school. I'd love to see this kid be the first recipient and then, from there, the school would pick a student every year. And, I want this scholarship to be available to all students—not just the jocks."

"Wow," Mary added. "That's beautiful, Blake. I remember those days of hoping we'd have enough money to keep food on the table. When you started to get bigger, the food started to go quicker!" she smiled. "Those days weren't easy, and they were filled with a lot of worries."

"But you guys did it," Blake said, smiling at each of them. "You managed to keep food on the table, the lights on, gas in the car. You even, somehow, managed to keep sneakers on my growing feet," he laughed.

"Oh, my God," Mary laughed. "I felt like every month you shot up to a new size! I couldn't wait for your feet to stop growing!"

"We wanted to do whatever we could for you," Ben said, reaching over to touch Blake's shoulder. "We saw the potential in you."

Blake nodded and looked down, feeling grateful, but also ashamed about his reason for being home right now.

"Thanks, I know I haven't been a model citizen lately, but I'm hoping I can make up for it, and repair my reputation while I'm here. I let a lot of shit go to my head. Being home, away from it all, has really made me see just how much of an ass I've been. Being around these kids has been great for me, too. I don't know why exactly, but this kid,

Alex, really got to me. I would love to try and make a difference in his life."

"He seems pretty special," Mary smiled.

"When are you meeting with Charlotte next?" Ben asked.

"I don't know," Blake answered, feeling bad that he hadn't reached out to her after the whole Piper situation on Wednesday night. "I feel badly, I actually happened to run into her Wednesday night at Finnegan's. I didn't realize she worked there," he said looking at his parents.

"Oh, I didn't know she worked there," Mary said. "Why do you feel bad about running into her?" she asked, looking at Blake.

"I didn't really run into her, she actually waited on me and Piper," Blake responded.

"Oh... " Mary said, not sure where this was going. "Was she a bad waitress?"

"No, not at all," Blake answered with a slight smile. "It's just that Piper was a little blunt with her, and I felt bad for Charlotte. I probably should have called her yesterday and said something, but I didn't realize Piper was staying as late as she did."

"So..." Mary said slowly, looking at Ben and then over to Blake. "Are you and Piper together?"

"Me and Piper?" Blake shot back. "No, not in that sense."

"We weren't sure. Especially when she showed up like that," Ben said, looking at Blake.

"I know what it looks like, but no... we're not together, at least not in a relationship."

"Does she know that?" Mary smiled and then winked at Blake.

"Geez, you could have asked me about this yesterday," Blake said, rolling his eyes to the amusement of his parents.

"We don't like to pry," Ben answered. "You're an adult, you have your life in New York. We know that. We don't want you to feel like you need to answer to us."

"But we do hope that when you settle down," Mary said, reaching out her hand to touch Blake's, "we won't be the last to know."

"It won't be anytime soon, believe me. Piper's a fun girl to hang out with, but I don't really see anything more than that with her."

Wanting to move the conversation away from Blake's personal life, Ben asked, "And how was she blunt with Charlotte?"

"It almost seemed as if she was trying to make her feel bad. She was telling her how hard it was to break into journalism in New York City, and stuff like that. Let's put it this way, she wasn't exactly warm and fuzzy when Charlotte mentioned her goal of working in New York City."

"How did Charlotte handle it?" Ben asked.

Blake smiled to himself, thinking back to Charlotte. He knew most women bowed down to Piper because of who she was and what she did, but Charlotte didn't give her that satisfaction. "She held her own," he said, "I'll give her that."

Mary smiled at her husband and then grabbed her water glass. She hadn't liked Piper the second she walked into her house, but she hadn't told Blake that. She stayed out of his love life. It was the opposite of high school when he had come to her all the time asking her advice on how to ask out girls. He had been so shy in high school; he could never work up the nerve. His looks attracted the girls, but his shyness prevented him from pursuing anything.

"I don't know," Blake joked. "Women still confuse the hell out of me."

"Amen," Ben laughed as he grabbed his glass to toast his son.

As Blake clinked his glass with his father's, his eyes were instantly diverted to a gorgeous blonde who had just entered Bluewater and was walking toward the bar. He couldn't see her face very well because she was far away, but he could see that every guy at the bar seemed to be thinking the same thing he was. She was turning heads left and right. He caught her profile and, from the looks of it, she had the most perfect, delicate features. He didn't often see women like her in Barrington, or maybe he had just been gone for so long that he hadn't noticed the beauties right here in his hometown.

As his parents continued to chat, he was only half-listening, jumping in here and there so as not to appear rude. He couldn't keep his eyes off this woman. Her blonde hair flowed halfway down her back. She was wearing a navy blue blouse and every time she turned her head to the side to talk with the redhead next to her, he tried to catch a glimpse of her full face, but he couldn't. As he continued to watch her, he noticed that the redhead was being distracted by the guy to her left, leaving an opening for anyone to approach the blonde. He watched an older man, who happened to be at the bar with four or five buddies, walk over to her and start talking. Just from her body language, it was obvious that the blonde had no interest. She appeared to be trying to get her friend's attention, but her friend seemed preoccupied with the guy she was talking with.

"Earth to Blake," Ben interjected.

Blake shook his head and looked at his dad. "Sorry, Dad. What did you say?"

"Your mom's asked you the same question three times, but you seem to be in outer space."

"Oh, God. Sorry, Mom. What did you say?"

"I just asked if your steak was good, that's all. You OK?"

"Yeah, yeah... I'm fine. I was just watching this older guy try and pick up a younger girl at the bar. She doesn't seem interested, so I was just thinking I should go over and help her out."

"Where?" Mary asked, turning around to see what Blake was talking about. "God, the bar is packed. How can you even see anything, especially this far away? Where's the girl?"

"The blonde girl on the end," Blake added. "But Mom, don't point or anything. Let's not make it obvious."

"Oh, God, Blake. What are you, fifteen?" Mary laughed as she looked over at the bar. "Oh... I see her. Ben, you know who is talking to her? It's that guy, Tony, from town, who lives down on the water. He's a piece of work and always has a new young chick on his arm. He's a... you know what!" She winked at her husband and son.

Ben laughed, "A what?"

"You know," Mary smiled. "He's an ass! Look at him trying to pick up that young woman. He's got to be 60 at least. Such a player. She's trying to ignore him."

"You can tell the girl isn't into him-- she keeps turning the other way and now he's got his buddies chanting for him to buy her a drink. It's obvious the guys have all been drinking. Even the bartender, and now her friend, are trying to get the guy to leave her alone."

"But if you go over, everyone will see you," Mary said.

"I guess that's a risk I'm going to take," Blake shrugged as he stood up. "Imagine if that was Molly."

As Blake started walking toward the bar, he heard a few tables whisper his name as he walked by. Normally he'd stop, but now, he just wanted to get to the bar. He might be known as a ladies' man, but there was one thing he never did, and that was pursue a girl who didn't want to be pursued. He couldn't help but think about his sister Molly and how he'd break a guy's neck if he did this to her in front of a bunch of people.

Blake was almost at the bar, and he wasn't sure how he was going to play it with the older guy. He obviously didn't want a fight or altercation, but he also wanted the guy to back off.

He walked up to the blonde, ignoring the older guy next to her, put his hands gently on her shoulders, and did the only thing he knew to do, "Hey, honey, you didn't save me a seat," he said loudly enough for the guy to hear.

"Oh, shit," the guy said, "you're Blake Manor."

Blake smiled at the guy, who had had too much to drink just by the smell of alcohol on his breath. "Sorry, man. I didn't know this gorgeous woman was taken." He smiled and staggered back to his buddies.

Everyone near the bar was stone silent. It was obvious that Blake had broken up what was turning into an altercation, but it was also crazy for everyone to see Blake Manor up, close and personal.

"Thanks, man," the bartender shouted. "That was getting rough. Appreciate you stepping in."

"No problem," Blake smiled, realizing he still had his hands on the shoulders of the woman in front of him. He quickly released his hands and looked down to introduce himself, but as his eyes caught her full face, he realized he knew the beautiful woman sitting in front of him.

"Charlotte?" he asked surprisingly.

"Hi, Blake," she smiled, with a nod. "Thanks for helping me out."

22

B lake felt as if the floor was going to collapse beneath him. The beautiful blonde was Charlotte? The woman who had caught his attention from the moment she had walked in until the second he saw her face, was Charlotte? How could this be?

"Charlotte," Blake said, trying not to sound flabbergasted. "I didn't realize it was you," he said quietly.

"Well... I hope you would have still come over to rescue me even if you *knew* it was me," Charlotte joked.

Blake let out a bit of a nervous laugh, "Of course, I would have. I just didn't recognize you with your hair down."

"My best friend," she said nudging Lindsay's arm, who was sitting speechless with her eyes wide open staring at Blake, "thought we should dress to impress tonight, and it looks like that old guy took the bait." She smiled. "Right, Lindsay?"

Lindsay nodded at Charlotte, trying not to appear starstruck at the sight of Blake, but was failing miserably.

"I don't know if you know Lindsay, her father is Frank

from the *View*," Charlotte said casually, as she introduced them.

"Oh, yeah," Blake nodded. "That's right. I knew Frank had a daughter. Good to meet you. Your dad is a great guy."

"Thanks," Lindsay managed. "Thanks for helping Charlotte out. I wasn't sure how I was going to get that guy, Tony, to back off."

"I don't want to interrupt your night," Blake added. "I was having dinner with my parents when I noticed the craziness going on over here and wanted to help out."

"Very chivalrous of you," Charlotte smiled. "Thank you, I appreciate it. We were actually going to try to get a table, but the wait is over an hour."

"You need to make a reservation next time," Blake nodded with a wink. "Works miracles."

"Noted," Charlotte laughed as she grabbed her wine glass.

"Are you able to eat at the bar?" he asked, trying not to stare, but he couldn't believe how beautiful Charlotte looked tonight. She was normally so prim and proper, right out of a J.Crew catalog, but not tonight. She looked stunning because she seemed so relaxed.

"Yes, I'm going to order something for myself. I think Lindsay has made a new friend," she said discreetly, pointing to Lindsay who was now laughing and giggling with the guy to her left. "I'll probably just get something and head home. I'm her wingman until she meets her soul mate," she laughed with a shrug.

"I can hear you, Charlotte, and you're not going home," Lindsay shouted, obviously eavesdropping. "You're not leaving this bar anytime soon. You look too good to go home!"

Charlotte smiled at Blake and whispered, "She'll be

begging me to leave her alone in ten minutes, just watch."

Blake laughed as he looked over to Lindsay. "I can't say I haven't been there," he said with his hands up.

"Funny," Charlotte added. "I can't say I'm surprised by that. But thank you for the help with that guy, Blake, I appreciate it."

"No problem, I guess that proves I'm not a total ass, right?" he said, trying to make a joke.

"I guess not," Charlotte nodded with a smile, "although I don't think I called you an ass, just a spoiled athletic brat."

"Oh, yeah, that's right..." he laughed back. "I'm going to head back to join my parents. I'll text you this weekend about connecting early next week. I have an idea I want to run by you."

"Oh," Charlotte said perking up, "that sounds great. I look forward to it."

"All right, well... I, ugh... I'll see you later," Blake smiled and walked back to his table. He couldn't believe his heart was pounding. This never happened to him. She had made him a little nervous while he stood there talking to her, and he didn't know why. She just looked so pretty, he found himself tongue-tied.

"How'd it go?" Ben asked. "Looks like good old Tony walked away, so whatever you said certainly did the trick."

"It was Charlotte," Blake uttered as he sat down, and Ben and Mary could tell he was stunned.

"Charlotte?" Mary asked. "Why didn't you invite her over?"

"Invite her over?" Blake asked.

"Isn't she by herself?" Mary asked.

"No, she's with a friend. Although... it seems like her friend is preoccupied with some guy at the moment," Blake responded, looking over and seeing her sitting alone while

Lindsay was talking to the guy next to her. "Charlotte said she was just going to order something and probably take it home."

Mary glanced over and saw Charlotte sitting there at the bar while her friend was chatting away. "Oh, Blake," Mary said, "invite her to come over and join us. She's all by herself right now. That's no fun, especially on a Friday night. At least she can have a little bit of fun with us," she smiled.

"But we've already eaten," Blake said, looking down at his empty plate, but liking the idea of inviting her over.

"We could get dessert," Ben said, shrugging his shoulders. "Might be nice for her to get to know you with us rather than just the guy who keeps showing up late to her meetings."

Blake looked at his mother and rolled his eyes, "Do you tell him everything?"

"Guilty!" Mary laughed. "Come on, Blake. Go on over, before she leaves."

Blake took a deep breath and walked back over. He hadn't felt this shy about a girl since high school. Not that he felt truly shy, but he had forgotten what it was like to have his parents encourage him when it came to girls. He couldn't believe it, but he actually had butterflies in his stomach and he found himself not wanting her to say no.

As he approached Charlotte, he noticed that she had now taken out a notebook and was jotting something down. This was something you didn't normally see at the bar, especially on a Friday night. It made him smile because he bet she was writing something about him and his newspaper feature.

"You working on a Friday night?" he asked, startling her.

Charlotte turned around to see Blake standing there again and, as much as she didn't want to admit it, he took her breath away. She had never been attracted to athletic-looking guys in her life, but there was something about Blake standing there in a baseball hat and a navy tee and jeans that did something to her chest.

"I was just writing down a few things I didn't want to forget," Charlotte laughed. "It's not like anyone is missing me," and rolled her eyes toward Lindsay.

"You know," Blake said, trying to keep it cool, "I'm with my parents over there," as he pointed toward Mary and Ben, who were sitting there waving across the room. "Why don't you come over and join us. We just finished dinner, but we're going to get dessert and stay a bit longer for the music."

"Oh, I don't want to hone in on your family time," Charlotte said, shaking her head.

"Not honing in," he added. "My mom was the one who sent me over. She would love to visit with you." He suddenly felt stupid, not wanting her to think that he didn't want her to come.

Charlotte looked over at his parents again, who were still waving.

"And I'm just warning you, they will keep waving until you come over," Blake added.

"You know," Charlotte said, looking over at Lindsay, who was still in la-la land with some random blonde guy, "I will, I mean... I'm all dressed up. I might as well enjoy dinner and some conversation. I actually just ordered, so I'll ask the bartender to send my food and the check over to where you guys are sitting."

"Great," Blake said, feeling a sense of excitement in his chest. "I'll let my parents know you're coming to join us."

And, as Charlotte smiled back at him, he felt something inside he'd never felt before: giddy happiness.

23

As Charlotte made her way to the Manor table, Blake noticed tables turning to look at her. She was that rare kind of beauty who didn't know what she possessed. One could just tell. There was a simple innocence about Charlotte that even made her more intriguing-- she was oblivious to the attention she was getting.

"Hi, Mary," Charlotte gushed as she sat down in the open seat between Blake and Mary. "And hello Ben," she said with another smile. "Thank you so much for having me over here. My ride or die has left me to die," she laughed.

"Oh," Mary said with a huge smile. "We're glad Blake convinced you to come over. Not to mention how he rescued you from Tony. My God, he's old enough to be your grandfather!"

"That's for sure," Charlotte nodded with a laugh as she tucked her phone away. She wanted to keep her phone out of sight for the time being. Lindsay had ditched her the second they sat down, and she had found herself obsessively checking her emails and she knew she should just take the night off.

"We can't wait to read the first article you have coming out on Monday," Ben stated. "I went with Blake yesterday to see everything get delivered at the high school. The gym looks incredible with all the new equipment."

"Yes, our photographer sent me the photos," Charlotte said. "Everything looks great. I hope you enjoy the article," she said, looking over at Blake. "You shared some important details on this one, including why it was so important for you."

"Thanks," Blake nodded.

"I'm excited to hear about your next idea. Do you feel like sharing?" Charlotte asked, looking hopeful.

Blake watched the excitement on her face, and it touched him that she cared so much about it. He knew he had given her a hard time initially about whether the *View* should have been given the story. He had been so annoyed when Frank showed up to the meeting with her without giving him a heads up.

"Oh, Blake," Mary glowed. "Tell her!"

Blake looked over at Charlotte, "I thought it would be nice to start a $3000 scholarship fund each holiday season to give to a student who is doing exceptional things for the community. My plan is that it will continue year after year, but we would start the first one this year...it would be the kickoff."

"I love that idea," Charlotte said enthusiastically, looking directly at Blake. "Are you thinking Alex would be the first recipient?"

"Yes," Blake smiled, knowing that she had really listened to him the other day. "He's exactly who I had in mind."

Mary watched the two of them stare at each other. When

it came to women, she knew her son was different than he had been in high school, but Charlotte was the kind of girl he had been attracted to back then. He had always fallen for girls with a head on their shoulders, and not just pretty faces like Piper. The parade of women he was photographed with made her stomach turn. They were always dressed in barely-there clothing, and always in full hair and makeup. Every time she grilled him about them, he would tell her he was just having fun right now, not looking for anything serious. She knew he was young, so she let it go, as much as it was tough to do. Whether Blake knew it or not, Charlotte possessed both beauty and a head on her shoulders. She was the kind of girl she pictured him with, not someone like Piper Saunders. Maybe this suspension was the best thing that could have happened to him. He might just figure out the importance of being with the right woman.

"Well, I think Alex is a perfect choice. I have a bunch of other ideas that you're welcome to choose from, but I think it's more powerful if the ideas come directly from you. It makes it much more authentic," Charlotte enthused.

"So, tell me, Charlotte," Mary smiled, looking around Bluewater with its gorgeous Christmas decorations. "Do you enjoy the holidays?"

"Um... " Charlotte started. "I, ugh... used to love them. It's been a little different for me over the last few years. I don't know if Blake mentioned it to you, but I lost my parents a few years ago, so the holidays haven't been the same since then."

"Oh, sweetheart. I'm so sorry. I didn't know," Mary said, looking at Blake. "He didn't mention anything to us."

"Oh, Mary. Please don't worry. It's not something many people know about, because I don't talk about it much. I mentioned it to Blake the other day in the context of something we were discussing. The holidays are a little different for me now but believe me... I'm sure Frank will keep me busy, and I'm sure they'll fly by quickly," she smiled, hoping to convince them.

"Do you have family nearby?" Ben asked.

"No, actually I don't. My extended family is in Pittsburgh. They're all anxious for me to come home, but I'm sticking around here. I'm going to make my place as festive as I can. If I'm not too busy, I'm getting my first Christmas tree next weekend!"

"Oh, that's lovely! There's nothing like the fresh smell of pine. It just says Christmas," Mary smiled.

At that moment Charlotte's food was delivered to the table, and Mary discreetly looked over at her husband and motioned for them to head out. She didn't want Blake to notice, and thankfully her husband picked up on her subtle hint.

"You know what," Ben added, "you two stay and enjoy the music. It's getting too loud and too late for us old fogies."

"Oh, please don't leave on my account," Charlotte pleaded. "I can easily get a to-go box."

"Oh, stop," Mary gushed. "The night is young, it's just that we're not," she laughed. She looked over at her son who knew what she was up to and knew he wouldn't try to convince them to stay. She figured he would want to spend time with Charlotte without the stress of the article. "Charlotte, it was wonderful seeing you again," she reached over and gave Charlotte a hug.

"Honey, I'll see you later," and she blew a kiss toward Blake.

"How are you going to get home?" Charlotte asked, as his parents darted off quickly.

"I met them here in my own car," Blake answered.

"Oh, well... I can wrap this up, Blake," Charlotte offered. "I'm sure you have other things you could be doing tonight," she laughed. "I don't want to hold you up either."

"You're not holding me up," he chuckled. "There really aren't that many places to go to; besides, it's nice listening to live music," Blake said, motioning toward the band.

"Blake, I know how this town works. Tomorrow everyone is going to be talking about the two of us having dinner at Bluewater." She laughed. "Just watch! This might put a crimp in your love life."

Blake looked over and shrugged his shoulders. "Hey, let them talk, who cares? Small towns live on gossip."

"I'm sure your girlfriend won't be very happy," she said taking a bite of her food.

"Who, Piper?" He asked, feeling bad about the other night again. "She's not my girlfriend."

"No?" Charlotte asked confused. "Oh, sorry. It looked like it."

"Yeah... it's complicated."

"Gotcha," she laughed and nodded as she swallowed a bite, and took a sip from her wine glass.

"Listen, Charlotte... about Piper," Blake started. "I hope she didn't upset you the other night. I felt bad that she came at you like that. She normally isn't like that."

Charlotte shook her head and did her best to pretend that it was no big deal. "Oh, it didn't bother me. I know I have to work extra hard to get where I need to be."

"But it didn't come across as nice as it should have," Blake added. "I just want you to know that she didn't mean it the way it came out."

Charlotte just smiled and nodded her head. She wasn't going to tell Blake that whatever he wanted to call her, his 'girlfriend' was a jealous bitch. He would eventually figure it out on his own, but she admired him for trying to smooth over her behavior.

"Well, thank you for telling me that," she lied with a smile.

"So, how do you like working at Finnegan's?" Blake asked.

"I'm not a huge fan of waitressing, but the tips are amazing," she nodded with a smile. "Waitressing was the only option I had, because of the hours. Finnegan's is a good place to work, the people are nice, and it's always busy."

"Yeah, that place is always packed."

"The good thing is that a lot of people from town don't go there, which helps because I hate waiting on people I know," she said frankly.

"Oh..." Blake laughed, leaning back in his chair. "So were you surprised when you saw me?"

"Truthfully? I was just hoping you wouldn't make fun of me!" Charlotte answered.

"I wouldn't do that," Blake said seriously. "No way. I commend hard work, and it's obvious you don't mind getting your hands dirty."

"I will say this, it's hard work, but it's definitely steady work, and I need all the extra cash I can get if I ever want to move."

"You really want to go to New York City, huh?"

"Yes, I do," Charlotte said, lighting up. "I know it's a shot in the dark, but it's a shot I need to take. I've been working on my portfolio, really trying to beef it up, and showcase what I can do."

"A small town isn't your thing?" Blake asked.

"It's not so much that," she shrugged. "I really do like it here in Barrington; it's just that I feel I'll have more opportunities in a big city. It was always where I wanted to be, and it was one of the last things I talked about with my parents. My dad told me that he and my mom planned to sell their house in Pittsburgh, and rent an apartment in the city, to be near me when I did eventually move. That meant a lot to me, and I kind of feel I owe it to my parents, as well. It was a dream we all shared."

Blake looked at her for a moment and then smiled, "I get it. You've got to go where your heart is. I can't fault you because I did the exact same thing. I haven't been back here for an extended stay in a couple of years, but I have to admit that there's just something about Christmas in this small town."

Charlotte smiled. "I have to say, Barrington makes it super special, that's for sure."

"Growing up here, Christmas was always my favorite holiday," Blake explained.

"Yes, I can imagine," Charlotte smiled, and then became serious. "Christmas did change for me quite a bit after I lost my parents. I know this sounds silly, but I didn't have anyone to buy gifts for. What I ended up doing was participating in 'Giving Trees' in the area. I never got to see the people open their gifts, but it felt nice to shop for someone."

Blake looked at Charlotte and smiled. He had her pegged wrong from the start. She wasn't boring at all; he just needed to get to know her a bit. She was like an onion, with every layer, he found something else.

"But what about gifts for *you*?" he asked.

"Oh, God," she scoffed, "I don't need anything. I love being able to give to someone else, but I don't need anything in return." Charlotte smiled at Blake.

She wanted to change the topic She didn't want to dwell on things she couldn't change. "So, tell me," she said, moving the food around on her plate, "where do you live in the city?"

Blake knew what Charlotte was doing, and he didn't want to pry or push anymore. There were things he didn't like to talk about, and she had respected that from the start. "I'm right on Central Park West," he answered. "I'm a suburban guy, so I wanted to make sure I had a good view of Central Park. That was my one must-have."

"Oh, wow! I bet it's a beautiful view. I used to love walking through Central Park as a kid with my parents," Charlotte said excitedly.

"It is beautiful. You'll have to come and see the sights from my place. It gives you a pretty expansive view," Blake answered.

"I'd like that," Charlotte answered. "Although I'm sure my apartment in New York City will have a much different kind of view," she laughed.

Blake and Charlotte continued talking for the next two hours about random things, oblivious to the band, the music, and everyone else. They talked about foods they liked, and foods they hated. They talked about movies and TV shows that they had seen. They also discussed places they'd always wanted to visit. Charlotte told Blake all about Pittsburgh, and Blake told Charlotte about his favorite Rhode Island spots. Blake shared a bit about his sister, Molly.

As the band packed up, and the Bluewater staff cleared the last of the glasses and plates from their table, Charlotte looked around and noticed that they were among the last guests in the restaurant.

"Oh, look at this place! We'd better get out of here," Charlotte said with a laugh. "I completely lost track of time. Looks like Lindsay took off," she said looking over at the bar.

"Even my new boyfriend, Tony, has gone," she said with a laugh that was hard to resist.

"Well, it's just after 10 pm," Blake said, looking at his watch. "I'm used to starting my night at this time!"

"I can't imagine," Charlotte said, shaking her head in amusement. "Listen, if you don't mind, I'm just going to run to the ladies room. I'll be right back and then we can head out."

Blake nodded as Charlotte walked off to the restrooms. They truly were the last people there. He felt bad about holding up the staff, so he thought it might be helpful to wait for Charlotte by the front door rather than at the table. As he got up, he looked down and saw her tote bag on the floor and, as he picked it up, on top, he noticed a small book called *Learning the Game of Football*. It had a bunch of post-it notes sticking out of it. He smiled to himself knowing she was reading it. Maybe she was a closet sports fan after all.

Then he heard her cell phone ringing. Every time he'd been with her, that phone was practically attached to her. As he looked down, he couldn't help but see she had a string of text messages from a Dylan, along with 4 missed calls from him, too. Now, the only thing running through Blake's mind was, who the hell is Dylan?

24

As Charlotte drove home, she couldn't seem to shake the butterflies in her stomach. She had had such a great time tonight with Blake. It wasn't anything she had expected, and certainly not anything she had anticipated. Blake Manor was Blake Manor, but he seemed to be two different people. He was the badass ladies' man/football God in New York City, but he was also this funny, kind, gentle giant in Barrington.

Charlotte was touched that he had waited for her with her bag, and had even walked her to her car, making sure she got in and then watched her pull away. Until tonight, this was a side of Blake she hadn't known existed. He was turning out to be a kindhearted, thoughtful person, too. When he shared his idea of starting a scholarship fund, it touched her heart. He had opened up to her a little bit about his upbringing, and she knew he didn't want it shared publicly, but it all made sense to her seeing the way he bridged his childhood with the present. He wanted to give back, and that was commendable.

She wondered what Blake had thought of her mini

transformation tonight, not that it mattered. He had a girl-friend, or whatever you would call Piper, but she wondered if he had noticed. He'd obviously seen the guy hitting on her and had walked over to be her knight in shining armor, but the look of pure shock on his face when he realized it was her was priceless. Even having his hands on her shoulders had sent shivers up and down her spine. It was a feeling she had never felt before. She had always played it safe when it came to men, especially after her parents passed away. In many ways, she'd put up a wall, not wanting to fall madly in love, because her heart couldn't take another crushing loss. She knew she couldn't lose someone else, or she would die, too. It was a tough realization to have so young, and one she knew she was doing to herself.

As she parked behind her building, she pulled down her mirror and looked at her reflection one more time. She had forgotten what it felt like to feel beautiful. She smiled at herself as she tucked her hair behind her ears and looked at her eye makeup one more time. She knew she was attrac-tive, but she also knew she didn't care enough to put energy into her hair and makeup. Her mother had always been a makeup-free, hair up in a bun type of woman, and Charlotte had followed suit. The one thing Charlotte concentrated on was her clothing. That was something she splurged on. She needed clothing that was professional, classic, and elegant, clothing that would allow her to be taken her seriously. That's what mattered to her, but she couldn't help but smile at herself in the mirror one more time.

It was a cold night, so as Charlotte turned off her car, she blew warm air into her hands and got ready to rush into her apartment. The winter in Rhode Island was no joke. You felt like an icicle in the evenings if you were outside for even 30 seconds. Charlotte opened her door and started to run when she heard a voice shout out, "Charlotte!" It was a male voice, and for a split second, she wondered if Blake had followed her home to make sure she got in.

"Charlotte!" She heard again, but it was hard to see where it was coming from in the dark. "Over here!"

Charlotte turned to see car lights turning on and off a few times and realized where the voice was coming from. She squinted her eyes to get a better look and realized it was Dylan.

"Dylan?" She shouted back, as she walked quickly to the car.

"Yes," he waved and jumped out of the car to meet her halfway. "I've been waiting here for over an hour. I've been texting you and calling you for the last few hours. I was beginning to wonder if you were ignoring me, or if you had changed your phone number," he said.

"Oh, Dylan. I'm so sorry. I was out with Lindsay, and then with Blake, and then just completely lost track of time. I haven't even looked at my phone since earlier tonight," Charlotte said as she went in to give him a hug. She knew they didn't have an over-the-top passionate relationship, but it felt good hugging him and being in his arms.

Dylan hugged her back. "You without your phone?" He laughed. "So wait, where were you? Out with Lindsay and then, who's Blake?"

Charlotte pulled back from his hug and shook her head with a chuckle. "I swear you don't listen to anything I say," she smiled at him, but always felt a little hurt since she had already told him all about Blake. "Blake Manor is the guy I'm doing features on in the paper."

Dylan still looked confused.

"Forget it," Charlotte said as she rubbed her hands

together. "Why don't you grab your things so we can get inside. It's freezing out here!"

Dylan turned off the car and grabbed his duffle bag. He had never surprised Charlotte before or done anything like this for her in all the time they had been dating. He was a routine type of guy and never seemed to deviate from any plans that he had in place.

As they walked into Charlotte's apartment, she looked over at Dylan as he put his stuff down and took off his jacket. She had missed him, that was for sure, but she was still confused about why he had randomly shown up. "I don't know what got into you, Dylan. I've never known you to surprise me."

"You really had no idea?" he asked with a sly smile.

Charlotte shook her head, "No, none. I tried calling you earlier today, but you texted me back to say that you would call me later. When I didn't hear from you, I just thought you got busy with work and forgot."

"Well, I was busy, and I know it's been a while since we've seen each other. I wanted to do something a little crazy, so I rented a car and drove here because the trains were booked solid."

"I can't believe you did this," Charlotte smiled. "It's so not like you."

"I know, right?" he joked. "I have to admit, it felt a little wild. So wait, where were you tonight? I know you were with Lindsay, but who is Blake again?"

"I just told you!" Charlotte said, exasperated. "He's the football player I'm interviewing for the paper over the next few weeks."

"Is this the football guy in New York who got suspended?"

Charlotte nodded, "Yes, that's the guy."

"Jesus. What a disaster he is. I don't follow football, but he has been all over the papers. Seems like a real bad egg," he said.

Charlotte shook her head, "Actually, he's not at all what I thought he would be like. He's a really good guy. I don't know why he let his reputation get so bad, but the Blake I'm interviewing is the polar opposite to the guy in the papers."

"So what?" Dylan added. "He's been getting in trouble with the police, and pulling crazy stunts for the last couple of years. I was just reading about him last week. The name didn't register when you mentioned it."

Charlotte didn't know what to say. She couldn't defend Blake's actions. He had done some pretty horrible things and had caused a lot of damage and embarrassment to his football team and his family. She only knew the person she had been assigned to interview.

"Well, so far, he's been a good guy," Charlotte replied.

"Just don't let him fool you. You're a good journalist, so I have faith that he won't pull a fast one on you. Just have your guard up. It seems like a guy like him will do anything to save his butt, and it's certainly on the line right now," Dylan reminded her.

"Listen," Charlotte smiled, trying to hide her irritation with Dylan. She didn't want to defend Blake, but she also didn't want to hear Dylan's opinion of him. "Let's not talk about work right now. Why don't I grab us some wine and we can relax."

"That sounds like a perfect plan," Dylan smiled as he watched Charlotte go to the fridge. "You know, I like your hair like that. Looks good down with all those curls."

Charlotte smiled at him and kept walking. Even Dylan wasn't used to seeing her all dolled up. "What about my makeup?" she asked from the other room.

"Ugh," Dylan laughed. "I'm not into makeup, but it looks fine. It kind of looks like you have two black eyes," he laughed.

As Charlotte returned with their wine, she stopped in front of her hallway mirror to look at her eyes. Her makeup still looked flawless. She didn't have black eyes at all. She just rolled her eyes to herself in the mirror and returned to the living room.

"I'm sorry I couldn't get here any earlier tonight. I wasn't able to leave the city until 6 pm and, for me, that's like leaving in the middle of the day, but Lindsay thought you would appreciate the visit," he added.

"Lindsay?" Charlotte asked, looking up at Dylan. "What does Lindsay have to do with it?"

"She didn't tell you?" Dylan asked, sounding surprised.

"Tell me what?"

"Oh, darn. I thought she told you I was coming."

"She didn't tell me anything. What are you talking about?"

"I got a text from Lindsay this afternoon telling me that I needed to come to visit you because it had been too long," Dylan said as he grabbed his phone to show Charlotte the exact text.

"So you came because you got a text from Lindsay?" she asked, looking down at the message.

"Not just because of the text, I mean... I know it's been a while," Dylan added. "It's not that I don't want to visit, it's just that you seem to have a little more free time on your hands than I do."

"Free time, Dylan? What are you talking about? I have a full-time job, and I'm also waitressing three nights a week," Charlotte responded.

"I don't want to get you upset," Dylan expressed, seeing

Charlotte's eyes getting wider. "My new job has me tied to my desk, so it's not easy for me to get away, that's all I mean."

"I know that," Charlotte nodded. "I haven't put any pressure on you to come to visit. My God, I'm working my butt off here, so I can hopefully get to the city myself."

"I know," Dylan said, walking toward Charlotte to hug her. "Listen, don't get mad. I thought it was nice of Lindsay to text me letting me know that you missed me. It certainly did the trick because I wrapped up work and headed out as quickly as I could. Not to mention sitting in the car waiting for you for an hour. I texted Lindsay, too, but she didn't get back to me."

Charlotte rolled her eyes and laughed, "You know Lindsay. She left with some guy, and so she was most likely preoccupied."

"That wasn't nice of her to leave you," Dylan said, rubbing her back as they were still hugging.

"Oh, please," Charlotte laughed, pulling herself free. "It's Lindsay, I'm used to it. She's on the hunt for a boyfriend."

"As always," Dylan laughed. "Come on, let's sit down and watch something on TV. You've got me until Sunday afternoon."

And the first thing Charlotte thought was, "Oh, God... that seems like an awfully long time for him to stay."

25

Y ou can tell it's Monday morning in Barrington because there's a line of people at the local gas station waiting to buy the *Barrington View*. The publication comes out every Monday morning at 5 am and people can't wait to get their dose of local news. As newspapers around the country struggle with ad buys and content, the *View* still had lots of loyal customers. Most people actually preferred the hard copy to the online version, and that wasn't something you heard every day.

Blake felt something jolt him out of a deep sleep. "Wake up Blake, your first article is out," his father shouted.

"What the hell time is it?" Blake asked, with a groggy voice.

"6 am," Ben uttered.

"Did I ask you to wake me up this early?" Blake asked confused.

"I just thought you'd want to take a look," Ben answered and pointed to the local paper on his nightstand.

Blake looked over and saw the *Barrington View*. He had forgotten how early people woke up to get this paper. As he turned over to take a look at it, he rubbed his eyes. He woke up right away when he realized he was the lead story. There was a large color photo of him standing in the high school Fitness Center with his hands on his hips, surrounded by the new equipment. The headline read, "Manor Brings Good Deeds to Town," and Blake couldn't help but smile when he saw the byline, *Charlotte Court,* at the top of his article.

Almost afraid to read the article, Blake took a deep breath as he scanned it. He didn't see the word 'suspension' upon a first quick read, for which he was thankful. Knowing that the nerves in his stomach weren't going to go away, he began to read.

Blake Manor is bringing holiday cheer home to Barrington while he's staying with his parents over the next few weeks. Though Blake hasn't called Barrington home in almost ten years, it's a place that's near and dear to his heart. Blake grew up here, and his famous football career started right on the fields at the high school. It's been heartwarming talking to his family and friends about how exciting it is to have him back but, more so, for seeing him do incredible things for the town he loves. His passion for this town, his passion for the people, and his passion for the local businesses is incredible to witness firsthand.

Blake has challenged himself this holiday season with a good deed challenge. Each week he's going to be doing one good deed for the community. As many locals remember, Blake put football on the map in Barrington. Games were sold out. College recruiters lined the sidelines. And kids around town suddenly became enamored with the game of football, all because of Blake Manor.

The first holiday good deed that Blake has brought to Barrington centers around the high school's Fitness Center. Not many people outside of the high school know that the fitness center hasn't had a refresh or upgrade in more than a decade. As

Blake shared, "The Fitness Center was where I spent hours upon hours of time building my strength and reaching my goals. It was, in many ways, another home for me because I felt at peace there. It was a place to better myself and push myself. All student-athletes deserve a place that gives them the tools to go after and attain their goals."

After Blake spent a morning working out with Coach John Gorman, it was clear to Blake that something needed to be done. The expense of an undertaking such as this was something that the high school didn't have in their budget. That was all Blake needed to learn, and he set out on his first good deed, to refresh the Fitness Center at the high school.

"I had a chance to visit the high school as soon as I came home because I knew I needed a place to workout. I could have found an expensive gym or hired a personal trainer to come to my home, but it was nice going back to my roots and being somewhere that I knew would keep me focused."

Much of the equipment and weights were dated or needed fixing. With more than 400 student-athletes who have the ability to utilize the fitness center, he knew it would be a perfect spot to start. He felt each student deserved to work out with equipment that was the best of the best, even state-of-the-art. Many student-athletes don't have the ability to join gyms in town, due to the expense. The fitness center at the high school is free for all students, a great destination for them to turn to when they're looking for instruction and training.

"The second we unveiled the new equipment, it was like magic for these kids. I hope that it helps these athletes go after their athletic goals and dreams. Sports opened so many doors for me, and my hope is that it will do the same for the kids. You need to start somewhere, and maybe this fitness center will be the beginning for someone. It's a good feeling to be part of their journey, even in this small way."

Coach Gorman was brought to tears by Blake's generosity. "I still can't believe he did this. I know this gym meant a lot to him, but now he's paying it forward for so many other kids. There's no better feeling than walking in here and seeing these athletes working hard, but knowing it came from Blake Manor is a special thing. I can't tell you how many of my athletes want to be the next Blake Manor. This will give them the motivation to go for it."

It's estimated that Blake gifted upwards of $10,000 worth of equipment to the school.

The high school honored Blake by naming the fitness center after him. It will be known as the "Blake Manor Fitness Center."

"That shocked me," *Blake said.* "That really got me. I've won a lot of games and been awarded many things in my career, but this one went right to my heart. This is a legacy that I'll be able to show my children someday, and that means something to me."

On a personal note, if there's one thing I've learned about Blake Manor over the last week is that he's a very generous man who cares deeply about this town. Football may be what he does for a living, but he's a hometown boy with roots that run deep here. Be on the lookout next week for Blake's second holiday good deed. It's going to be another good one.

Blake sat up in bed and reread the article one more time, and he felt the nerves that had been built-up in his stomach slowly start to disappear. Charlotte had done it. She had written a solid first article without mentioning the suspension, or really even much about his football career with the Skyscrapers. He wasn't used to reading things about him without stats or plays being attached to them.

He saw his bedroom door open and his dad poked his head in again, "You read it?"

Blake nodded, holding up the paper.

"What do you think?" he asked with inquisitive eyes.

"It's good," Blake answered. "I'm not used to reporters actually listening to what I say," he chuckled.

"I think it's a great first article," Ben said. "She set it up beautifully and included some wonderful quotes. This is exactly the kind of press you need and, to be honest, you and Greg should try to get more articles like this one."

"How do you mean?" Blake asked.

"You're showing the Blake Manor I know and love," his father responded. "It's nice to see."

"Dad, I haven't been that bad."

"Oh, yes, you have, so don't let one article go to your head." Ben was totally serious. "It's just nice, for once, seeing you get excited about doing good things for this town. You have drawn a lucky hand in life with football and earning good money. Your mom and I love seeing you do good with it."

"Thanks, Dad, I appreciate your honesty. I just wish you and Mom would let me do more for you guys," Blake answered.

"We have all we need, Blake. Money doesn't buy you an easy life; I think you're beginning to learn that firsthand. My hope is that you continue to make positive changes in your life. Paying it forward is a great thing to be able to do. Did you know that even when your mom and I didn't have a pot to piss in we still did our very best to give back? We knew we couldn't donate money, but we could donate our time."

"I actually do remember that," Blake said with a fond smile. "We used to go once or twice a month to help out at the soup kitchen."

"Yes," his father responded. "It always felt good to be able to do something for other people. Too bad that a shitty circumstance prompted it, but you need to start somewhere. I think you've been wearing blinders for too long."

"Dad," Blake said, trying to reason with him. "I've just been a normal twenty-five-year-old guy."

"Well, maybe it's time for this twenty-five-year-old guy to start acting like an adult. Feels good when you do it, doesn't it?"

Blake nodded and smiled, "Yeah, it does." Blake looked up at his father and knew he needed to tell him what was on his mind. "You know Dad, I owe you and Mom an apology. I've been living my life hard in New York, obviously too hard. I've got to be honest, it's been fun because I never knew what it was like to let loose and have fun. My partying never affected my performance at work, so I never thought much about it.... until now, when all of this shit happened. I'm sorry you and Mom had to watch from afar. I hope I didn't embarrass you too much."

"Thank you, son," Ben replied, nodding his head with a smile. "It hasn't been easy, and I knew deep down it most likely had a lot to do with you never knowing what it was like to be a normal high school and college kid partying and letting loose. You were always so focused on getting to where you are now, you didn't let anything distract you."

"I didn't," Blake added. "But I know it can't go on, it's clear to me."

"Make sure you tell your mother this, too," Ben nodded, looking at his son as a way of accepting his apology. And do me another favor," Ben said as he turned to leave his son's room. "Let Charlotte know she did a great job when you talk to her."

His mind flashed to Charlotte and their time together on Friday night. He hadn't been able to get her out of his mind all weekend. He tried, Lord knows, but he kept thinking how comfortable it was having dinner with her. It was cool to get to know her on a more personal level. She was smart, witty, and she listened. Normally, the women he dated just talked about themselves, but she was different. She opened up little by little, and she asked questions that had nothing to do with football. He couldn't remember the last time he'd had a conversation with someone that didn't revolve around football.

He also remembered how gorgeous she'd looked on Friday night--her hair down, her makeup done perfectly, and her outfit. She didn't need a cropped top or cleavage to look sexy. She was able to make a bow tie blouse look stunning, and he didn't want to admit how many times he had thought about what she was wearing beneath that blouse. She looked that good. It was also bizarre spending time with a beautiful woman who had no interest in being with him. She had no agenda. She had no intentions of hooking up. In a way, that was driving him even more crazy.

Blake couldn't believe it, but he found himself a little excited about spending time with her today. They had planned to talk about the annual scholarship fund, but first, he wanted to thank her for the incredible article. He didn't want to let the morning go by without acknowledging it. As he grabbed his phone to text her, he thought surprising her with a Monday morning coffee and some pastries might be nicer.

Blake looked at his watch. It was still early. He didn't want to wake her up, but he also banked on the fact that she was most likely an early riser. He grabbed his phone and quickly shot off a text asking when she wanted to meet today. He figured if she got back to him quickly, he would know that she was up. As he got ready to hop in the shower, he heard the text and looked at his phone with a smile. He saw Charlotte's name pop up with the message, "*Morning! How does 11 work? I'm meeting someone at the Town Hall for an interview at 10. Want to meet there and sit outside? It's supposed to be a beautiful day.*"

He figured he wouldn't text back, instead just quickly shower, get dressed, grab her coffee, and head to her place. But then he heard another text come through.

"*You see the article?*"

Blake smiled, he knew she must be chomping at the bit for his feedback. He quickly fired back, "Yes," knowing it would annoy her, but hoping that before she left for work all would be smoothed over.

Blake thought about his life in Barrington. He had been at his parent's home a little over a week, and he had fallen right back into the small-town groove. He had always loved the holiday season at home. There was something magical about seeing the town come together to celebrate. According to his mom, businesses had started to decorate immediately after Halloween. Barrington looked like something out of a picture book, everything seemed too picturesque to be true, but it was. He realized he had missed the familiar feeling of being part of a community and a hometown. He knew New York City treated him as one of their own, but the truth was that was solely based on performance. There wasn't any loyalty attached to it. It was all smoke and mirrors.

"Hey, Blake" his mother called from downstairs. "I hate to interrupt you while you're getting ready.

"What's up, Mom?" Blake laughed to himself, thinking how crazy it was to be back home. He had forgotten what it was like to be back with his parents.

"Our phones are going off like crazy with people texting

us about the article!" She yelled with excitement in her voice.

The article must have hit the airwaves, and there were probably both good and bad reviews. The naysayers would say he was just doing it to look good, which was true, but there was more to it. He knew what he was doing would have a lasting impact. That meant more to him than anything.

He grabbed his phone and headed downstairs scanning the texts and missed calls, most from Greg.

"So?" Mary asked, hoping it was good feedback as she was head down in her own phone.

"Seems like Greg's happy with it. He says Charlotte did exactly what he was hoping for."

"Anyone from the team reach out yet?" his mom asked.

Blake shook his head, "Not yet. Piper sent me a bunch of texts."

Mary looked at her son as he scanned something on his phone. "What did she think about it?"

Blake shrugged his shoulders, "She has some feedback," he said. "I'll call her later. I don't have time right now."

"You heading to the gym?"

"First I'm going to head to Charlotte's to thank her for the article. I think it came out great, and I appreciated her holding back on some of the negative things," he said.

Mary smiled and nodded her head, "Yeah, I think it was nicely done. She didn't mention anything about our interview either."

"She interviewed you?" Blake asked, surprised.

"Yeah, the day you were late for your first meeting she asked me a bunch of questions. You know me, I get nervous. She was nice enough to put her notebook down and just listen. But the second I finished talking I couldn't remember a thing I said, although I know after all this time not to say too much to anyone."

"And you've done a great job, Mom," Blake answered as he walked over to give her a hug. "Listen... I'm going to head over to her place real quick. If anyone calls or stops by, just tell them I'll be back soon. OK?"

Mary nodded with a smile, "Tell her I said hello."

He didn't dare go into any coffee shop because he would get pulled into conversations, so the drive-thru was his only option right now. With this weekly coverage in the paper over the next few weeks, it was going to be a little tougher getting out. Most people were respectful of his privacy while he was home, but with everything going on, he had a feeling people would want to stop and chat.

As Blake pulled up to Charlotte's apartment, he smiled when he saw Charlotte's car in the parking lot, confirming that she was home. He looked at the multifamily house where she lived and hoped that her name would be displayed above the doorbell, or on a mailbox, so he would know which unit she lived in. He had ordered her a large, hot black coffee with cream, milk, sugar, and sweetener on the side. He wanted to make sure she had options. He also purchased a dozen donuts, choosing the variety pack, not knowing what she would like.

He noticed Charlotte lived in unit #1, which was downstairs. He felt nervous to see her. Without giving it too much thought, he pressed the button next to her name. A loud bell rang behind the door. Almost on cue, he heard movement and suddenly hoped that she wouldn't be pissed that he'd done a random morning drop by. As the door slowly began to open, Blake found himself face to face with a guy in a black turtleneck about four or five inches shorter than he was. He seemed just as surprised to see him.

"Oh, shit," Blake answered, "I think I rang the wrong bell."

"Are you looking for Charlotte?" the man asked.

"Yeah," Blake nodded. "Sorry to bother you, man."

It was then he saw Charlotte walking up behind the guy with a surprised smile on her face. "What are you doing here?" she asked.

Blake locked eyes with Charlotte and smiled back, "I... uh... came by to thank you," and held up the tray of coffee and box of donuts.

"You must be Blake Manor," the guy said, looking at Blake and then over at Charlotte.

"I am," Blake said, nodding his head. "I'd shake your hand, but I don't have a free one at the moment."

"I see," the guy responded. "Here, let me grab something."

"Thanks," Blake said, handing him the box of donuts, looking over at Charlotte who appeared thankful for his gesture by the look on her face.

"I'm Dylan," the guy said as he held out his free hand to shake Blake's. "Charlotte's boyfriend."

In that moment, Blake felt his stomach turn, almost dropping the coffee.

26

"Here, come on in, Blake," Charlotte suggested. "It was sweet of you to come over and deliver this," she said, gesturing to the coffee and donuts.

"Oh, no," Blake responded. "I won't come in. I don't want to disturb you two." Charlotte took his breath away standing there in the morning light with grey joggers, an oversized white tee, and her hair down. She wasn't wearing a trace of makeup, but she looked beautiful, more so than she had on Friday night.

"You're not disturbing us," Charlotte answered quickly. "Dylan was just about to head out. He had planned to leave yesterday, but ended up with a migraine which left him on the couch all day."

"My boss is going to kill me," Dylan responded, looking at Blake. "I'm a trader on Wall Street, and my boss doesn't believe in sick days."

"But there was no way he could have driven," Charlotte interjected.

"I finally gave up trying to convince her otherwise."

Dylan tried to joke with Blake, but it was obvious Blake didn't really care. He was more interested in Charlotte.

"Well, I just wanted to thank you for the article. It came out great," Blake smiled at Charlotte.

Charlotte beamed and looked over at Dylan, "See, he liked it!"

"You didn't think I would?" Blake asked, feeling bad as he looked over at Charlotte.

"Honestly? I didn't know for sure. Well... I hoped you would," Charlotte answered. "Dylan read it this morning and thought it was fluffy with not enough substance, so I got worried."

"Well, in defense of myself," Dylan said, annoyed, looking over at Charlotte, "I know your writing tends to be more hard-hitting, that's all. This was more of a feel-good piece. I don't actually think I used the word fluff. I mean, she didn't mention anything about your career."

Blake looked at Dylan and immediately hated the guy, which he knew wasn't fair, but he knew this type of guy. He was the kind of guy who had excelled in school, and probably hated the jocks. He was the guy studying while he assumed guys like Blake were partying, and this went up his ass.

"For what it's worth," Blake said, looking at Charlotte and ignoring Dylan, "it was exactly what I hoped it would be."

"Did you hear from anyone else?" Charlotte asked, with hope in her voice.

"I did," Blake answered. "Greg texted me to say he liked it. So did my parents, but they don't really count. I left my phone in the car, but I know I have a bunch of texts and messages."

"I'm glad," Charlotte nodded. "I couldn't believe it, but Frank only edited one small thing. Normally he makes a few changes, but he kept this one pretty much as is."

"Well, there you go," Blake chuckled.

"See," Dylan said looking over at Charlotte, "that's all you should care about--Frank and Blake liked it. Don't listen to me, I know nothing about journalism." He looked at Blake, "I always feel the pressure when she asks me to read what she's written."

Charlotte smiled politely and Blake could tell she looked defeated. He didn't know the history or the dynamic between the two of them, but he sensed it was off. Dylan didn't seem like the kind of guy you head to a bar and have fun with. He seemed uptight standing there in his khakis, white button-down, and Vineyard Vines sweater vest. He looked like a preppy guy you find at the country club, not at football games. He knew he needed to get out of there before he said anything he would regret.

"Well, it was good to meet you, Dylan," Blake said, his voice a little tight. "Charlotte, I'm heading to the gym and then I'll see you at 11 am, right?"

She nodded with a smile, "Yes, I'll see you at 11. Don't be late! And thank you for the breakfast surprise."

Blake turned to walk toward his car as Dylan and Charlotte headed back inside. As Blake was about to get into his car, he turned and saw the door was still open a crack and he shouted, "Hey, Charlotte!"

He saw the door open again and their eyes locked, "Yeah?" she answered.

"How do you take your coffee?"

"How do I take my coffee?" she laughed. "With cream and sugar. What about you?"

"Oh," Blake smiled deviously, "I don't put that stuff in my body!" Then he winked and hopped in his car, leaving Charlotte standing in the cold feeling hot all over.

"He's flirting with you, Charlotte," Dylan stated for a second time. "I don't know how you can miss it."

"For the second time," Charlotte said, looking at Dylan, "he's not. He has a girlfriend, or I should rephrase that, *many* girlfriends."

Dylan grabbed his last few things and looked over at her again. "I don't know," he said with a shrug, upset. "Maybe this is fun for him while he's home, then. You're obviously not the type of girl he normally dates, but you should be careful."

"What's that supposed to mean?" Charlotte asked, feeling hurt.

"You said yourself that he normally has parades of women around him. You're not exactly groupie girl material. He goes for that sexy type," he said bluntly.

"You don't find me sexy?" she asked, wondering what he was really trying to say.

"Charlotte," Dylan answered, realizing he walking into a minefield. "Of course you're sexy--in your own way. You're not the kind of girl who needs attention. I love the way you dress, and how you don't fuss and constantly worry about your hair and makeup. People take you more seriously that way. You know that."

Charlotte stood listening to Dylan, not sure how to respond. She knew she wasn't a sex pot, but men had noticed her the other night. For Pete's sake, Blake had noticed her the other night. She never worried about her appearance with Dylan. Not to mention, she had always thought he was cute in that academic kind of way, and those were always the types of guys that she was normally attracted to.

"I can tell you are upset," Dylan said. "I don't want you to be. I just want you to be careful. You're not the kind of girl a professional athlete falls for--the bubbly, blonde cheerleader type. You're the brainy, smart blonde that I love," he said as walked over to hug Charlotte. "That's all I'm trying to say."

The truth was she knew instinctively that Dylan was right. She wasn't the kind of girl a guy like Blake Manor goes for, which was why she knew he wasn't flirting with her. He had Piper breathing down his throat, and she was certainly no Piper. Nevertheless, she couldn't help tears from forming in her eyes listening to Dylan break it down so pointedly. She knew their relationship wasn't built on hot sex and crazy romance, but she also knew why she'd chosen someone like him. He was a safe choice. She knew she could build a life with him, and feel some sort of love for him knowing, at the same time, she was protecting her heart from the pain of losing someone she couldn't live without. She would love nothing more than to fall crazy in love with someone. The kind of love where you can't breathe or live without them, but she wasn't sure she would ever let herself get to that point. What scared her was that she was thinking about Blake a lot lately, and she knew she needed to guard her heart.

"I better get going. I might be able to spend a few hours in the office if I leave now," Dylan said as he pulled back from their hug and kissed her forehead. He grabbed his bag and walked toward the door, "I hate leaving you like this, but please know I didn't mean it rudely. I promise. I love you, and I will try to give you a call tonight, OK?"

Charlotte smiled and nodded her head, "Sounds good, Dylan. Have a safe trip and thanks for coming."

27

Charlotte's 10 am ended earlier than she expected, so she had time to sit outside by herself and enjoy the warm sun on her face. She sat thinking about her first article about Blake, and she felt good knowing she had received positive feedback so far. Greg had personally reached out to thank her. Frank had called to say that the online comments had all been fairly positive. As well, he said the article had been shared by a dozen online sports publications, and already had thousands of shares from fans. This was incredible for the *View*. It was crazy to see that a simple article could be shared so widely in such a short amount of time, truly the Blake Manor Effect.

She grabbed her notebook and began jotting down a few notes for Blake. Her notebook possessed all of her thoughts and notes on Blake, including things she would never, ever mention in her articles, but they were things she didn't want to forget. She wasn't out to ruin his reputation. She liked seeing this different side of Blake that not many people got to hear about.

She had been reading about the game of football, trying

her hardest to understand the game. It wasn't too complicated once the core principles were understood. She even watched a game on TV while Dylan was sleeping, feeling proud of herself that she understood what was going on. She knew it may seem crazy to some, but she kept a section of her notebook devoted to football terminology.

"You're always writing in that notebook," a friendly voice said. Without turning around, she knew it was Blake.

"How else do you expect me to write about you, or anyone else for that matter?" she responded, holding it up with a laugh. "I can't remember everything people tell me, so all of my notes have to go somewhere."

"Well, you certainly write fast enough. Do I dare ask to see what's inside?" He asked with curious eyes.

"Nobody touches my notebooks," she said, trying to sound serious as she noticed Blake carrying two cups and a little white bag. Her heart soared thinking that he may have thought of her again.

"I hear you," he nodded. "Nobody touches my playbooks. They're my work bibles."

"Then you get what I'm saying," she answered, looking down at her notebook. "I write down more than just the things people tell me. I write about my feelings, and random things I pick up from them. It's the best way for me to connect with a story. Sometimes I even write down what people are wearing, just so I'll have a mental picture again of our interview."

"Impressive," he nodded, sitting down next to Charlotte and handing her one of the paper cups.

"What's this?" she asked with a hesitant smile. Blake was wearing different workout clothes than he'd had on that morning, and it was obvious that he must have gone home to shower because she could smell a fresh soap scent on him. She couldn't help but notice how good he looked in his navy hoodie and joggers, along with a grey wool beanie.

"Hot cider and homemade apple danish from my mom," he answered. "She wouldn't let me leave without bringing something for you."

Charlotte smiled, thankful for the kind gesture. "Well, please thank her. I haven't had hot cider in forever, and the danish looks incredible," she said, peeking into the bag.

"Hey, listen," Blake said, "I hope your boyfriend wasn't upset with me for stopping by this morning."

"Oh, Dylan? Oh, no, don't worry about it. I mean, how would you have known he was going to be there?" Charlotte smiled, feeling her stomach turn. Dylan's words were still fresh in her mind about how a guy like Blake would never go for a girl like her. "I really appreciated it. It was a nice surprise."

"Good," Blake smiled. "I'm glad. So how long have you and Dylan been together?"

"For a couple of years now," Charlotte answered. "We met in college, but after graduation, he moved to New York City."

"Another reason to move there?" Blake asked, looking over at Charlotte.

"Yeah," Charlotte nodded hesitantly. "It will be nice to be in the same place again. I'm sure it's the same thing for you —it's tough not being with all of your lady friends while you're here," Charlotte chuckled, trying to change the subject.

"Oh, my lady friends," Blake nodded. "Is that what we're calling them?"

"Believe me, I'm sure they're missing you, too," Charlotte winked.

"I guess we'll see," he said shrugging his shoulders. "I've

still got a couple more weeks at home, so they're going to have to manage."

Charlotte laughed "Hopefully, they'll see the article."

"I hope everyone does. That article has gotten some good attention today. I shared it on my social media right before I came over, so I'm hoping that will give it an extra push," Blake said as he grabbed his phone to see who was calling him. Charlotte happened to notice Piper's name pop up, but he hit the ignore button and just continued talking.

"I can't believe the number of shares it's getting online," Charlotte answered, the heat of his body sending shivers up her back. She didn't want him to have this kind of effect on her because she knew, at the end of the day; it was all about Piper and the ladies back home. Her job was interviewing Blake, plain and simple. There could, and would, be nothing more. She had Dylan, and Blake had his posse of women. She wasn't his type, and she wouldn't be stupid enough to fall for a football player. Everyone knew they had a new girl each week.

"Well, believe it," he said. "I know not all the feedback has been positive. I knew people would call me out saying I was just trying to sweep the arrest and suspension under the carpet, but I was expecting that. All in all, it's been really good and I have you to thank for that."

"In all fairness, Greg certainly knew what would be good for you," she said.

"Greg knows his stuff," Blake said, shrugging his shoulders. "He's not the kind of guy to beat around the bush. He actually wants me to do more stuff like this in New York City when I get back. See what you've inspired?"

"I'm glad… which brings us to the scholarship fund," Charlotte said, trying to sound professional. She had worn her hair down today, knowing that it was silly, but she couldn't help it. Blake had mentioned how different she looked the other night with it down, so she thought it would be nice to wear it that way today. She had added a headband, just to keep it a bit more professional-looking. "Let's dive in," she said, looking down at her notebook, ready to write.

"Before we get going," Blake said, looking at Charlotte, "I wanted to tell you that I've come up with a third idea, and you were the one who inspired it."

"I was?" she said, sounding confused, but anxious to hear about it.

"Yeah, I want to start a Holiday Giving Tree in town. I had my dad look into it and nobody does this type of thing here, so I thought it might be nice to start one, and then have all the gifts delivered on Christmas Eve."

Charlotte felt her throat catch, not wanting to show any emotion, but she couldn't help it. She loved the idea and knew that it would be an amazing holiday good deed. As much as a lot of people in Barrington had money, she knew firsthand that there were people in town who would really benefit from this. "Oh, Blake," she said as her voice cracked a bit, "I think that's a great idea."

Blake heard the emotion in Charlotte's voice and knew that it meant something. She was the reason he'd thought of it. The second she had mentioned that she didn't receive any holiday gifts from anyone, he felt bad. He knew it was because she didn't have a family, but he didn't think anyone should have that happen to them at Christmas.

"I'm glad you like it," Blake answered with a smile. "I figured it would be a great way to not only give back, but to inspire others to do the same."

"It's perfect," she said, composing herself. "Hey listen, if you have time right now, why don't I interview you for both of them? Kill two birds with one stone. It won't take too much extra time, I promise."

"Whatever you want," Blake said, smiling. "I'm all yours."

Charlotte smiled, knowing there were thousands of women who would love to hear Blake Manor say that to them.

She didn't have to say much to get Blake talking--so different from their first meeting. She sat, furiously taking notes, as Blake talked about his idea on the scholarship fund. He talked about Alex and told Charlotte that he had been just like him growing up, having to utilize everything he could that didn't cost his parents extra money. He asked her not to share Alex's personal background story because it wasn't his to share, but he talked about the scholarship fund and why Alex would be his first recipient. Blake talked about leaving a legacy and wanting to create something that he could look back on years from now and know that it helped and that it mattered. This conversation rolled seamlessly into the Holiday Giving Tree for the town, and why it was important.

"You really love this stuff, huh?" He asked with a smile as he watched Charlotte smiling as she jotted down note after note. She had been difficult to not stare at while they worked today. She looked so much more relaxed with her hair down. She looked pretty with it any which way, but he liked it down. She was wearing jeans, ankle boots, and a green puffer jacket that made her eyes look even bluer and her hair even blonder. She had a classic, natural beauty about her that drew him in. She was the exact kind of girl he would have fallen for in high school, although he knew she wouldn't have given him a second look back then. He was the big, quiet jock, and she must have been the beautiful, studious editor of the school newspaper—and someone who judged guys like him before they knew them.

Charlotte looked up at smiled at Blake as she wrapped up her notes. "Yes, I do and I think I have it all. There is more than enough here to write the next two articles."

"Well, you know where to find me if you need anything else," Blake said.

"Off the record," Charlotte said as she shut her notebook.

"Oh, she's getting serious with me now," Blake laughed. "Off the record, this better be good."

"Oh, stop," Charlotte laughed. "But seriously, what's the biggest misconception about you that's out there?"

"The biggest?" Blake asked as he sat back on the bench to think about the question.

"Yeah, what's the biggest thing you're known for, but that's not really true?"

"Well, you probably won't believe me," he said.

"Why's that?" Charlotte asked, very curious to hear his answer.

"Biggest misconception is that I've always been this ladies' man. You know that... you've pegged me that way."

"Well, aren't you?" Charlotte shot back.

"What most people don't know is that I never had a girl-friend in high school. I didn't have the nerve to talk to girls," he admitted.

"Stop it!" Charlotte laughed. "You're pulling my leg!"

Blake laughed, shaking his head. "I kid you not. Girls were not my forté in high school."

"But you must have gone to your dances and proms," Charlotte said.

"I went, but not with anyone serious. Never with a girl-friend. I was always so focused on football that everything else seemed like a distraction to me. Not to mention, I was shy as hell," Blake admitted.

"This is unbelievable to me," Charlotte gushed. "I never would have guessed that about you."

"What can I say?" he laughed. "I was a late bloomer."

"You continue to surprise me, Blake Manor," Charlotte said as she stood up to pack up her things. "Just when I think I've figured you out, you drop something else."

"But none of that goes in the articles," Blake shot back with a wink. "After all, I do have a reputation to maintain."

"Not one word," Charlotte smiled, "and don't worry, your secret is safe with me. I wouldn't want to ruin your reputation or anything." Charlotte picked up her tote and started to walk toward her car. "And now, I have an article to write while everything is fresh in my head, and then I'm off to Finnegan's."

"You don't give yourself a minute, huh?" Blake asked.

Charlotte shook her head looking at her watch, "Not really, but it keeps me busy, and Monday nights are normally good tip nights. I wanted to try to grab a Christmas tree today, but it doesn't look like that's going to happen."

"Wow," Blake said in a surprised tone. "We're a solid week into December and you don't have a tree yet? I thought everyone in town had decorated by now."

"I haven't had the time, but it will happen this year. This will be my first tree," she said.

"I normally have a staff of people come and decorate for me," he laughed. "My mom hates it."

Charlotte smiled, wishing she had the money to do something like that, at least this year when she was so busy. But decorators aside, she was just happy her car still started.

It had been giving her so much trouble lately. She was lucky enough to be able to walk to work if necessary.

As they approached the parking lot, Blake looked at her and said, "Hey, if you're free Wednesday afternoon, you should come when we give out the first scholarship. They're having a ceremony at the high school. It might be nice for you, especially knowing the backstory."

"I would love that," Charlotte gushed. "Thank you. Maybe I'll grab a quote or two from Alex and add it to my article."

"I'm sure he'd be fine with that," Blake smiled. "I'll look for you on Wednesday."

"Great, it's a date," Charlotte said without thinking, not meaning to imply *date* date. She looked at Blake with a horrified and embarrassed look on her face. "Oh, my God, not a date. I don't know why I said that. I didn't mean date, I meant it's a set date for the scholarship thing."

Blake stood watching Charlotte's cheeks turn red as she tried to double talk her way out of her mishap. He knew she didn't mean date--she wasn't like that, and she had a boyfriend. Not to mention, he knew from experience that girls like Charlotte never fell for guys like him. They were smart enough to stay away from the circus that came with dating a professional athlete.

28

The Barrington High School gymnasium was filled with students, staff, and townspeople all excited to be part of the 1st Blake Manor Scholarship Fund ceremony. As soon as word spread around town, everyone wanted to be there.

Charlotte was told that it started at 4 pm, so she arrived at 3:30 pm, thinking it would be plenty of time to find a seat, situate herself, and even grab a quote or two from Alex. She didn't think she'd be late for the ceremony, but she had been wrong, dead wrong. The place was packed solid and as she walked in and looked around, it seemed clear that she wasn't going to get a seat. The only thing she could do was stand in the back and watch from afar, wishing she had arranged a press seat for herself.

She found a spot in the back, put her tote on the ground, and pulled out her notebook. She spotted Blake on stage, walking around greeting people, and she found herself smiling. He knew how to take charge and deal with fans, and it was pretty neat watching him go from person to person with a smile and a handshake. He was dressed in a dark gray suit that hugged his body perfectly, obviously expensive. He was wearing a white button-down underneath along with a navy blue tie. As much as Charlotte wanted to push the thought from her mind, he looked good enough to eat. Even his hair was gelled back to give him more of a polished look, making him appear as if he'd walked right out of the pages of a magazine.

She saw Blake motion to his watch at someone across the room, most likely signaling that he wanted to start getting things ready. She laughed to herself, knowing that he wasn't a stickler for time when it came to her. Blake then walked over to a couple of people sitting in the front row and bent down to talk to them. Charlotte couldn't see who they were, but she assumed it was his parents, or friends, or maybe even Alex. She watched Blake stand up and look out into the sea of people, obviously looking for someone. She flipped to an empty page in her notebook and jotted some notes about the gymnasium, and the sea of people.

"Excuse me," an older woman standing next to her said loudly.

Charlotte looked up and smiled, "Yes?"

"Looks like someone is trying to get your attention," the woman said, pointing forward. "I certainly know he's not trying to wave me down," the woman laughed.

Charlotte looked up and saw Blake waving at her. Charlotte pointed to herself and mouthed the word "me?" making sure that she was who Blake was trying to flag down. He laughed, saying something to the person sitting in front of him, then shook his head up and down and waved for her to come down to the front.

Feeling a little extra pep in her step about being called out of the peanut gallery, Charlotte tossed her notebook into her bag and headed down to the front of the gymnasium. As she walked down the aisle, heads turned to see who it was that Blake was calling down to the front. She kept her eyes focused in front of her, trying not to let the attention embarrass her. She knew that Blake was a big deal, but she didn't want to call attention to herself.

"What were you doing back there?" Blake said as she got closer.

"There were no open seats," Charlotte responded.

"There's one next to my mom," Blake motioned. "Come and sit down next to her. You'll get a good view of the ceremony."

"Are you sure? I don't mind standing," Charlotte added, not wanting to take an open seat if it was meant for someone else. She turned to where Blake was motioning and saw Ben and Mary smiling and waving at her. They were sitting next to Greg, and who she assumed was Alex and his family.

"I told you I would be on the lookout for you," Blake whispered, "I'm a man of my word. Grab it before someone else snatches it. We're about to get started."

Charlotte didn't waste another second and walked over to the empty seat next to Mary. This was better than standing in the back.

"Hi, Charlotte," Mary smiled as she sat down. "It's wonderful to see you."

"Hi, Mary," Charlotte greeted her back. "So great to see you. This should be pretty exciting, huh?"

Mary nodded and looked over at Blake who was heading back onto the stage. "He's been looking forward to this all morning, a little nervous I think, but don't tell him I said that. I don't see him before football games anymore, but he used to pace the house all morning with nervous energy. I know he's excited about starting this fund."

"I can't imagine Blake gets nervous about anything," Charlotte responded, grabbing her notebook.

"Oh, he hates public speaking," Mary quickly answered back. "He puts on a good front, but this is probably his least favorite thing to do in the world."

"But he plays football in front of millions of people," Charlotte said, surprised by Mary's words.

"He does, but that's football. When he's in the zone, everything else just fades away. It's not like this," she said, glancing all around.

Charlotte looked at Blake who was getting mic'd for the ceremony and saw him looking down at his notes. He didn't look nervous, but that didn't mean he wasn't nervous. Moms always know their kids the best, she knew that. She smiled watching Blake run his lines to himself. He always seemed so confident about things, and it was sweet seeing yet another side of this football God.

"Looks like they're getting ready to start," Mary excitedly whispered to Charlotte as she saw Blake quickly adjust the microphone on his jacket and hand his notes off to someone on stage. "This is so exciting!"

Just as the ceremony was about to begin, she heard voices coming from the side of the gymnasium and wondered what was going on. The voices weren't loud enough to be disruptive to Blake as he began his introductions, but they were getting closer. She innocently turned her head to the side to see what was going on and froze when she saw Piper only a few yards away. She was walking along the far side of the gymnasium with an older gentleman, and they were heading towards where she was sitting.

"Are you expecting Piper?" Charlotte whispered to Mary.

"Excuse me?" Mary asked confused, as she was trying to listen to Blake's introduction to the crowd.

"Piper," Charlotte whispered again and then tilted her head toward Piper.

Mary looked over and shook her head *no*, "I didn't know she was coming. Unfortunately for her, there are no open seats down here," Mary nodded.

As Piper got closer, the gentleman pointed directly at Charlotte's chair and whispered something to her. Piper smiled at him and nodded her head, and then she carefully tiptoed over to Charlotte, appearing to enjoy the attention of the people watching her. Oddly enough, Blake seemed unaware of the disruption.

Charlotte smiled as Piper walked over, not sure what she wanted. Her escort had already started back toward the back of the gymnasium.

"I think you're in my seat," Piper whispered to Charlotte in a matter-of-fact tone.

Charlotte looked confused, "This is your seat?"

Piper nodded with an over-the-top fake smile, "Blake was saving me a seat."

"He was?" Charlotte whispered back, not believing her, but having no way of knowing if she was telling the truth.

"Yes," Piper answered. "He told me that he was saving me a seat next to his parents. Looks like you're in it," she winked. "Let's swap?"

"Swap where?" Charlotte asked, not sure what she was getting at.

"Just get out of my seat," Piper stated with another fake smile. "I'm sure there are plenty of open seats somewhere else, or you could just stand at the end of the aisle," she pointed. "I don't want to miss this, and I'm already late. Thank you for holding it for me, though. You're a gem."

Charlotte felt hot from head to toe. She wanted to scream. She was annoyed and outraged. She had just sat down and was now getting kicked out of her seat by Piper. Why the hell would Blake invite her to sit there if he was saving it for her?

"What's going on?" Mary whispered to Charlotte, trying to not make a scene as she watched Charlotte pack up her things.

"Apparently, Blake invited Piper to sit here," Charlotte said, obviously frustrated. "So I'm just going to sneak toward the back."

"What?" Mary said, mad that Piper had butted in. "Can't she find another open seat?"

Charlotte shook her head and whispered, "I guess not." Then she quickly excused herself and walked along the side of the gymnasium toward the back.

The lights in the gym had been dimmed at the start of the ceremony, and she knew that with a large spotlight on him Blake wouldn't be able to see a thing. She was upset about having to move for Piper Saunders. She was also pissed that Blake had invited her. It was obvious they had some sort of fling going on.

The moment Charlotte got to the back of the gymnasium, she took a deep breath. Thankfully, she was able to find a spot in the back, but she couldn't see much. She grabbed her notebook for the third time and stood taking notes for her article. It was tough to clearly hear everything Blake was saying, so between Piper, her poor sight lines, and the noise she was frustrated. Blake seemed to be doing well because the audience was laughing and clapping continuously. She definitely wanted to get a quote or two from Alex, so she was stuck here for a while.

When the ceremony ended, and people began to file out of the gymnasium, Charlotte waited to see Blake, who would be able to introduce her to Alex. As the crowd cleared, she peered down toward the stage and saw Piper walking over to Blake to hug him. He seemed to accept her embrace, which made her stomach turn.

Piper was dressed to kill, too, and she knew it. She looked perfect in his arms, wearing a tight black off-the-shoulder sweater with tight black jeans and tan suede ankle boots. Her long brown hair cascaded down her back in big, loose waves and her makeup was flawless. There were twenty or so people snapping photos of the two of them on stage, and she was loving every second. It was also clear that Blake was enjoying the good press and was clearly not going to put a stop to it.

Charlotte scanned the gymnasium and spotted Alex. She took a deep breath, knowing that she might have to have another interaction with Piper, but knew her future meant more to her than dealing with a devious woman. As she walked down the aisle toward the stage, she kept focused on Alex.

"Alex?" Charlotte asked, smiling at the young man in front of her who was flashing a smile from ear to ear.

"Yeah, that's me," he responded excitedly.

"I'm Charlotte from the *Barrington View*. Do you mind if I ask you a couple of questions?" Charlotte asked.

"Sure thing," Alex said with bright eyes. He looked to be sixteen or seventeen years old. He was a good-looking young man with an athletic build. He had about ten people with him who were all beaming and seemingly very happy for him.

"How does it feel to be the very first recipient of the Blake Manor Scholarship?" she asked him.

"Oh, it feels great. I can't believe that Blake chose me for the first one. I can't tell you how much this $3000 will help out."

"How do you plan to use it?" Charlotte asked with a smile, hoping Alex would divulge a little on that topic.

Alex looked down at his feet and then back up at Charlotte. "I'm not like a lot of the kids here. Money is tight for our family, so anything extra helps out when it comes to new sneakers or cleats, workout clothing, books, things like that. I know Blake started this because he wanted to give back. I just hope he knows that I plan to pay it forward, too."

Charlotte smiled at Alex who was just a young teenager, and she was impressed at his maturity and wanting to do good from what he was given. If only there were more kids like Alex in the world. "I think I've got what I need, Alex. I just wanted to grab a quote or two and this is perfect. Thank you for talking with me," Charlotte nodded and shook his hand. "Congratulations."

Alex thanked her and then turned back to his family. She could tell he was a little embarrassed by the attention, but that made her like him even more.

Since Charlotte had what she needed for the article, she grabbed her stuff and quickly slipped out of the gymnasium without running into Blake or Piper. The last thing she wanted was to deal with Piper again. She hated seeing Blake and Piper together and watching them play to the crowd. He seemed like a completely different guy when he was with Piper.

Who *was* the real Blake Manor?

29

"So, she's here in Barrington? Again?" Lindsay asked as she sat at the bar in Finnegan's, chowing down on a plate of mozzarella sticks. "What the hell is she doing here? I thought they weren't serious?"

Charlotte rolled her eyes, "Who knows! She must be here for work."

"Or pleasure, more like," Lindsay said with a frown on her face.

Charlotte made a grossed-out face and laughed. "All I know is that Piper kicked me out of my seat, and I had to freaking move to the back. All this while the ceremony was going on."

"I mean, who the hell would pull a stunt like that?" Lindsay asked angrily.

"This must be standard operating procedure for Piper Saunders. She didn't even hesitate. Blake's mom was shocked by the whole thing."

"Well, in all honesty, Blake should have told you she was coming. I mean, the whole thing is crazy. I blame Blake," Lindsay said firmly.

Lindsay had a free night, so she had come to visit Charlotte at work. She sat at the bar and just chatted with Charlotte every time she came over to grab drinks. Thankfully, Finnegan's wasn't packed solid, and Charlotte had been able to fill Lindsay in on her entire Piper Saunders encounter.

"I'm telling you right now, I wouldn't have moved," Lindsay laughed as she took a sip from her wine glass. "My ass would have been glued to the seat. I would have ignored her."

"Oh, please," Charlotte laughed back. "You would have done no such thing. Besides, I couldn't ignore her. I didn't want to distract Blake or the ceremony."

"Well, he was the jerk who invited her, so it would have been his fault, too."

"I don't know, I guess so. I just can't stand her. She talks down to me, and I freaking hate it."

"I'm sure she does the same thing to everyone," Lindsay added. "She's not the kind of woman to get where she is without being a shark."

"I don't know why Blake didn't ask *her* to write the articles on him. I mean, she has the means and the right audience," Charlotte said.

"Well, since they're dating, or hooking up at the very least, maybe it was a conflict of interest. Like I told you, Blake wasn't the one who pitched this idea to Dad. This was all Greg and his team. Blake just had to go along for the ride," Lindsay explained.

Charlotte remembered. Greg and Ben Manor were the ones to really push the local press idea with the hopes of it getting picked up by national news outlets. Since the first article accomplished what they had hoped, she knew the next few would, too. People loved Blake Manor and whether they were curious about him, or a true fan, they shared whatever they could about him. His haters would always hate, but she was pretty sure his supporters far outnumbered the anti-Blake contingent.

"I'm just glad I didn't have to deal with them afterward. I booked it the hell out of there after I interviewed Alex," Charlotte said.

"So you didn't see Blake after the ceremony?"

"Nope," Charlotte answered. "I grabbed my things and left. There was no reason to stick around and watch the two of them hanging all over each other."

"So, what? Did it turn into the Blake and Piper show?" Lindsay asked. "What about Ben and Mary? What did they think?"

"He's a grown man," Charlotte said, shrugging her shoulders. "He can date whomever he wants without his parents' permission. But, ugh... she was on the stage with Blake and loving every second."

"And he didn't try to stop it? This was supposed to be all about Alex and not Piper." Lindsay asked. "He is really pissing me off."

"Oh my God, Lindsay. You should have seen the two of them posing for photos on the stage. It was a photo opp for her, nothing more. It just left a bad taste in my mouth because the Blake *I* know doesn't seem to care much about stuff like that. I thought he would have had Alex up on stage for the photos. But, I guess, Piper's a different beast. She was hanging all over him in the photos; it was... I don't know... ridiculous. Obviously, he's with her and I guess she needs to make sure everyone else knows, too."

"She's marking her territory," Lindsay laughed.

"What is she, a jealous puppy?" Charlotte added with some gusto in her voice.

Lindsay stared at her friend. She had wondered if Charlotte would fall for Blake. No one could deny that Blake was hot as hell. You would have to be blind to be immune to his good looks. She knew that Charlotte had Dylan, but she also knew that wasn't a relationship built on heat and passion. Charlotte never talked about her sex life, which made Lindsay wonder if it was a good one. For all intents and purposes, Dylan and Charlotte were perfect together on paper, but that's all it seemed to be. Charlotte had always been so preoccupied with studying and the school news-paper that she never got out there to meet other guys. When she and Dylan started to date, it was almost like she had checked off that box in her life. No need to look anymore. She had never confided in Lindsay about her relationship, but Lindsay had always been an open book about the guys she dated. Charlotte wasn't like that at all. It seemed out of character for Charlotte to be so bothered about someone like Piper, and it made Lindsay a little curious.

"Wait a second. Am I sensing a little jealousy?" Lindsay said with a subtle laugh. "Cause that's what it sounds like..."

"Me?" Charlotte asked, shocked by Lindsay's question. "Oh my God, no way. Jealous of Piper? Are you kidding me?"

"I don't know," Lindsay shrugged. "She seems to have gotten under your skin. I've never seen you like this."

"She's got to be one of the fakest people I've ever met."

"And..." Lindsay egged her on.

"And, she's obnoxious, and she thinks she's better than everyone else."

"OK..." Lindsay said, hoping Charlotte would say some-thing else.

"And, she doesn't deserve a guy like Blake," Charlotte interjected.

Lindsay smiled at her friend, knowing that particular answer revealed her true feelings. Charlotte felt something for Blake, but she wasn't going to admit it to Lindsay, at least not yet. Maybe Charlotte didn't even know what she was feeling. Lindsay didn't want to push her friend, not while she was working, and not while she was pissed. There were two things she knew Charlotte didn't often talk about, one was her parents, and the other was her love life.

"Well," Lindsay said, trying to keep things light because she saw Charlotte was becoming more agitated. "Blake seems to be a bit of a mystery, but there is no mystery about the fact that he seems to go for girls dressed in barely-there clothing," she said disparagingly. "That seems to be his thing."

Charlotte looked down at her Finnegan's uniform, remembering the night he and Piper came in for dinner. She would never forget the look Piper gave her --a cross between pity and satisfaction. She couldn't describe it, but she had felt Piper's eyes boring through her.

"I'm sure he'll figure her out at some point," Charlotte nodded and then looked over at her tables and the customers she had ignored for the last ten minutes. "Crap! I gotta go check on my tables. I'll be back."

Lindsay watched her best friend rush off. Charlotte was one of the kindest, most hard-working people she had ever known. She also knew that Charlotte had no idea how beautiful she was, and that men constantly stared at her wherever she went. Her natural beauty drew people in. Her features were perfect and her personality, though serious, was warm and welcoming.

As Charlotte rushed back to the bar to drop off another drink order, Lindsay quickly popped off her barstool and gave her a kiss on the cheek. "I'm going to head home. Hey, listen, Friday night I've actually got a date!"

"Ohhh... with whom?" Charlotte asked, excited for her friend.

"His name is Peter, and he's a teacher at one of the elementary schools. I met him last week while covering a Town Hall meeting."

"OK, so no dinner Friday night dinner with you. No prob, I'll have takeout at my place," Charlotte said as she added some prepped drinks to her tray.

"I'm actually looking forward to it."

"Look at you," Charlotte smiled. "You're blushing."

"I am not," Lindsay laughed. "Let's just say I'm excited about this one. He's a great guy and really funny. I'm trying not to overthink it."

"I'm happy for you," Charlotte smiled. "I will miss our usual Friday night date, but I totally approve of the cancellation. I'll need full details on Saturday morning," she winked. "And don't go texting Dylan to come for a visit again! I know it completely messed up his routine all this week."

"Oh my God," Lindsay laughed. "As I told you before, I was just trying to do something nice."

"And it was," Charlotte added. "You know Dylan, he's not one to deviate from his normal plan. But have fun on Friday!"

"You know I will," Lindsay laughed back. "It's been a while since I've actually been excited about a date. I don't know, there's something about this guy. I forgot what it felt like to have real butterflies over a guy."

Charlotte smiled, grabbed her tray of drinks, and walked off thinking to herself, same here.

30

Charlotte felt the urge to walk to work on Friday morning, but was completely upset with herself as the late afternoon rolled around. It was dark by 4:30 pm, so although it was still afternoon, it felt like night-time. The temperature had dropped to just above freezing, but since she only lived a 1/2 mile away, she knew she could make it home without freezing to death. It was almost time to head home.

She was the last one in the office and, although the quiet was nice, she felt lonely. Lindsay took off early to get ready for her date--she had booked a blowout and a manicure. Frank left early for a meeting at the Town Hall, and said he would call it a day afterward. The rest of the team had slowly filed out once 4 pm rolled around.

Knowing that Dylan most likely wouldn't pick up his phone, she thought she would try him anyway. He had texted her to say he made it back to the city on Monday, but they hadn't talked or caught up all week. She listened to his phone ring, expecting it to go to voicemail, but she was shocked when she heard him pick up.

"Hey, Charlotte," Dylan answered. "What's going on?"

Charlotte could tell he was at work and most likely in the middle of something, but she was happy he picked up. "Nothing much, just wrapping up stuff at the office and heading home."

"Lucky," Dylan chimed back. "I don't know when I'm going to get out of here."

"Oh, that stinks," Charlotte responded, holding back her annoyance. Dylan always needed to make sure she knew either how hard he worked, or how long he worked.

"Goes with the job," Dylan answered, not having a clue that Charlotte didn't want to hear about it. "Good thing is that when I stay past a certain time, they cover dinner and my car service home."

"Not too shabby," Charlotte added.

"What are your plans tonight? Heading out with Lindsay?" Dylan asked.

"No, not tonight," Charlotte shared. "She has a date with a guy who works at one of the local schools here, so my night is free."

"What do you plan on doing?" Dylan asked, but she could tell he was typing away at his computer, only half listening.

"I'm going to order takeout and watch some movies. My goal for the night is to relax. I'm going to enjoy my night without crunching a deadline or waitressing. I know the next two weeks before Christmas will be super busy at the paper."

"So you're eating dinner, huh?" Dylan asked.

Charlotte pulled her phone from her ear and stared at it. Had she hit the mute button by mistake?

"What?" Charlotte asked back confused.

"What?" Dylan asked.

"I didn't say I was eating dinner, Dylan," Charlotte said. "Did you hear anything I said?"

"Yeah," he shot back. "I thought you said you were eating dinner and watching a movie."

"No," Charlotte responded, unable to hide her annoyance this time. "I'm still at work. I was telling you what I had *planned* to do tonight."

"Sorry, Charlotte," Dylan replied. "I'm in the middle of a project but didn't want to miss your call. I know we haven't talked much over the last week."

"Much?" Charlotte shot back. "Not at all."

"I know," Dylan added, sensing Charlotte's frustration. "I'm paying my dues like you right now."

"Yeah, but I still try to find the time to reach out. You don't," she answered quickly.

"Did I just not come to visit you last weekend?" Dylan asked.

"Because Lindsay told you to come," Charlotte shot back.

"Why does that matter?" Dylan asked. "For the record, my boss was super pissed that I missed work on Monday. I told you he doesn't care about migraines or sick days."

"Well then, next time you can go back sick as a dog," Charlotte replied. "Be my guest."

"Charlotte," Dylan said, as she heard the typing stop on his end. "Listen, I'm sorry. I was doing something when you called, but I'll stop so we can talk for a minute."

"Honestly, Dylan. It's no big deal. Get back to your work."

"What's got into you?" he asked. "I'm not used to you acting like this."

"Like what?" Charlotte asked, curious how he would answer.

"I don't know... needy," Dylan responded.

"Needy?" Charlotte laughed, shocked that he would say that. "Me? Needy? Dylan, for Pete's sake. I'm the polar opposite of 'needy'. I was just calling to check in, that's it. Call me crazy, but when someone calls you—your girlfriend for example--normally you stop and listen. Or don't bother picking up the phone in the first place."

"I didn't want you to be mad if I didn't pick up," he responded honestly.

"Forget it," Charlotte stated. "You go. I'm going to head home and relax for the night."

"I don't want you to hang up angry," Dylan said.

"You know what, Dylan...? I'm actually not angry. I'm just tired. I thought it would be nice to chat and talk a bit about work, but you don't even ask or listen when I do tell you something."

"Your job is a stepping stone, so it's not really the important kind of stuff you'll do in the future," he answered.

"Well, you're wrong. And, quite frankly, everything I work on is important to someone. As much as I want to get out of this small town to be in a bigger market, I take what I do seriously."

"You mean the Blake Manor stuff?" he asked.

Charlotte shook her head and rolled her eyes, "You don't get it. That article, and the other ones that I'm writing, are very good for my career. Do you get that?"

"Yes, I get it," Dylan responded. "I just don't want you to put too much pressure on yourself about them."

Charlotte exhaled. The truth was that Dylan wasn't trying to be mean; he was just laser-focused on his own life and work. It was part of the reason she thought he would be a perfect boyfriend and potential husband someday. He didn't coddle her or love her the way some women want to be loved, and she appreciated that. It had worked for her in college because it was exactly what she needed, but now? She wasn't so sure. She didn't miss him the way you should miss a boyfriend. She didn't love him the way you're supposed to love someone.

"I'm not," Charlotte answered. "I'm just doing what I need to do for my career."

"I know you are," Dylan responded, knowing this wasn't good, and fearing where this conversation might lead. "But listen, I can tell you're upset. Let's talk again this weekend. Nothing good will come from the two of us going back and forth right now."

"Yes, I know. You're right on that one," Charlotte said. "I'm around this weekend. Call me when you're free." And with that, she ended the call.

Charlotte grabbed her stuff and tossed it into her tote bag. Although she knew the temperature outside had to be around 40 degrees, she knew her body heat right now would make it seem a lot warmer. She wasn't necessarily mad at Dylan; she was just annoyed about their relationship, and that she had allowed it to get like this. He was oblivious because she had never really let him into her heart. Hearing she was upset was out of the ordinary for him, because she always made everything look and seem okay.

Walking the 1/2 mile home went by in a flash. The cold air felt so good. There was a slight winter flurry in the air, which added beauty to the cold night, making it seem magical. Just breathing in and out, and looking up at the dark starry night sky calmed Charlotte. The holiday decor and lighting also brightened her spirits as she walked along the streets. By the time she rounded the corner to her building, and had thought about her and Dylan along the way, she realized that he was creating *his* own perfect life in New York, and it was time for her to do the same.

Feeling better, and knowing that she needed a night to forget about everything, she stopped short the second she approached her door. There was a beautiful Christmas tree leaning against the door with a red bow attached on top, along with a note addressed, "Charlotte."

She looked around quickly to see if anyone was still there, but all was quiet. She walked up to the tree and immediately smelled the delicious pine scent. It made her smile, reminding her of being back home with her mom and dad. She reached for the white notecard and flipped it over.

"I know you've been busy, so I thought I would make sure you got your tree." -Blake

And suddenly she was hot from head to toe again, but this time it was not from anger.

31

Charlotte normally didn't cook or bake for herself, but with Friday night being open, she thought it might be nice to attempt to make something for herself. After her talk with Dylan, and then coming home to find the Christmas tree, her emotions were all over the place. She wanted to do something different. As much as ordering takeout would be an easy option, she thought it might be fun to try to make homemade pizza and chocolate chip cookies.

Thankfully, the grocery store was empty around 7 pm, allowing her to walk up and down the aisles and take her time without feeling rushed. She was normally always rushing to be somewhere, so it felt great walking each aisle without looking at the time.

"Fancy meeting you here."

She turned around, knowing exactly who it was. "I could say the same about you," she responded, unable to hold back a smile. Blake was wearing a baseball hat and a grey Adidas tracksuit, looking relaxed and cool as ever.

"Looks like someone's cooking and baking tonight," Blake said, glancing inside her cart.

"I got the Christmas tree," Charlotte beamed. "Thank you."

"I hope you haven't bought one yet," Blake said hopefully.

Charlotte shook her head, "I haven't had the time, so I appreciate it. The smell has already overtaken my apartment and I love it."

"Good," Blake nodded. "I dropped it off around noon and I was hoping nobody would take it."

"Nope," Charlotte answered. "I got it and was even able to get it inside and standing up all by myself."

"Look at that," Blake laughed. "So... what are you making tonight?"

"I'm making pizza and cookies. I don't know how they will turn out," Charlotte said looking at him, "but we'll see."

"You know, that surprises me about you," Blake answered with a glimmer in his eyes.

"What's that?" Charlotte asked.

"I think of you as a domestic goddess," he laughed. "I bet you make a mean cookie. You seem to do everything well."

"Well, I'm about the furthest thing from a domestic goddess there can be," she laughed back. "I never got the domestic gene. Homemade pizza and chocolate chip cookies are about as far as I go." Looking at Blake she couldn't help the pull she felt toward him. It was something that happened without thinking about it, and her heart beat faster every time she was with him now.

"Oh... that actually sounds good," Blake added. "My mom used to make homemade pizza for us all the time."

"So, tell me," Charlotte said, grabbing her cart to keep

moving. "What is Blake Manor doing at a grocery store on a Friday night?"

"I was grabbing a few things. My mom forgot how much I eat during the course of a week. She's trying to keep up, but I thought I'd help her out. I don't want her paying for extra grocery bills. What about you? I thought you said you normally spend Friday nights with Lindsay."

"You remembered," Charlotte nodded in approval. "I'm surprised."

"I do know how to listen," he laughed.

"I'm kidding with you," Charlotte added. "Actually, Lindsay has a date tonight, so I'm running solo this Friday."

"Kind of like last Friday, too," Blake added with a shrug and wink.

"Yes," Charlotte nodded. "But apparently this date is promising, so I couldn't stand in her way."

Blake nodded and smiled, "What about you? Dylan coming for a visit this weekend?"

"Me?" Charlotte asked, feeling her heart beat faster. "Oh, no. Dylan's back in the city. I probably won't see him until the holidays."

"What about you and Piper?" Charlotte asked, feeling her body tighten as she asked.

"She's back in New York," Blake answered, looking at Charlotte with a half-smile. "Listen, I'm sorry about the seat mix-up. My mom told me what happened. I honestly didn't realize she was coming. I did invite her and told her I'd reserve her a seat if she was coming, but she never confirmed anything with me. I figured she was taking a pass."

Charlotte smiled, "Yeah, well... honestly, I was surprised by the whole thing. It was embarrassing. I tried not to make a fuss, but Piper was not backing down, so there was nothing I could do but give up my seat."

Blake looked embarrassed. "Yeah, she's not known for being discreet. She said she wanted to surprise me, so that's why she never let me know she was coming. But, again, I'm really sorry. This never should have happened."

"Whatever," Charlotte said, still a bit annoyed. "I ended up getting what I needed from Alex, so all was good," Charlotte responded.

"I'm anxious to read it on Monday. If it's anything like the last one, it's gold."

"I hope so, too. It was crazy to see how many shares that first one got. I keep telling Frank that it's the Blake Manor Effect--you've got some major pull with your fans."

"I like that term, 'the Blake Manor Effect,'" he nodded. "I'm going to use that one."

Hearing his text messages going off she said, "Sounds like someone is trying to reach you, so I'll let you go. Thanks for the tree, and I'm glad everything went well for you on Wednesday. You were right: Alex is a great kid. I'll call you next week about getting together to discuss your 4th article." With that, Charlotte grabbed her cart and left him standing by himself.

"It was good to see you, Charlotte." Blake watched her walk away with a look of guilt on his face. Tree or no tree, he had messed up big time the other day at the scholarship fund ceremony.

∼

BLAKE GRABBED his phone and looked down to see who was texting him. It was Piper. There had been a barrage of texts from her in the last five minutes. She was back in New York with her girlfriends and wanted to FaceTime, most likely to show him off. Instead of getting back to her, he silenced his phone and kept moving, an idea forming in his mind. He just hoped he wasn't too late.

Walking quickly through the market, he couldn't get over how shocked Charlotte had looked when she saw him. She was normally open and friendly, but she was pretty cool, and he wasn't even sure she was happy to see him. He hadn't been able to get her out of his mind since Wednesday. He felt horrible about what had happened with Piper and, because Charlotte hadn't stayed around after the event, he assumed she had been angry. Blake wanted to try to make it up to Charlotte, which was why he thought surprising her with a Christmas tree might be a start. He could tell she appreciated the tree, but it was obvious that he should have called her after the ceremony.

Charlotte had looked adorable tonight, walking around with her shopping cart. She had been wearing a black beanie with her hair down, along with an oversized grey University of Rhode Island sweatshirt, a puffer vest, and tight gray joggers. She looked beautiful standing there with her list, and he had given himself an extra second to watch her before he interrupted her.

He knew he needed to push thoughts of her from his mind, but there was something about her he couldn't shake. She was driving him crazy, but in a good way. He felt this magnetic force to her that he had never felt with any woman before.

As he rounded the aisle to head to the cash registers, he spotted Charlotte reading the label on a jar of sauce. He stood there smiling again, feeling his heart swell.

It was now or never so, without hesitation, he walked over to Charlotte. "Hey. I want to apologize again for

Wednesday. I want to try to make it up to you. I know it's last minute, but do you want to grab a bite?"

Charlotte turned around quickly, "Oh, it's you again. You scared me. You want to grab a bite? Tonight?"

"Yeah," Blake nodded. "It's only 7 pm. You haven't started cooking yet," he said, pointing to the sauce in her hand. "Let's go get something to eat."

"I don't have my notebook or anything on me," Charlotte said with a confused look on her face. "I'll have to record everything on my phone, which I guess I could do. I was planning to kick back tonight, but if this is the only time you're free I'll make it work."

"Charlotte," Blake said seriously. "Turn it off, just like you did last Friday night. I'm asking you out to dinner, not to interview me."

"Oh. I...could do that..." Charlotte nodded, surprised by the offer. "I mean, I don't want to cause any problems with you and Piper. And what about people seeing us?" she continued.

"I'm not worried about that, and I'm not worried about Piper. Despite what you may think, she is definitely not my girlfriend," Blake said, being completely honest. "Everyone knows you're writing about me. Besides, when is it a crime for people who know each other to grab a bite?"

"Well, yes then, if you're sure," Charlotte confirmed one more time.

"Great," Blake smiled, which sent shivers up Charlotte's back. "You up for any particular kind of food?"

Still a bit confused and unclear about why he was doing this, Charlotte quickly responded, "What about pizza? Pepperoni's is open till 10 pm. They do mostly takeout, so I bet the restaurant will be empty."

"God, I haven't had Pepperoni's in years!" Blake said,

lighting up, which made Charlotte laugh. "They have the best crust, or at least they used to. Sounds great, let's head over there."

"I'll meet you there in thirty minutes. I'm just going to drop these groceries at home."

Much to their surprise, Pepperoni's was packed when they arrived. There must have been a middle school dance because there were tweens everywhere. The second they spotted Blake all hell broke loose. There were about thirty kids who all wanted selfies with him. Charlotte watched as each kid came up and snapped a photo. She noticed Blake took time with each kid.

"You make each kid feel like a million bucks," Charlotte told him when they finally had a second to get to the counter and order their pizza. "That took you about thirty minutes, and you didn't flinch once."

"It's always nice to chat with the kids," Blake smiled. "I never mind posing or doing autographs for kids. I remember being that age. Thanks for your patience."

"Well, you can tell it meant a lot to them," Charlotte added. "I snapped a few photos on my phone."

"Alright, so now let's feed you," Blake said while clapping his hands. "Now the kids will have to wait," he winked. "I pulled you away from your cooking plans, and even held you up with all this paparazzi, so let's figure out what we're going to order. What would you like?"

"I'm about as boring as they come with pizza," Charlotte joked, looking at the menu. "I'm good with cheese."

Blake looked over at her and laughed, "What? You're not going Plain Jane on me, are you? Let's order a few pizzas to try and get your honest reaction. How about a meat lovers, a veggie plus and, just for you, a basic boring cheese?" He winked.

As Blake ordered the pizzas, Charlotte walked over to find a booth. It was cute seeing the middle school kids enjoying themselves. They were playing video games, some were doing TikTok dances, some were taking selfies, and some were on their first dates. It was just sweet watching them and, of course, seeing them sneak glances at Blake. Charlotte looked over at him and couldn't help but stare. He had this magnetic way about him. He was saying something funny to the older man behind the counter and shaking hands with a couple of the teenagers helping him. People were drawn to him, part of the "Blake Manor Effect." It wasn't just about football, although that had put him on the map. He took the time to engage, smile, and listen. Maybe *this* was the real Blake Manor.

"Pizza order is in," Blake announced as he joined her in the booth. "They said it could be a while since we're behind all these kids," he said as he pointed toward the mass of kids. "But the good news is that the kids have calmed down and are no longer asking for photos. I think we're good. And tonight? No working, Charlotte Court. It's Friday and you deserve a night off."

"Oh, come on," Charlotte said, rolling her eyes. "I'm not always working."

"Um, yes you are. You're always on the clock. I like this version of you better," he joked.

"How do you mean?" Charlotte asked, not sure if she should be insulted by his statement or not.

"It's nice when you're just chill and not worrying about asking the right questions, or getting the best answers out of me."

"I'm chill," Charlotte said, leaning back and putting her hands behind her hand.

"You're getting better," Blake shared. "Maybe my definition of chill, and your definition of chill, are two completely different things."

"That's fair," Charlotte agreed. "Your kind of chill is sitting back with a beer, eating pizza, and watching football. Right? My kind of chill is reading on the couch."

Blake stared at her, wondering if he should bring it up, but decided to nonetheless. "So talking about reading. I happened to notice the book, *Learning the Game of Football* in your bag last week. New reading?" He asked with an innocent smile.

Charlotte's eyes shot wide open and her mouth got wide in complete shock. "Wait a second, were you snooping through my bag?"

"No, not at all... I just happened to see it in your bag when you were in the restroom at Bluewater," Blake nodded with a grin.

"Oh, OK. I've been doing a little reading about football. I figured it might be a good idea to understand the game, since I was interviewing you."

"And?" Blake said with a grin, enjoying the fact that he had her in the hot seat.

"And..." Charlotte answered. "I still don't understand the game completely, but I'm getting better at it. You're one of the guys that tackle people, right?"

Blake flashed his million-dollar smile and nodded. "Yes, I'm one of the guys that tackle people."

"Like I told you," Charlotte added, "I didn't grow up in a sports home, so this is all new to me. It's not the most riveting reading I've ever done, but it's an easy read, and I'm almost done with it. I normally prefer a Danielle Steel book, but I'm getting through it. And, for the record, Danielle Steel writes romances, so this football book is the complete opposite of what I would even pick up."

"Well, still," Blake grinned. "I'm impressed. And I do know who Danielle Steel is. My mom's a fan and always has her books around the house."

"Yeah," Charlotte smiled. "She's my favorite. I started reading her books in high school. My mom and I would read them and then discuss them. It kind of became our thing."

"That's sweet," Blake nodded, knowing it must be tough for Charlotte not to have her mom anymore.

"Yeah," Charlotte grinned. "My father would surprise us every Christmas with her new hardcover book. I mean, it wasn't exactly a surprise because we always knew it was coming, but it was our tradition and then we would spend all Christmas Day reading to see who would finish first." Charlotte looked up at Blake and smiled. "That's the kind of stuff I miss," she shrugged.

Blake reached across the table to touch Charlotte's hand. He just wanted her to know she wasn't alone. His touch startled Charlotte and she jumped for a second, and then looked up into his eyes.

"I can't imagine how tough the last few years must have been for you," Blake said sincerely. "I hope you know that you've got people here for you, myself included."

"Thanks, Blake," Charlotte smiled, wiping away a single tear from her cheek. "I appreciate that," she said as she grabbed a few napkins to blot her eyes. "Your mom actually reminds me of my mom a bit, which is nice."

"She would love to know that," Blake smiled back.

It was this side of Blake she preferred, not the guy on the stage with the fake smile next to Piper Saunders. How could one person be two different personas?

As Blake sat staring at Charlotte, he instinctively wanted to hold her in his arms and let her know that everything would be OK—that he'd make sure of it. But the sad reality was that he couldn't do that, and he needed to remember that. The thoughts and feelings he was having needed to go away. Being back at home was cluttering up his head. This wasn't his real life; this was just a momentary detour until his suspension was over.

Blake grabbed his phone to distract himself and to give her a minute to compose herself. He'd had his phone on mute and hadn't seen or heard the new texts, and the three missed calls. As he began to scroll through everything, he noticed that they were all from Piper. He rolled his eyes. He didn't have time for this tonight, and he certainly wasn't doing FaceTime. The second he was about to put his phone back in his pocket, yet another call from Piper came through.

"Charlotte, could you excuse me for a minute? I need to get this. It's Piper," Blake said quickly. "She hasn't stopped texting me all night. I've gotten about twenty texts from her since we've been here, and maybe it is something urgent. Just give me two minutes, OK?"

"Sure," Charlotte said and grabbed her own phone pretending to be fully immersed. But she was trying to listen to his conversation. She couldn't tell exactly what Piper was saying, but she was talking a mile a minute, and she sounded agitated and pissed about something. Charlotte smiled to herself.

"Piper," Blake finally said. "It's nothing. You know that. It's just a joke. You know it's just people trying to stir shit up."

Blake looked over at Charlotte and whispered, "Sorry," as he pointed at the phone.

"You know how these things go," Blake said into the phone. "I'm telling you right now, it's nothing. People would never believe it anyway. Come on. Think about it, it's ridiculous. It will blow over."

Charlotte tried to keep herself distracted, trying hard not to eavesdrop. She discreetly looked over at Blake and saw him readjusting his hat. He seemed frustrated about whatever Piper was saying.

"Fine," Blake breathed loudly to her. "I'll let her know."

Charlotte quickly shot a glance over at Blake, wondering what on earth was going on.

"I said I would," Blake said firmly this time. "I'm telling you right now, it's not a big deal. I told you, people will never believe it. But listen, I've got to go. Let's talk about this later, OK?"

And then Blake tossed his phone on the booth next to him.

"Everything OK?" Charlotte asked, wondering what the hell had just happened.

Blake looked up at Charlotte. "Well, that depends."

"Depends on what?" Charlotte asked.

"You know how you like to say I have a lot of lady friends?"

Charlotte looked at him confused, "Yeah…"

"Looks like you're one of my new lady friends."

32

Charlotte needed a second to process what Blake had just said. She knew Piper had been ranting and raving about something because she had been talking in a high-pitched tone that was hard to ignore, but she wasn't sure what was actually going on.

"What are you talking about?" Charlotte finally asked, staring back at Blake.

"Apparently one of the kids here must have snapped a photo of us tonight and posted it on Instagram... and it's circulating."

"Define circulating," Charlotte shot back, not sure what he meant.

"It's been shared on a couple of sites."

"How did that happen?" Charlotte asked, confused as hell.

"I don't know. All I know is that Piper said I was tagged, and that's all it took," Blake announced, noticing Charlotte looked uncomfortable.

"What are you talking about? We're in Barrington for

God's sake. Who the heck would have access to a kid's account?"

"She's going to send it to me, but it's a shot of you and me in this booth. It looked like we were on a date, so it started to go viral."

Charlotte sat there feeling as if her entire body was on pins and needles. She didn't know if she was shaking, or just staring into space. She had just listened to Blake tell Piper that it was no big deal, and nobody would believe it. He had been talking about her. He had been referring to dating someone like her, and how it was obviously just a joke. She felt like she wanted to vomit.

"Charlotte?" Blake asked. "You OK?"

"I...I... don't know," she said, trying to compose herself. She didn't want Blake to see that she was upset. But she couldn't believe he would say that nobody would believe they were dating...and right in front of her. What was she... chopped liver?

"Charlotte, it's no big deal. I promise everything will blow over tomorrow. I bet if Piper hadn't seen it, we wouldn't even know it was out there. It was just one of these little gremlins," he said joking, as he pointed to all the kids at Pepperoni's.

"Piper is upset because you are her boyfriend," Charlotte stated, trying to remain calm.

"That's not true, it's just Piper being Piper," Blake nodded, seemingly calm.

"You seem pretty calm about this," Charlotte said, stunned. "But I have no interest in being drawn into your complicated relationships."

"Charlotte, please, just relax. I promise you this will blow over. A couple of gossip sites have it on their Instagram accounts, but that's it. Piper's freaking out because she doesn't want it to look like I'm cheating on her which, obviously, I'm not."

"Is my name mentioned?" Charlotte asked, still wondering how one of these kids could have snapped a photo of them together without her knowing.

"I don't know," Blake answered honestly. "Piper's going to send it to me."

Blake looked down at his texts and saw that the photo had come through. "Here, come and look at this," he said.

"No," Charlotte shook her head. "I'm staying right here. I don't want any other incriminating photos taken."

BLAKE STARTED TO BELLY LAUGH, "Jeez... I've never had that kind of reaction from a girl before, at least not since high school!"

"Oh, is that right? Let me see it," she said, as she grabbed the phone right out of Blake's hand. It was a photo of the two of them laughing together in this very booth. If you didn't know any better, it did look like they were on a date, although they were sitting opposite one another in the booth, and they weren't touching or anything. It looked like they were just having fun.

"See," Blake said with a reassuring smile. "And it's not a bad photo either, so there's that, too," Blake stated with a grin.

Right then a text from Piper came through and Charlotte happened to catch it: *I'm coming to Rhode Island tomorrow to squish these rumors. I bet Charlotte arranged for this photo to be released. I wouldn't trust her at all.*

Charlotte let out a deep breath, and handed Blake his phone, "Piper just texted you."

Blake looked down at his phone and read the text. "You know I don't believe this, right?"

"I certainly hope not," Charlotte answered, hurt.

"Piper's all bark and no bite, I promise you. She's a little bit of the jealous type," Blake shrugged.

"Sounds more like a *big* jealous type to me," Charlotte said, pointing at his phone. "I would never do something like that... to anyone—I hope you know that. You're the one who invited me out, not the other way around."

"Charlotte, I know," Blake said, trying to calm her down.

"Well, tell your girlfriend," Charlotte shot back, feeling her heart pound with frustration. "It's humiliating, and not who I am... at all. I've dealt with Piper two times now, and both times she has gone out of her way to crap all over me. I'm over it." Charlotte grabbed her bag and her phone and darted for the door, not caring who was watching.

Blake jumped up and followed her.

"Please don't get upset, Charlotte," Blake yelled in the parking lot, clueless about how things had gotten so bad so quickly. "Let me call her right now and smooth this over. You can tell her yourself that you had nothing to do with any of it."

"Are you delusional? I have *nothing* to say to her! She's the one who should be apologizing to me," Charlotte yelled back.

"Please, Charlotte. Just stop for a second. I don't want you to be angry."

"Angry?" Charlotte interjected back. "You just told Piper that nobody would ever believe we could be dating and, that people would think it was a joke."

Blake didn't know what to say. He was in the middle of a shit show.

"You were talking about me? Right?" Charlotte challenged him. "And just in case you didn't hear me the first time, let me remind you. You actually told Piper that dating someone like me would be seen as a *joke,* and that nobody would believe it." She was now standing beside her car.

"Wait a second, you're taking it the wrong way," Blake replied. "I mean, clearly people wouldn't put the two of us together."

"OMG, fucking stop!" Charlotte demanded as tears formed in her eyes. "I don't want to hear it. I'm looking at the New York City version of Blake Manor and, let me tell you...he's a jerk."

"What are you talking about?" Blake asked, trying to close the gap between him and Charlotte.

"Oh, don't play dumb with me. You're one guy when you're home in Barrington but, in New York City, you're nothing but a playboy asshole. Who *are* you? Who is the real Blake Manor? You can't be both!"

"That's not fair," Blake said, shaking his head. "You're reading way too much into this."

"You know what? I'm just glad I wasn't tagged in that photo because I wouldn't want anyone to think I would be stupid enough to fall for a guy like you," Charlotte shot back. "This is exactly why I didn't want to interview you in the first place."

"So then why did you take the assignment to interview me?" Blake asked, not sure he wanted to hear the real answer.

"Because I needed you just like you needed me. You needed articles to polish up your shitty reputation, and I needed your name in my portfolio. You were my ticket to get out of this town."

"I'm your ticket out of here?" He asked.

Charlotte stood there with tears in her eyes, but she refused to let them fall. She held her head high and nodded her head. "God, I hope so."

33

Charlotte didn't move out of bed all day Saturday. A day off from life had been exactly what she'd needed. She ordered takeout. She binged on TV shows. She even put her phone on mute and didn't bother to look at it. She hadn't done anything like this since her parents died.

Friday night had left her feeling felt numb. It had hurt to hear Blake say those things about her, and the reason it hurt was that she had started to have feelings for him. She knew she wasn't his normal sexy, sultry type, but she also knew a lot of men found her very attractive. The only difference between her and Piper was that Piper had big boobs, brunette hair, and a pushy attitude.

She was mad at herself for telling Blake the truth about why she had taken on the assignment in the first place. She knew she shouldn't have lashed out at him like that. Piper was the bitch, not her. She was a professional, and professionals don't behave that way.

As much as she tried, she couldn't get that photo of her and Blake out of her head. She had tried to find it online, but couldn't find it anywhere. She was pretty savvy about using the Internet, but she found it odd that the photo wasn't popping up anywhere. She had no idea how Piper had found it-- she must have alerts set on her phone for Blake's name. What had struck Charlotte most about the photo was how comfortable they looked together. They had huge smiles on their faces, obviously laughing at something the other had said, enjoying the moment.

She was in dangerous territory with Blake. She refused to go there, but she wasn't stupid. She had denied it long enough, but the reality was she couldn't get him out of her mind. Hearing Blake say those things about dating her had hurt her to the core, because it confirmed what Dylan had told her, as well.

The truth was, she never had that kind of fun with Dylan, not even when they were in college and life was simpler. They had never even done something as simple as a date night at a pizza place. Their dates centered around work, planning, and routines. Dylan was an amazing man - she couldn't deny that - but he didn't set her heart on fire. She didn't daydream about Dylan. She never thought about tearing his clothes off. She didn't lose herself thinking about him or what she wanted to do to him. He brought her stability and companionship, and for the last few years, that's exactly what she'd needed. Her life had been uprooted when her parents died, and Dylan had been a solid and steady foundation for her. He helped her put herself back together, and she loved him for that. She had needed someone who wouldn't play games or abandon her. She had needed someone who could help guide her professionally and give her sound advice. And she had needed someone to care about her, but... not be crazy in love with her. And that was why Dylan had been a perfect fit. But she was not being fair—to Dylan or herself. If she did nothing else, she needed to end things with Dylan.

The sound of her doorbell startled her, and she froze. Who could be calling on a Sunday morning? She wasn't expecting anyone, and the last thing she felt like doing was dealing with anyone. She hadn't showered, she was in her pajamas, and she looked horrible. She hoped that whoever was there would just go away once they realized she wasn't going to answer the door. She pulled her comforter over her head hoping to block out the sound.

Finally, after the eleventh or twelfth ring, Charlotte got up to see who the hell needed her so badly. She knew they weren't going away. They knew she was here because her car was parked outside. Hopefully, whoever it was would be scared off by her bad breath, messy hair, and dirty pajamas.

Fully expecting to see Lindsay or, God help her, Blake, she was shocked speechless when she opened her door to find Piper Saunders standing there.

Piper stood before her in full makeup wearing a black wool pom pom hat, a Canada Goose red puffer jacket, black jeans, and black shearing boots. She looked like she was about to hit the slopes in the Alps, not visit Barrington, RI.

"Charlotte," Piper nodded, and then slowly looked Charlotte over from head to toe.

"What, may I ask, are you doing here?" Charlotte asked cuttingly, feeling a blast of cold air on her face from the December wind.

"Blake asked me to come and apologize to you," she stated bluntly.

Charlotte stared at her in confusion. Piper Saunders was standing on her doorstep apologizing? "Blake asked you to apologize, so you came all the way over here for that?"

Piper shook her head in agitation, "Oh, no... not for you.

I came on Friday night to see Blake. He said I upset you the other night when I called about the photo."

"Considering you accused me of having someone else post it, yes... you could say I was upset." But that wasn't all she was upset about.

"He told me you would never do something like that," Piper responded, as she blew air into her gloves.

"And do you believe him?" Charlotte asked annoyed. She was so sick and tired of people like Piper acting like spoiled brats and using it as fuel to get ahead in life.

Piper nodded, "Yes, I believe him. Listen, can I come in for a quick second? It's freezing out here."

Charlotte felt her teeth chattering just from standing in the doorway. She wasn't sure what else Piper needed to talk about, but she opened up her door to let her in. "Yeah, come on in."

Piper walked into Charlotte's apartment and gave it a full sweep and nodded in approval. "Feel free to take a seat," Charlotte said, pointing to her couch.

"Blake explained to me that it was just a big misunder-standing."

"Oh yeah?" Charlotte asked, looking directly at Piper.

"You have a boyfriend," Piper said smiling at Charlotte.

Charlotte looked at Piper, "And what does that have to do with anything?" Knowing that she wouldn't have one much longer, because it wasn't fair to Dylan to stay with him when she had feelings for someone else.

"Well, obviously, you're not trying to get with Blake," Piper said in a matter-of-fact tone.

"No," Charlotte said, trying to stay composed. "I'm not trying *to get with Blake*."

"I should have known," Piper said with a smile. "And I'm sorry my claws came out. You can imagine how many women I have to deal with—all trying to get with him. It's like a job within itself," she joked. "I guess I'm just not used to meeting a woman who doesn't have an agenda with him."

"I don't know who you associate with, Piper, but I have a job to do, and that's what I'm doing," Charlotte stated. "You might have an agenda, but I don't."

"That's what Blake said," Piper responded. "And I know he would *never* go after you, but he said you were upset the other night after I called, and he made me come here to apologize."

"He made you come here? How interesting." Charlotte commented, annoyed, feeling her body heat up with anger.

"Yes," Piper said rolling her eyes. "Can you believe that? I told him that women just get over things like this, and that he should relax... but he wouldn't hear of it. So, he made me come over and apologize. And again, after he explained everything, I know you didn't have someone run that photo on purpose."

"I don't even think it's online anymore," Charlotte said, shrugging her shoulders.

"Oh, it's not," Piper laughed. "I had it taken down. Only two outlets had picked it up, and I was able to have them take it down immediately."

"Really? How did you manage that?" Charlotte asked surprised.

"Oh..." Piper smiled coyly. "I have my ways."

She looked over at Piper sitting there as if she owned the place, and then looked down at herself. Granted Piper had come by unannounced, but Charlotte couldn't afford a J.Crew puffer jacket, never mind a Canada Goose. Piper was always on, that was how she was, and how she always would be.

"Listen," Charlotte said. "As much as I have enjoyed our

little visit, and I appreciate you coming by, I have never been accused of doing something I didn't do. So, this was a first for me. But, let me tell you something, Piper. I'm over you. You didn't need to come by, and I didn't need to invite you in. Just don't confuse me with you. If I'm with Blake it's because I'm working. Nothing else."

Piper just stared at Charlotte and then slowly looked around her living room again. "I like your space. You've got a good vibe here."

Charlotte didn't respond as Piper continued to look around her living room, and she couldn't get over how out of touch with reality Piper appeared to be.

"Do you mind if I have a glass of water?" Piper suddenly asked.

"Water?" Charlotte asked, thinking it was a random thing to ask for. It was time for Piper to leave, and she didn't want to give her a reason to stay.

"Yeah," Piper responded. "My throat always gets super dry in cold weather like this."

Charlotte walked to her kitchen to grab a glass of water. What was with this woman? She wasn't picking up on any of Charlotte's social cues. What else could they possibly talk about? Piper came over because Blake made her, that was it. Obviously, Blake just wanted Piper to be reassured that he would never date Charlotte. So, everything was settled. She needed to put all this behind her and move on, and job one was getting Piper Saunders the fuck out of her home.

"Here you go," Charlotte said handing the glass to Piper.

"Oh, you're a gem!" Piper gushed as she grabbed the glass and took a sip. "Oh my God, so much better!"

Charlotte smiled to herself. Piper was a Valley Girl trapped in an east coast body. How she could go from perky to annoyed to mean to perky again so fast was scary. She reminded Charlotte of a mix between Lindsay Lohan in *Mean Girls* and Alicia Silverstone in *Clueless*.

"Anything else you need to talk about?" Charlotte asked, expecting Piper to take her leave. "Because I've got some place to be in an hour, so if there's nothing else..."

"Oh, no," Piper said as put her glass down on the coffee table. "I don't want to eat up your morning. Silly me. At least Blake knows I came by, that's got to count as extra brownie points for me!"

"Yeah brownie points are always good," Charlotte offered, not sure Piper picked up on her sarcasm.

"I mean, I bet your boyfriend was glad those photos didn't go viral," Piper added as she walked toward Charlotte's door.

"Oh, Dylan's not on social media," Charlotte responded with a shrug.

"You're kidding? How does he manage?" Piper shrieked, shocked by the information. "Everyone *has* to be on social media nowadays."

"Not him," Charlotte answered, opening her door wide so the cold air would speed up Piper's exit.

Piper kept talking, but Charlotte tuned her out. She didn't care what she had to say. She said her piece, and that was all that she cared about. As Piper walked outside, she turned around and smiled at Charlotte, "Thanks for inviting me in. I'll tell Blake you said hello!"

"Oh, don't bother. I have to see him this week."

Then Piper turned around and air-kissed Charlotte from a foot away in the freezing air.

At that moment, there were two things Charlotte knew for sure... she detested Blake Manor...and she was falling in love with him... and she hated herself for both.

34

Blake Manor has made another important and special mark on this town by creating the Blake Manor Scholarship Fund. The $3000 scholarship will be given out every December to a worthy Barrington High School student who is making a difference in our community.

This year's recipient, and the first, is Barrington High School junior, Alex Andrews.

"I can't believe that Blake thought of me for the first one. I can't tell you how much this $3000 will help me out," Alex shared.

Because Alex does so much for the community, and his impact has had a positive effect on so many, Blake Manor was highly supportive of the decision, "It wasn't just me who chose Alex. I worked with the high school to select a student who is not only working hard, but is doing great things in the community, too. We wanted to find a special student who is leaving his mark on this town."

Born in Barrington, Alex Andrews started a free tutoring program for middle school kids, on top of achieving top grades in *high school. Alex is also a valued member of the high school football team. He also works part-time.*

Blake Manor knows firsthand that it's not always easy for kids to do well in school, excel in sports or other activities, and find time to help out in the community.

"The second I met Alex, I knew he was the kind of student that needed to be acknowledged. We need more kids like Alex because these are the kids who will help and inspire others. He works hard, doesn't complain, and does everything he can to help out in the community. That deserves some recognition.

It was incredible to see the community support that Blake Manor had on Wednesday at the award ceremony. The gymnasium at Barrington High School was packed with students, staff, and people from all over the town to see Alex be presented with his scholarship. Seeing members of the community happy for Alex is a testament to his character.

"There aren't always awards for kids who simply work hard all year long. There are awards for achieving high grades, and awards for excelling in sports and other specific activities. But there's nothing for kids who are doing it all, and I think it's important to shine a light on them," *Blake shared.* "Alex is that kind of kid. As everyone has said, he's always got a smile on his face. There are a bunch of reasons he stands out."

As many know, Blake Manor had his own success here in Barrington as a member of the high school football team. He watched his parents work very hard to make sure he was able to fulfill his hopes and dreams in high school, and says he owes all of his determination and dedication to his parents. "It either makes you stronger or not. There's no in-between. You can't look at your circumstances and use it as a crutch. You take what you're given and work hard to go after what you want. I'll never forget watching my parents rush to my games, still in their work clothes, because they didn't want to miss anything. Seeing that kind of work ethic at home makes you appreciate everything you have."

Blake hopes that kids like Alex will look to him as a mentor. He shared that he was lucky enough to have core people in his life, in addition to his parents, who helped him along the way. Mentorship is something that's very important to Blake and he knows it's a role that can't be taken lightly.

"The mentors I've had in my life have changed my life for the better, and I hope to do that for Alex and other kids, too. I can't stress enough how crucial and important it is to have someone who can help you dream big about yourself."

We all know Blake Manor, the football player; but it's been a privilege to meet the man under the helmet. He has a heart of gold.

Greg held up his phone on the ZOOM call and shouted, "I mean, Blake. This is pure gold! This is fucking fantastic!"

Blake nodded in agreement, but not with as much excitement as Greg had on his face. "I know, this one is better than the first article."

Blake was sitting at his kitchen table with a cup of coffee. He had woken up early to read the article, hoping that Charlotte hadn't changed anything since their blow-up over the weekend. He knew she wasn't like that, but he wanted to be sure.

"As soon as you're back in the city we start a mentorship program," Greg stated. "I didn't even know stuff like this was important to you. I'm telling you, this is the kind of press we need to keep getting."

"Noted," Blake responded.

"What's wrong with you? Are you not happy about this?"

Greg asked, trying to figure out what had crawled up Blake's ass.

"Just personal shit going on," Blake answered, not wanting to discuss his love life with Greg.

"Well, whatever it is... let it go. Today's a good day and, believe me, this is going to get you a lot of play. Wait till the League and the Skyscrapers see this. I'm going to pitch this mentorship program to the entire team. I have a feeling, they're going to be all over this, too."

"Any chance you think they would lift the suspension?"

"Because of a little good press?" Greg joked. "This isn't high school, Blake."

"Just figured I'd ask," Blake shrugged.

"You're ready to get back, huh?" Greg asked, sensing Blake's anxiousness.

"Yeah, I gotta get out of here soon. It's been a long couple of weeks," Blake said rubbing his hair.

"You've got, what? Two more good deeds to do before you leave?"

"Charlotte's already interviewed me for the 3rd one, so that's taken care of."

"Oh, that's right. You decided to do the Giving Tree thing for Barrington," Greg said.

"Yeah, that one is about to kick off. Thankfully, my mother stepped up and helped with the planning with the people at Town Hall. That one needed a few more hands to massage things since I needed to use a tree that was already being used by the Town Hall."

"What does that mean?" Greg chuckled. "I'm not used to all this small town talk."

"They put up a tree every year at the Town Hall. I needed special permission to use it as the Giving Tree this year. My mom got all that arranged for me."

"Look at you delegating like a boss, and making things work there," Greg teased.

"You know my mother, she loves stuff like that. It's much easier to use the Christmas Tree that is already set up. People can add their wishes and then, for a week or so, they have the opportunity to pick a wish and then buy that specific gift."

"This will be a good one, too," Greg said with a smile. "This is another idea that we could start. Maybe we can pitch the idea of a Giving Tree to be set up at the stadium."

"That's not a bad idea," Blake nodded. "Always thinking of that angle, aren't you Greg?" Blake was teasing but knew, in reality, it was the truth.

"For my clients? It's my job. I'm always angling, you know that. You're one of my biggest pains in the asses," Greg laughed. "Although the last couple of weeks have been pretty tame without you here."

"Listen, man," Blake said seriously. "I know I can't go back to that lifestyle. It embarrassed too many people I love and respect, not to mention seeing myself in a different light made me see the light," he smiled. "You wanted that suspension to be a wake-up call for me. Well, consider it done. I won't be acting like a dick anymore, believe me. Those days are over. But I'll tell you what, I don't think I'm made for small-town life anymore."

Greg knew something was weighing on Blake, but he didn't want to push. He knew well enough to leave things alone when it came to certain things with Blake, "If you want to head back to the city, just come back. I don't want you miserable at home, that's not good either. My advice to you is if you come back before the suspension is over, you've got to stay put at your place with your head down. No going out, and no partying. Can you do that?"

Blake sat up in his seat and took a sip from his smoothie, answering him by saying, "Doesn't really seem like I have a choice, do I? Besides, I just told you. Those days are over for me."

MARY MANOR DIDN'T MEAN to eavesdrop on Blake's ZOOM video call with Greg, but it was hard not to hear what was being said just one room away. She knew that Blake had seemed a little different over the last couple of days, and it didn't help that Piper Saunders came for a visit. Thankfully they stayed at a hotel in Providence again and she didn't need to deal with Piper.

She hadn't been impressed with her the first time she met her, and she certainly lost points when she kicked Charlotte out of her seat at the scholarship ceremony. She loved her son to pieces, but she wanted to shake him when it came to the women he chose. She also feared if she told Blake how she felt about Piper that he would stay with her just to prove her wrong and try to show her how great Piper was for him.

She missed the shy and reserved teenage boy he'd been in high school. He spent hours working out, watching football tapes, and teaching himself the game. He'd known that football was his ticket to a better life, and nothing got in his way. Seeing the transformation of Blake over the last few years was still shocking to Mary. She hated seeing the stories about him when he was out having fun with his friends. It was too much. She knew he was having the time of his life, but he was also creating a bad reputation for himself. Fame certainly had its pros and cons, but the bad boy reputation was one that Blake had brought on himself, and it still shocked her to the core to think about it.

"You itching to get home?" Mary said quietly as she walked into the kitchen.

"You heard all that, huh?" Blake asked, feeling badly because he knew his mom loved having him home.

"I wasn't trying to eavesdrop, but when you have a house this size, and a video call on speaker, it's tough not to hear what's going on," she smiled and then went over to sit next to Blake at the kitchen table. "What's going on, Blake?"

"I don't know, Mom. I just think it's time for me to head back. It's got nothing to do with you or Dad, I promise. It's been great spending time with you, and it's been nice being present in your lives again. I've missed that," he smiled at her.

"So, what's the problem then? You seem to be enjoying the early morning workouts with Coach Gorman. People have been wonderful about leaving you alone. You've done such incredible things for the town, especially with the Giving Tree kickoff this week. And you certainly have made a nice impression on the students at the high school."

"I know," Blake nodded with a smile, knowing his Mom knew there had to be something wrong. "Everything's been great here, it's just... I don't want to upset anyone, and I have done just that, and I don't really know how to fix it."

Mary stared at her son and for a split second; she saw a glimpse of the confused, shy teenage boy she once knew. He was referring to a girl, that much she knew, but she thought everything with Piper had been squared away after her weekend visit. She knew Blake was an adult, and probably didn't want to confide in his mother, or even talk about women with her, so she figured taking it slow with him was best.

"The one thing I've learned in life, Blake, is that honesty is always the best policy. If there's something you need to get off your chest, then do it. Is this someone a she?" Mary asked with a smirk, knowing the answer already.

Blake laughed, "Yes, it's a she. I feel bad as to how certain things went down recently, and I don't want her to think that's how I really am."

"And does she?"

"Does she what?" Blake asked.

"Does she think that's how you really are? Seems to me like she knows you pretty well."

"I thought she did, or at least I was beginning to think so," Blake said, sounding frustrated. "That's why I think going back home and getting back to my real life is the best thing I can do right now. She's going to think what she wants about me. I can't help that."

"I guess so. But is that how you really want to leave it?" Mary asked. She hated that he was so hung up about Piper--the girl wasn't worth it. She wasn't the kind of woman she pictured her son ending up with, but she knew he had to figure that out on his own. "Besides, I thought you two settled everything this weekend. Isn't that why she came to visit?" Mary asked confused, hoping she hadn't overstepped too much.

Blake looked over at his mom with confusion on his face, "Who are you talking about?"

"Piper," Mary shot back, wondering why Blake would even ask. "Why? Who are you talking about?"

Blake looked down at his hands, not wanting to make eye contact with his mother. "Charlotte," he said

35

Lindsay couldn't get Charlotte to snap out of her funk at work on Monday or Tuesday, so when Wednesday rolled around, and she was still down, she knew she needed to say something. It wasn't like Charlotte to be so quiet, especially around her.

"Everything alright with you?" Lindsay asked as she plopped herself onto Charlotte's desk Wednesday morning.

"Other than you messing up all these papers on my desk?" Charlotte half-smiled while shaking her head.

"You haven't been yourself for two days," Lindsay said, looking at her friend with caring eyes. "I know you well enough to know when something's wrong. Everything OK with you and Dylan?"

Charlotte looked up at her friend and nodded, "Dylan's fine. Actually, I never told you, but we talked the other night. I think it's safe to say we're taking a little bit of a breather right now."

"WHAT?" Lindsay shouted. "Did you guys breakup?"

Charlotte nodded, motioning to Lindsay to quiet down. She didn't want anyone else in the office to hear about her love life. "I just didn't think it was a good idea to keep things going with Dylan. Honestly, though, I'm OK... it's for the best."

"He doesn't rev your engine?" She joked with a wink.

Charlotte looked at Lindsay dramatically, "Really? Only a best friend can make you laugh about a breakup."

"Hey, if he doesn't do that, he's not worth it."

Charlotte sat there, thinking about it for a second, "You know, I don't know if he's ever rev'd up my engine that way. I think I'm seeing it for the first time."

"Or maybe the first time you're admitting it to yourself," Lindsay added. "So this has been the problem? I've been wondering."

"Actually, what I've been dealing with has nothing to do with him."

"So there is something!" Lindsay said with hope in her voice. "Why are you holding out on me? I can't believe you let me go on and on the other night about my amazing first date with Peter, and kept quiet about everything that's bothering you!"

Charlotte sat back in her desk chair and looked up at the ceiling before looking back at Lindsay. "I'm sorry, Linds. I'm not trying to hold out on you."

"Well, is everything OK?" Lindsay asked, sounding concerned.

"It's just that I don't think I can write my 4th article on Blake, so I was planning on asking your father to pass it along to someone else."

"What? Why not?" Lindsay asked, looking directly at her friend. Charlotte had gotten great feedback from her second article, and that it had created even more buzz for Blake. For all intents and purposes, Charlotte had hit a work home run.

"I just don't think I can do it, that's all," Charlotte responded, trying to mask any emotion in her voice.

"What's going on, Char?" Lindsay asked. "Is it something to do with that online photo of you and Blake? Did something happen between the two of you?"

"No!" Charlotte exclaimed. "Not at all, you know that."

"Well, stop worrying about that picture. Nobody saw it. Believe me, I tried my hardest to find it online, but it is gone. Whatever magic Piper Saunders has, she made it work."

"It's not that, Linds," Charlotte said, feeling defeated.

"And he's an asshole for saying it would be a joke for people to think you were dating. You know that, too. You're gorgeous. You're smart. You're talented. Don't let words like that affect you. It's not worth it. Look at the women he entertains. And, for the record, Piper Saunders has nothing on you. Well, except for boobs," she laughed, trying to sound positive.

Charlotte looked at her best friend who had turned into family. She loved Lindsay like a sister and appreciated that her friend had her back. "I love you, you know that?" Charlotte responded as she got up to give her a hug.

"Is that it?" Lindsay asked, looking at her friend, feeling her heartbreak. "Is that what's been bothering you?"

"That, and knowing I have to see him tomorrow for the Giving Tree kickoff."

"And he still hasn't reached out at all after Piper stopped by to supposedly apologize?"

"No," Charlotte answered. "And that's what is confusing to me. I was pissed about her accusing me of planting the photo, but I'm upset that he never apologized for what he said. He claimed I had interpreted it the wrong way, but come on... why even say something mean like that?"

"Men are idiots, just forget about it. He doesn't know

what he's talking about. You've used him exactly the way he's used you--to further your careers. Just leave it at that."

Charlotte loved how cut and dried Lindsay could be. She never let too much bother her, and she never dwelled on things or overthought them. She wished she had a piece of that in her.

"Why don't you just skip the Giving Tree kickoff tomorrow night and let me go with the photographer," Lindsay offered. "There's no reason for you to be there. Besides, Blake is just going for the photo opp, and to be seen. I can take care of everything that you would need to do. The article is done, right?"

Charlotte nodded her head as she put her hair up in a messy bun. "I was planning on adding a few details about the event itself, but the meat of it is complete. You sure you wouldn't mind?"

"Not at all," Lindsay said with a caring smile. "And listen... you have two great articles published about Blake Manor, and one more to come. I'll do the last one for you if that's what you want. I'll explain everything to my father. Don't even worry about it."

"I would love you forever, Linds," Charlotte gushed, relief on her face. "I just can't face him right now. I don't even know what his last holiday good deed is going to be, so you would be doing it from start to finish. You sure you don't mind?"

"Mind?" Lindsay smiled deviously. "I'm anxious to give Blake Manor a piece of my mind."

"Don't you DARE! I don't want him to know that I'm in love—" and then Charlotte cut herself off, knowing she had just admitted it out loud, wishing she could rewind the last three seconds.

Lindsay's eyes shot open wide and her mouth dropped open, "WAIT A SECOND!"

"Shhhhh..." Charlotte pleaded. "Lindsay, please. I don't want anyone to hear you!"

"Are you telling me what I think you're telling me?"

"I didn't mean to say a thing," Charlotte said looking down feeling defeated. "Please... please, just forget what I said."

"No way in hell, Charlotte Court!" Lindsay said, moving closer to Charlotte's face. "You fell for Blake?"

Charlotte looked at her best friend and knew she couldn't lie. She wanted to, but she knew she didn't have it in her to lie directly to her face. "I didn't mean to..."

Lindsay smiled at her friend, knowing she protected and guarded her heart like a mother protects her baby. "That's the problem with love, you don't have any control over it."

"I know it doesn't make sense, because he's the polar opposite of anyone I've ever been attracted to, and I know I'm not his type, but--"

"Stop saying that!" Lindsay snapped. "You can't help who you fall for in life."

Charlotte shook her head, "Regardless... I know he won't understand. I don't even understand it. I know nothing will happen with Blake, but it's clear to me that I can't see him, or even be around him. And truthfully? I know now, more than ever, that what I felt for Dylan is nothing compared to what I feel for Blake. I just need time to get Blake out of my head, and out of my system."

Lindsay smiled and hugged her friend, "Well... if there's one good thing to come out of this, it's that your heart is alive and well."

Charlotte nodded and tears formed in her eyes. "The

Blake Manor Effect, that's how I've been describing every-thing he touches."

"Ohhh... touches," Lindsay winked.

"Oh, stop," Charlotte laughed as she wiped a tear.

"So this is why you've been so upset. Hearing Blake say those things about you actually did hurt you," Lindsay said, connecting the dots.

Charlotte nodded her head.

"Well, screw Blake Manor," Lindsay laughed. "It's time for you to close this chapter in your life, and get your butt onto the next one. If he doesn't appreciate you the way everyone else does, then he's not worth it. Do you hear me?"

"Yes, I hear you." Charlotte laughed. "You're crazy, but I love you for it."

"Listen, Charlotte, in less than one month it will be a new year. You're going to make it the best one yet. Do you hear me?"

"God, you're like a bossy cheerleader," Charlotte teased. "Yes," she said wiping her eyes. "I hear you."

"Good, because we're spending the next hour sending out your writing portfolio to every publication we can find —whether they have an opening or not."

36

The Town Hall looked gorgeous all lit up with white holiday lights. Poinsettias lined the steps of the Town Hall building. Red bows were wrapped around each tree. It looked like a winter wonderland. The Giving Tree itself was displayed in the front foyer of the Town Hall and it looked spectacular. The glorious twelve-foot Fraser fir tree stood as townspeople gathered around, anxious to include their holiday wishes.

Blake and Mary had set up a table filled with cardboard ornaments in the shape of a star, along with Sharpies. Everyone was welcome to come and write down a wish for themselves, or for someone else. The only restriction was that wishes had a $50 limit to keep the cost reasonable for all. What Blake hadn't disclosed was that he was going to match the value of each wish, and the money would be donated to a variety of charities.

As expected, the town hall was packed, and this fun event had brought extra excitement to the town. Not only that, but having this be another Blake Manor good deed was making it even sweeter.

Blake knew he would spend the evening having photographs taken, and chatting with fans, but he didn't mind. He knew that tonight was an important night for the town, and he wanted it to be special for his mother, too. She had helped him put everything together, and he was grateful for her support and love. Even Ben Manor was manning the wish table, helping out and doing whatever he could to make the night a success.

"You alright, Blake?" Mary asked as she watched her son scan the crowd from one of the side rooms off of the lobby. She could tell he was looking for someone, and she had a feeling she knew who it was.

"Yeah, I'm fine," Blake said as he continued to look around, but obviously not having any luck. "I don't know if she's going to show tonight or not."

"She will," Mary smiled, trying to reassure her son. "Give her time. She's probably here already, but with this many people here, how could you spot anyone?"

Blake nodded and smiled at his mom. "You're probably right." They were waiting to be announced by the mayor. Blake had been asked to prep a small speech and explain the details about the Giving Tree. He knew that someone from the *View* would take photos, but he was hoping Charlotte would be there, too. He had been afraid to reach out to her, knowing she was still upset at the things he'd said, but he wasn't sure how to make everything right. He wasn't used to trying so hard with women, and he wasn't used to caring about trying with a woman. He just needed to see her tonight and talk to her.

"You should have called her, Blake," Mary said with a knowing look on her face.

"I know, Mom," he said, looking out at the crowd. "But it's a little too late now."

"It's never too late, remember that. She was hurt and I don't blame her. You wouldn't want to hear anyone say those things about you."

"But I didn't *mean* them," Blake confessed. "I only said them to get Piper off my back. I didn't think Charlotte would take it seriously, and when I tried to explain, she wouldn't listen."

"Well, you know what that means, right?" Mary said with a smile.

"What's that?" Blake asked, turning his head to look at his mother.

"You need to try harder."

"I know," Blake nodded in an annoyed fashion. "As soon as I'm done with my speech, I'm going to go find her. I don't know what good will come of it, but I owe it to her to tell her the truth."

"Are you going to tell her how you feel?" Mary asked with hope in her eyes.

"She has a boyfriend, Mom," Blake shared. "I don't know if it's right for me to mess that up, but I do know that I need her to know how I feel about her. Like you said, I need to be honest."

As Mary was about to say one more thing, the mayor's assistant walked in and asked Blake and Mary to follow her. It was time for them to greet the crowd and unveil the Giving Tree. Mary was honored to be working on this with Blake. Giving back and doing good in the community were things she loved to do, but the fact that she was doing it with her son made it even better. She was happy that he had taken these holiday good deeds so seriously.

The crowd went wild as Blake stepped out of the side room with his mother. He had worn a suit again tonight, this time in navy blue, with a red tie for a little extra festive flair.

"Hello, everyone!" Blake said into the microphone. "It's great to see so many of you here for the unveiling of the Giving Tree."

As the crowd erupted again with cheers and clapping, Blake found himself scanning the crowd again for Charlotte. He figured she might be somewhere up front, but he hadn't laid eyes on her yet.

"As you all know," Blake said, "I've been having some holiday fun in town and this good deed is special to me because I got to work with my mother on this one. Growing up here in town, I always loved and appreciated how my parents would take time each holiday to give back. Over the next four days, we're asking people to share their holiday wishes and hang them on the Giving Tree. We're asking that these wishes be tangible things that can be completed by the people in our town. Since townspeople will be trying to fulfill all the wishes, we're asking them to stay beneath a fifty dollar max. We know the holidays can be financially challenging, so we're hoping to not only fulfill some wishes, but to help out. With that in mind, I will match every donation made, and the money will be donated to charity."

As Blake looked at his mother over the screaming crowd, she smiled and nodded at him. "I want to dedicate this Giving Tree to my mother, Mary Manor. She's the heart and soul of this effort, and I know she's worked very hard behind the scenes making everything come together."

The crowd erupted as Mary walked over to Blake and gave him a huge hug. Cameras were snapping away, and people were enjoying the tender moment between a mother and her son. "

"She's not a fan of public speaking, so she begged me not to make her talk," Blake laughed into the microphone. "But I would like to give her one more loud round of applause for bringing everything together tonight. Have a wonderful evening, everyone, and make sure you get your wishes on the tree!"

Blake looked into the crowd and happened to see Lindsay standing next to a guy taking photos, presumably from the *View*. He looked to her right and to her left, but didn't see Charlotte. As Blake handed the microphone back to the mayor, he knew he needed to get to Lindsay before she left for the evening. Their eyes locked and he gestured for her to walk over to him, hoping she got the message. There was no way he could get to her without being stopped a hundred times.

As the mayor continued his announcements, Blake walked to the side of the room with his mother, trying to disappear. He needed the mayor to keep speaking so as to keep the crowd at bay, hoping that Lindsay would walk over. Then he saw Lindsay walk through the crowd and finagle her way over to him.

"Glad you understood what I mean," Blake smiled as she walked over.

"I was hoping I understood correctly," Lindsay nodded, trying to stay professional because she wanted to give Blake a piece of her mind. "This is my photographer, Ray. He took a bunch of great shots of you. Did you want us to get something else?"

Blake shook his head, 'No... I, ah... I actually wanted to see if anyone else was here with you."

Lindsay stared at Blake, knowing exactly who he was asking about, but not willing to give him an answer without making him sweat first. Since they didn't need any more photos, Lindsay told Ray he could pack it in for the night.

"Do you mean my father?" She asked, trying to sound confused as Ray took off.

Blake shook his head, "No, not Frank."

"No?" Lindsay asked, just to be a little bit more of a ballbuster.

"Actually, I was just wondering if Charlotte was here with you."

"Oh, Charlotte," Lindsay said with a gleeful nod. "Yeah, she's not here."

"Not here yet? Or not coming?" Blake asked, looking up at Lindsay, not even trying to mask his hope.

"She asked me to fill in for her tonight, and actually..." Lindsay said, looking directly into Blake's eyes, "She also asked me to write up the last holiday good deed."

"She what?" Blake asked shocked.

It took all she had not to show her happiness at the questionable look on his face. Nobody messed with her best friend and, if you did, she would make it her business to go after you.

"Yeah," Lindsay said with a devious smile. "Looks like you're stuck with me for the last one."

"But what about Charlotte? Did she say why?" Blake asked, sounding desperate. "I thought she needed it for her portfolio."

"Honestly, Blake, she's got all she needs for her portfolio," Lindsay replied, and then added, "Are you seriously asking me why?"

"You know, don't you?"

"Of course I know," Lindsay said directly. "She told me the whole story, including how you sent Piper to her door to apologize! How lame is that? But, for whatever reason, you never did."

"I never did what?" He asked sounding confused.

"You don't understand women, do you? Let me spell it

out for you. You. Never. Apologized. To. Her!" Lindsay said, frustrated.

"Shit," Blake said, rubbing his hand through his hair. "My mom was right."

"About what?" Lindsay asked, feeling annoyed. "That you just shit on one of the nicest people in the world? Or that you tried to make her feel small and insignificant?"

Blake stood there stunned, not sure what to say to Lindsay. He knew he'd upset Charlotte, but that had never been his intention. "I never meant for her to feel that way. I was just trying to get Piper off the phone so that I could get back to Charlotte. I didn't think she would react the way she did, I swear on my life. You've got to believe me. I tried telling Charlotte that, too, but she wouldn't listen."

Lindsay just stared at Blake, wanting to believe him, but she knew he was a master when it came to talking himself out of stuff when it came to women. "Do you make a habit of using other people to make yourself look good? And, as a matter of interest, what about Piper? Does she even know her current status with you?"

"We're not together," Blake said, trying to pull himself together after the dressing down he was getting from Lindsay. "We were never together."

"Well, your definition of together and her definition of together are a lot different."

"Geez," Blake said smiling at Lindsay. "You're no bullshit when it comes to Charlotte, huh?"

"She's one of the best people I know, Blake, and she did not deserve to be humiliated, insulted, and ignored by you. And the worst of it? She was just trying to help you. She did nothing wrong. But you, on the other hand..." Lindsay took a deep breath. She was not finished. "You owe her, Blake. Big time, and I won't be happy until you man up and make things right with her and do it without relying on someone else to do your dirty work for you."

"I know," Blake said, looking at Lindsay seriously. "She's one of the best, most honest people I know, and I want to make it up to her. Just so you know, Piper thought there was much more to our relationship than there was, but I set her straight this past weekend."

"So, Piper is out of the picture. For good?" Lindsay asked.

"No more Piper," Blake said seriously.

"So how did the New York City Barbie doll take it?" Lindsay asked with a straight face.

Blake chuckled and let out a deep breath, "Probably just as well as you can imagine. Let's put it this way, she's not my biggest fan right now."

"And so Charlotte?" Lindsay said staring at him. "Is Piper going to trash her in the press, as well?"

"Not at all," Blake said looking hopeless and defeated. "I just want to talk to her, that's all. I need to see her. Is she at home?"

Lindsay stood there staring at him, taking in everything she was seeing. "My God, you like her, don't you?" Lindsay asked with a knowing grin. "You do, don't you?"

"What about Dylan?" he asked, trying to be respectful, but knowing he really just wanted the guy out of the picture.

Lindsay looked directly at Blake, "I don't think that you need to worry about Dylan anymore."

Blake cleared his throat and rubbed his hand through his hair, and smiled his Blake Manor million-dollar smile, "You really think so?"

He might be smiling, Lindsay thought to herself, but he was nervous as hell.

"Yeah, I think so, but this is something you need to

discuss with her. It's not my place to talk to you about her relationships," Lindsay said, nodding slowly.

"Well, I hope it's true, " he said, looking hopeful.

"Let me ask you this, why the hell are you standing here talking to me and not to Charlotte?" Lindsay responded. Jesus, did this guy need a playbook?

"I should go tell her, right?" Blake asked hesitantly.

"Yes!" Lindsay shouted. "For Pete's sake! Are you that clueless? You need to go tell her, preferably right now! She's at home!"

Blake's phone started ringing, but he ignored it and planted a kiss on her cheek. "Thank you!"

As Blake darted off into the crowd, Lindsay smiled. Charlotte deserved a crazy, unexpected romantic gesture like this; she just hoped that she would be home to appreciate it.

As Lindsay was about to disappear herself knowing she got everything she needed for the paper, Mary Manor rushed over looking a bit frantic. "Is Blake still here?"

Lindsay shook her head, not sure what the emergency was, but Mary looked like she had seen a ghost. "What is it, Mrs. Manor? Is everything OK?"

"No," she said, shaking her head. "I need to find Blake immediately."

"He just left to go to Charlotte's apartment, but I'm sure you can reach him on his cell. He literally just left less than two minutes ago. What's happened?"

Mary held up her phone to show Lindsay the article that was displayed on her screen. She saw a photo of Blake, along with the headline, "The Real Blake Manor Effect." As she scanned the screen a second longer she noticed the words, by Piper Saunders.

"What the hell is this?" Lindsay asked, trying to process what Mary was showing her.

"It's an exposé on Blake on one of the biggest sports blogs out there, and it's horrible," Mary said, holding back the tears. "And guess who Piper's source was?"

Lindsay stared at Mary, not sure who would do that to him, "Who?" Lindsay asked.

"Charlotte," Mary said, with tears streaking down her cheek.

37

Lindsay took a moment to settle Mary into a room off the main foyer at the Town Hall. The place was crammed with people, and it was obvious Mary needed somewhere quiet. Once that was done, Lindsay pulled out her phone, found the article, and began reading...

Blake Manor might be superman on the field, but off the field, not so much. Recently Blake Manor was suspended from the New York Skyscrapers for four weeks due to violating a Personal Conduct Policy. The team needed to set an example to the players that this type of behavior and antics would not be tolerated any longer. Blake Manor is currently serving a three-game suspension. Instead of staying in New York City, Blake returned home to Rhode Island to wait out his suspension. It would appear that, for someone like Blake Manor, there are fewer temptations in a quiet New England town, not to mention that his parents can babysit him.

His personal management team and family knew he needed some good PR as a way to counterbalance the recent string of bad press. They orchestrated one of the best PR stunts of all time for a disgraced professional athlete: they turned him into a modern-day Santa in his hometown. The result was that he looked like a God to the people who love him the most.

Putting on a big smile, he began dishing out his own money as a wonderful way to give back and contribute to his community. But, behind the scenes, he could have cared less. His only goal was to get back on the football field.

Charlotte Court, the reporter from the Barrington View who was assigned to interview Blake, disclosed everything to me, including the fact that Blake was often late for meetings. As well, Charlotte had to sign an NDA before he would sit down to talk with her. Did he have something to hide? Apparently so.

What Blake Manor likes to hide from the public eye is the fact that he grew up poor, knowing that his only ticket out of his hometown was to play football. He was lackluster as a student, so he wasn't able to rely on his brains, only his body. Since his parents weren't able to afford to pay for him to join a gym, attend football camps, or work with private trainers, he relied on his high school's gym and his local coach to get him to where he needed to be. It's no surprise that Blake chose to redo his local high school gym as one of his first PR stunts... let me walk you through the various holiday good (ahem) deeds and dissect the real motivation behind each one of them...

Lindsay stopped reading and took a moment to collect herself, and to comfort Mary. This blog of Piper's was among the worst she had ever read. It was full of vitriol and, in her mind, it was libelous. She shuddered when she thought of her dad and Charlotte reading it.

She scanned through the rest of the article and came to the end...

...this alone violates so many things when it comes to journalistic integrity, although I'm sure people will throw stones at me, too. Here's the thing, I just don't care. This is an Op-Ed piece

on a blog. So, yeah, come after me. It is finally time to speak the truth.

Some men will never change and Blake Manor is one of those men. My advice to the ladies out there with an inkling of intrigue, like Charlotte Court, he's not worth it. It is ironic that the man who couldn't utter a word to a girl in high school could morph into such a playboy as an adult. Just remember ladies, there's always an angle when it comes to Blake Manor. There's always something shinier, better, and nicer whether it's an apartment, a car, a vacation spot, or a potential girlfriend.

My advice to Blake Manor fans? Stop blurring the lines between the superman on the field and the real man off of it. They are two different guys.

～

CHARLOTTE OPENED the door to her apartment and came face to face with Blake. He stood there holding up his phone in front of her. He didn't utter a word, he just held up his phone waiting for her to say something. He had come to Charlotte's place with a distinct purpose in mind, but that changed when he read Piper's article while sitting in Charlotte's parking lot.

"I just read it myself. I was wondering if you saw it," Charlotte said in a shocked voice. "Saw it?" Blake answered back, clearly very upset. "Yes, I saw it."

"Did you tell her these things?" Blake asked in a shaky voice. "Did you freaking tell her these things about me?"

"Blake...Blake, come on... let me explain—" Charlotte said, trying her best to hold herself together. "I absolutely *never* told her those things about you. I swear."

"No?" Blake said, shaking his head and taking a step back. He looked like he was going to lose it. "Well, then how the hell did she know so much? Such intimate details? The girls in high school? The NDA?"

Charlotte looked just as shocked, "Blake, I don't know. I have no idea. I'm as shocked as you are."

"Did you tell her all this stuff when she was here the other day?" Blake shot back. "I mean, she's not a mind reader, and *I* certainly didn't tell her that shit."

"No, I didn't say a thing to her—Piper Saunders is the *last* person on earth I would trust with any information," Charlotte said again, knowing he didn't believe her. "I wouldn't do that to you—I wouldn't do that to anyone."

"I would hope so," Blake said, looking completely stunned. "This blog post will go viral in an hour. It's been live for 20 minutes, and it's already spreading like wildfire. Do you get that? Piper's going to share this with every single person she knows, all just to shit on me."

Charlotte stood there, "I have no idea how she got that information, and I certainly don't know why she dragged my name into it. Frank sent it to me fifteen minutes ago. And, just so you know, this has the potential to ruin my career, too."

"Your career?" Blake said shocked.

"Yes," Charlotte nodded. "*My career.*"

"You've got to be kidding me right now. This is scathing for me," Blake expressed. "This is the kind of thing I can't shut down. I just have to fucking ride it out. Your career will be fine, believe me... this might actually help you!" He said, taking a step back and putting his hands on his head in frustration.

Charlotte looked at Blake and shook her head slowly. It was all about him. He didn't give a rat's ass about how it would affect her. "I don't know what to tell you, Blake. I don't know where she got the information, but it certainly wasn't from me. She's after you, and she's just dragging me along for the ride."

Charlotte didn't want to say anything else, but then she couldn't contain herself, "You date a woman who is a ticking time bomb. She shows up here, unannounced, twice. She's rude to me, not to mention to your family. She accused me of planting a photo of the two of us together, so God knows what else she is capable of. What do you expect from a woman like her? All you see is tits and ass, but she's out to get you! Wake the fuck up!"

Blake started at Charlotte's anger, "You know, for someone who met me a little over two weeks ago, you have some nerve."

"Oh, is that right?" Charlotte said, feeling her voice shake.

"Yeah, because I didn't do this to myself. Someone violated my trust, and it kills me to think it was probably you."

"You're out of your mind," Charlotte yelled back. "If you don't believe me, so be it. It's sad to think that you would even think that of me."

"I don't know what to think, Charlotte. The personal things she knew were things I only shared with you. How the hell else would she find out?"

"I don't know," Charlotte yelled back again, but this time with tears in her eyes. "Why don't you call Piper and ask her yourself?"

"Oh, believe me, Piper will hear from me and Greg and... maybe even my lawyer."

"So, I'm the first one you decided to blame, huh?" Charlotte said, feeling hurt and incredulous.

"I was on my way here to talk to you when Greg called to

tell me what was going on. This had nothing to do with the reason I was originally coming over, believe me."

"But the fact is that you came to me before you even called her for an explanation," Charlotte said, looking Blake directly in the eyes.

Blake put his head down and shook his head. He didn't know what else to say. The wind was knocked out of him. All the great things he had done for the town had been wiped out in a matter of seconds by Piper's blog post.

"You know what? I think you should go, Blake. Enough damage has been done, and you obviously don't believe a word I'm saying, so just please leave. And, one more thing, make sure you know this... Piper has one thing wrong, she keeps insinuating that I've fallen for you... I haven't," Charlotte shouted and slammed the door in his face. Lying was the most difficult thing to do, but she needed her ties cut with Blake one and for all.

∽

"SHE DENIED IT, ALL OF IT!" Blake shouted at Greg into the phone. "Charlotte said she has no idea how Piper knew any of that stuff."

"That's bullshit, Blake, and I hope you know it," Greg shot back. "You don't come up with shit like that out of thin air. Charlotte must have said something to her when she was with her. Or..."

"Or what?" Blake asked, feeling like he was on fire.

"Did Piper bug your phone or something crazy like that?" Greg asked, pulling at straws.

Blake picked up a stack of papers that were on his bed and tossed them across the room. He couldn't calm down. He had tried taking deep breaths, but nothing was working. Piper's blog post was up to over 6000 shares at this point and growing. All the work he had done over the last couple of weeks had been wiped out. And even worse? People were thinking he didn't care about his hometown, or the people in it.

"I have no idea what to do now," Blake uttered as he rubbed his face. "She is trying to destroy my reputation."

"Trying?" Greg pointed out. "She's halfway there. Do you know how many people follow Piper, and tune into her segments? This hasn't even hit the airwaves yet and, I'm sorry to say, this is about to get bigger and juicer."

"What the hell do I do?" Blake shouted.

Greg took a deep breath and shook his head. "You've got to let me figure this one out."

"At least let me call Piper, and see what the fuck she's up to with this shit."

"This is a revenge post. She even acknowledged it herself. She knows people are going to come after her for writing it, but she doesn't care. She wanted to get her story out and that was it."

"But what about my side?" Blake asked, feeling defeated.

"Your side were the articles Charlotte put out," Greg responded. "This was just her way of adding her two cents. I think she is pissed about not getting the exclusive with you in the first place."

"But none of it is true," Blake replied.

"I know that, and you know that," Greg said, understanding the dilemma Blake was in. "We just need to figure out the best way to respond. Our lawyer looking at it to see if there's anything we can do in terms of slander."

"Be straight with me," Blake said seriously. "Can this mess up anything else with me and the team?"

"I don't think so, but I don't know for sure, Blake.

Nobody from the team has reached out to me yet, so hopefully, they'll see this for what it is... a disgruntled ex-girlfriend."

"I knew breaking things off for good the other night was going to come back to bite my ass," Blake said, feeling upset. "She handled the news all too well. She pretended to understand, but I knew deep down she would try to get back at me someway or somehow."

"It would have been more helpful if Charlotte had been straight with you, too," Greg responded. "We could have at least gotten her side. It all seems fishy to me right now. You end things with Piper, and then you have Charlotte upset at you over the things you said about her. Maybe they conspired."

"Geez, I think that's a stretch. Charlotte can't stand Piper," Blake interjected. "I just want to say again that I didn't mean any of the things I said about Charlotte. I was just trying to get rid of Piper—she wouldn't stop emailing and texting. Plus, I had no idea Charlotte would take what I said seriously."

"Well, you're an ass, then, and know nothing about women," Greg huffed back. "Regardless," Greg shared. "You have two women who are pissed at you, and who would love nothing more than to get a little revenge."

Blake sat there processing what Greg was saying, "I hear you, but I don't know. I came at Charlotte hard with that accusation, and she looked equally shocked and surprised about the blog post."

"Well, like I said, Piper got the information somehow. Unless you told her everything and forgot... the only common denominator is Charlotte."

Blake shook his head again, wishing it wasn't the case, but knowing there couldn't be any other explanation. As much as things never surprised him when it came to loyalty and trust in his world of fame, this one stung. He had started to fall in love with a woman who he believed had his back, and it hurt like hell to think that she had stabbed him.

"I know what I need to do now," Blake said seriously as he looked at Greg on the other end of the FaceTime call.

"What's that?" Greg asked.

"I'm going to New York to talk to Piper—"

Without listening to Greg's protest, he ended the call, grabbed his keys, and took off.

38

Charlotte stood in her kitchen feeling like her head was going to explode. How dare he come to her home and accuse her of sharing those details with Piper. She couldn't stand Piper. Never, in her wildest dreams, would she confide or share anything about Blake with someone as sketchy and fake as Piper Saunders.

A knock at her door made her jump, and her blood quickly started to boil with the thought that Blake was back to say something else about the blog post. Without even hesitating, she ran to the door, getting herself ready for round two.

"Lindsay!" Charlotte exclaimed once she realized it wasn't Blake.

"Oh my God, Charlotte. What the hell is going on? I just saw the blog post," Lindsay said as she barged past Charlotte.

"Please don't tell me you think I would actually tell Piper Saunders any of that," Charlotte shot back, following Lindsay into her apartment.

"No, of course not," Lindsay yelled. "But why the hell

would Piper Saunders write that stuff about you, number one. And, number two, how the hell did she know so much about him?"

Charlotte shook her head as she walked into her kitchen to grab her glass of wine. "I have no clue, Lindsay. How did you hear about it? Did your father send it to you?"

"No," Lindsay said, shaking her head. "Mary Manor told me."

"Oh my God," Charlotte said, feeling sick to her stomach. "Mary saw it? Crap... everyone's seen it, haven't they?"

Lindsay nodded her head, not wanting to sugarcoat it. "Yup, Piper went after Blake and there was no stopping her. She made sure to do whatever she could to make him seem like an asshole. The post blew up and Mary saw it right away. I felt so bad for her—she was really rattled. I just left her and Ben at the Town Hall because I wanted to come check on you."

"But none of it is true!" Charlotte protested. "I don't know how Piper can get away with publishing so many lies."

"They think you're the source, Charlotte," Lindsay said, wanting to be straight with her friend.

"I'm going to be sick, I mean... is it possible to get something like this taken down? Can you do it?" Charlotte cried.

"I'm sure Blake's management team is all over it."

"What the hell prompted it in the first place? I mean, who does this to their boyfriend?" Charlotte asked, feeling confused and overwhelmed.

Lindsay stopped for a second realizing Charlotte had no clue about what set Piper on fire. "Wait a second. You don't know, do you?"

"Know what?" Charlotte asked, shaking her head. "What else is there?"

"The reason Blake came over here in the first place," Lindsay said, walking closer to Charlotte.

"Yeah, I know," she nodded in disgust, "to accuse me of plotting with Piper!"

"He didn't tell you anything else?" Lindsay asked.

"What else could he have to say?" She shouted back, obviously upset.

"He broke it off with Piper," Lindsay said, trying to quiet her down for a second. "He said he told her there was nothing between them, and there would never be anything."

"He broke it off with her?" Charlotte asked shocked. "So that was what prompted this?"

"Well, there's more," Lindsay replied.

"What? Was he cheating on her, too?" Charlotte scoffed.

"No, no..." Lindsay said, shaking her head. "He told me he broke up with her because he has feelings for you."

Charlotte's body froze and it took her a second to realize what Lindsay had just said. She looked over at Lindsay with a look of utter confusion, "Bullshit."

Lindsay just nodded, "Yes, I'm not kidding. That's what he said."

"How do you know this?" Charlotte asked. She felt like everything was spinning out of control in front of her right now, and she couldn't stop it.

"Because he told me himself," Lindsay said with a smile as she walked over to Charlotte. "He told me tonight as he was searching for you at the Giving Tree."

"He was searching for me?" Charlotte asked.

"Yes, he was," Lindsay affirmed. "He kept looking at me and Ray tonight while he was giving his talk, but it was clear that he was looking for you."

Charlotte took a deep breath and exhaled. Blake had feelings for her? She couldn't believe it. How could this be possible? She had hoped deep down that maybe he might feel something, but she never let herself dare to dream that it was actually possible.

"Blake broke up with Piper this weekend, and I don't know if he mentioned you or not... but Piper heard him out and didn't say much," Lindsay went on.

"But everything is all messed up right now. He accused me of giving her the information in the blog post," Charlotte said, looking at Lindsay.

"I know," Lindsay said, nodding her head. "I just want you to know what was going on before all of this shit happened. He was racing around trying to find you. He looked like a parent looking for their lost child."

"He literally hates me," Charlotte said.

"Listen," Lindsay said, reaching out to touch Charlotte's hand. "He feels blindsided right now, as are Ben and Mary... but when the truth comes out, it will be clear it wasn't you."

"I just want him to know that I had nothing to do with Piper's blog post," Charlotte responded, looking over at Lindsay.

"He will," Lindsay nodded.

"But then where the hell does that leave us?" Charlotte asked, feeling hopeless. "We both just left each other seeing red!"

"I wish I knew what to tell you, Char," Lindsay smiled as she went over to hug her. "Just so you know, I went in like gangbusters on him about the shit he said about dating you. I gave him a super hard time about it and pulled no punches. After ten minutes of busting his balls, he told me what was going on. It's you he wants. It seems like it's been you since he first met you."

"Oh my God," Charlotte said, not even sure what to do with that information. "And now he freaking hates me because of Piper Saunders. What do I even do now? He was so upset thinking I violated his trust... and now I know why it upset him even more."

"Listen, the truth has to come out," Lindsay said encouragingly. "It always does. There's no way Piper knew that stuff on her own. She either bugged your apartment, or she's a freaking psychic. Because I'll tell you what, she's not smart enough to pull this shit out of thin air!"

~

BLAKE DROVE DIRECTLY to New York City without stopping once. His phone buzzed and rang the entire way, but he ignored it. There was only one person he was interested in talking to tonight.

Normally the drive takes forever, but the three hours went by at warp speed. He had rehearsed a dozen different scenarios as to how he would approach Piper, but all of them went out the window the second he stood in front of her apartment ringing her doorbell. Piper lived on East 81st Street and 3rd Avenue in a high-rise with a doorman. Thankfully her doorman was a big fan and obviously hadn't seen the blog post because he let Blake breeze right through the lobby directly to the elevators, without even buzzing Piper's apartment. The doorman bought Blake's story of wanting to surprise her, and surprise her he would do.

After the third ring, Blake heard footsteps coming toward the door. Then there was an obvious delay when Piper looked through the peephole to see who was on the other side.

"Open the door, Piper. We need to talk," Blake said firmly.

Within a few seconds, the door slowly started to open

and Piper stood there with a mischievous grin on her face, trying her best to have the upper hand. "Is that all I needed to do to get your attention?"

"Can I come in?" Blake asked firmly again.

Piper stepped to the side, so Blake could come in. Her apartment was decked from head to toe in golden tones. Everything was modern and perfectly placed--the ultimate girly girl pad, but with a comfortable relaxed vibe.

"You really went to town on me, huh?" Blake asked, trying to stay calm.

"I just wanted to share the truth," Piper shrugged. "Besides, it is a blog post, so I can write whatever I want. I don't have to answer to anyone."

"So you're OK with printing lies?"

"Lies?" Piper laughed. "Tell me one thing that isn't a lie."

"For starters?" Blake shot back. "The fact that I did all of those good deeds purely for the PR."

"Oh, please, Blake," Piper shouted. "You know that's bullshit, so let's not even pretend that the town was your first priority."

"I certainly was thinking about the town," Blake confessed. "Was it good PR? Absolutely. Do I not care about Barrington? Absolutely not."

"Well, just so you know... everyone believes me, and not you. So, you can tell yourself whatever you want, but the truth is you had an angle, and you're just pissed I shit on it. Plain and simple."

"And then you had the balls to drag my mother into it," Blake said, staring directly at Piper. "You can call me all the names you want, but going after my mother is something else. You actually attached my mother's name to the blog post."

"She'll get over it," Piper said, dismissing Blake's feelings. "She's had to get over all the other shit about you, so this is nothing."

"And what about the kid Alex you mentioned?" Blake asked.

"What about him?" Piper said, rolling her eyes.

"That scholarship was created with him in mind, that's nothing I'm ashamed to hide. That kid works harder in a day than you do in a year. And who the hell are you to use his name?"

"Oh, please," Piper laughed. "His name was in Charlotte's article. My God... it's just so easy for you to dish out money to make people love you, isn't it?"

"That money was a big deal for him and his family," Blake shot back. "You know that, so don't dismiss it. It's shocking to me that someone like you has no boundaries, even when it comes to kids."

"It's all a farce and you know it," Piper shouted. "You think a few good articles are going to change how people see you and view you?"

"Well," Blake said with a shrug. "Seems like you thought so, or you wouldn't have written the blog post about me."

"People have a right to know about the real Blake Manor, not just the one you create for the press."

"People can think whatever they want about me, but when you drag in other people... that's when I draw the line. You brought in my mom, Alex, the town, and Charlotte."

"Oh, that's right. You're precious little Charlotte."

"Is that why you started all of this? Because of Charlotte?" Blake asked looking at Piper with questioning eyes.

"I knew something was up with the two of you the first time you introduced me to her," Piper shot back.

"Where? At Finnegan's?"

Piper nodded, "Just the way you looked at her, I knew

that you were going to work your Blake magic to make some pathetic, small-town girl fall for you, and I was right. You did just that."

"What are you talking about?" Blake asked. "Nothing ever happened between me and Charlotte."

"You know what, Blake?" Piper laughed. "You're the biggest liar on this planet, which is why I had no problem writing that blog post about you."

"How am I lying?" Blake interjected. "Nothing ever happened between us."

"Because she's in love with you, you asshole!" Piper yelled. "She wrote everything down." Piper picked up a notebook from her coffee table and tossed it at Blake, "So if you want to keep standing there lying to me, go ahead. She was stupid enough to put it all down on paper, and I was stupid enough to think you were serious about me."

Blake looked down at the notebook and froze. It was the notebook that Charlotte carried around with her everywhere. She used it to take meeting notes, and it never left her side. It was her work bible.

"Where the hell did you get this?" Blake whispered looking down at it, and then up at Piper.

Realizing she had revealed too much, Piper immediately started to backtrack. "Get what? Her stupid notebook?"

"Yeah," Blake said as he held it in front of her. "Where did you get this?"

"She gave it to me," Piper shot back, trying to sound confident.

"Charlotte personally gave you her private writing notebook that she keeps all of her notes in?" Blake said with a dismissive look. "That's a lie. You stole her notebook and manipulated everything in it, and that's how you got all those details about me."

Piper just looked at Blake and rolled her eyes. "What fool keeps notes like that anyway? She doesn't know how to record on her phone? She even wrote down what you wore at every meeting. It's creepy. Come on..."

"I can't believe that you would steal something like this from her," Blake said seriously. "What did you do? Take it from her apartment?"

Piper didn't answer him, so he knew that's exactly what had happened.

"So the day you went to apologize to her, you helped yourself to her personal notebook."

"The fool didn't even realize it was missing," Piper chuckled.

"No, you're the fool. Charlotte would never expect someone to steal it, never mind do it in her own home," Blake shot back. "And once the truth gets out as to how you really scored all of your inside info, you're going to have a lot of explaining to do."

Piper stood there glaring at Blake with her arms crossed across her chest.

"I can't believe you would stoop so low, Piper. Actually, no... I can believe it. All because you have some crazy idea she's in love with me."

"Crazy idea?" Piper shot back. "Take a look at what she wrote about you in the back. You certainly did a number on her." Blake looked down at Charlotte's notebook and fanned through the pages till he got toward the end. There were three or four pages filled with hand-written notes. "Go on, read it," Piper responded. "She's pathetic."

"There's only one pathetic person in this room, Piper," Blake said walking toward the door. "I hope you do the right thing and make it right with her. Taking down that blog would be a start. Hate me for whatever you want, but leave Charlotte and my family out of it."

"Nobody's going to believe you when you tell them I stole her notebook," she laughed with a shrug, as Blake opened Piper's door to leave. "It's always going to be your word against mine," she shouted.

"It might be," Blake nodded, "but at least I know the truth."

Blake raced directly to his car holding Charlotte's notebook in his hand. The second he shut his car door, and before turning his car on, he flipped to the pages in the back of the notebook and read:

Being assigned to interview Blake Manor might be the pinnacle of a sports writer's career, but for someone like me who doesn't know much about football or sports in general, I could have been interviewing the guy next door. Blake Manor wasn't even a name on my radar. I was raised knowing authors, journalists, books, and libraries.

I wasn't sure what to expect before meeting Blake Manor, so I spent the time I had before our first meeting to researching him. It had seemed clear to me that I needed to prepare myself for an overly confident, cocky, famous athlete.

Putting it lightly, our first two interviews didn't exactly go smoothly. He was late to both of them, and it was clear he didn't want to open up too much to me. Initially, he was what I had expected, but I've always felt that you can easily judge a man by how he treats his mother, and one thing was for sure, he treats her like gold.

There are many things you can find out about Blake Manor by simply looking online. Most of it concerns his football stats. But what you can't find out is who the man under the helmet is, in and out of the spotlight. This is the man I got to know over the last couple of weeks.

Blake Manor came alive in front of a group of high school athletes as he talked about playing sports and being coached under his high school team lead, Coach Gorman. I saw him talk, listen and give advice to athletes in the school gym until every last one of them seemed satisfied. I saw his passion. I saw him connect with one special individual and make him feel like a million bucks. I saw him go from a professional athlete to a mentor in a matter of minutes. I saw him single-handedly change a student's life with the gift of a scholarship. I saw Blake Manor want to give back to his community. There was lots more, including the way he stepped in to help me when I needed it.

The Blake Manor Effect--he has the ability to bring people together and change lives. He can inspire and motivate. He shows people that with hard work, dedication, and determination, you can be anything you want to be in life.

People forget that people like Blade are just regular human beings, too. I saw him as a son, brother, friend, and regular man. He also showed me his kindness and generosity, as well as how he exhibits compassion and understanding for others. He showcased the good he could do with his resources. These are the attributes that make heroes true superheroes.

The Blake Manor I've gotten to know has turned out to be one of the most genuine, kind, empathetic people I've ever met. I hope he sees in himself what I, and so many others, see in him. You can see how it would be easy to fall in love with Blake Manor, not the football superstar, but the guy from Rhode Island.

Blake sat in his car, stunned silent.

Was Charlotte in love with him? What had she planned

to do with these pages? Was this going to be one of the articles? As much as he didn't know what she planned to do with them, they were the best words to read. He was sick to his stomach about how they had ended things. All he could do now was try to see her again.

～

CHARLOTTE WOKE up at 6 am feeling like she had the worst hangover of her life. Her head was still pounding. Her eyes were still puffy from crying. Even her cheeks were flushed. She had finally fallen asleep around 1 am but had woken up every hour feeling sick to her stomach. She kept refreshing her phone to see if Piper's article was still live on the blog, hoping it had been taken down, but it hadn't. It made Charlotte want to vomit thinking about everyone reading it.

The worst was knowing that Blake didn't believe her. He didn't believe in her enough to side with her, and that killed her. This was exactly why she had sworn off falling in love with anyone. It took you down a lonely path when things went wrong. She had fallen in love with Blake, quickly and without forethought. She never understood what people had meant when they referred to falling madly in love with someone. It had finally happened to her, but with the wrong guy.

The only thing Charlotte felt she could do right now was to leave Barrington. She needed to make a move and start making things happen for herself somewhere else. She was young enough to start fresh somewhere, whether it was New York City, or somewhere up in the mountains of Maine. She just needed a job, a chance, and a new start.

As she walked to her kitchen to make herself a pot of coffee, she happened to catch her reflection in the mirror.

She had forgotten that she had fallen asleep in the same clothes she had on yesterday, an oversized grey sweater and black leggings. She looked about as good as she felt, which was horrible. And even though she knew she should change out of her clothes, she didn't have the energy. She needed coffee, and energy to somehow get her day moving.

She wasn't sure what was going to come of Blake's last article, especially now that she had checked herself out of the Blake Manor loop at the *View*. Major damage control was going to be needed. This debacle would be the topic of conversation at the office today, which was something she didn't want to deal with either.

As much as Charlotte knew Blake didn't want to hear from her, she kept wondering how he was doing. When Lindsay told her that Blake was originally coming here to tell her how he felt about her, she felt like she was floating on air. But then, just like that, it was gone. Life had snatched one more thing away from her, and it was too difficult to even process at the moment.

Grabbing a mug from her cabinet, she heard her doorbell ring and knew it was Lindsay. She had stayed with Charlotte until midnight last night and said she would be back first thing in the morning so they could head to work together.

"Coming!" Charlotte called out as she rushed toward her door. As she opened it, the cold air hit her face immediately, but there wasn't anyone there. She looked to her right, and to her left, but nobody was there. She thought she had heard the bell ring, or maybe she was so tired and delirious from lack of sleep that she was hearing things. She closed her door, feeling confused, and walked back to her kitchen to drink coffee that smelled incredible right now to her.

Charlotte heard the bell ring again, knowing this time

someone had to be pranking her. She rushed over to her door again to find nobody there on the other side.

"Hello?" She called into the morning air, looking around. Not seeing anyone, she stepped outside but tripped over something. As she looked down, she noticed a small package wrapped in brown paper with a beautiful red bow tied around it.

Charlotte bent down to pick it up, not sure what to make of it. There wasn't anything written on it, so she wasn't even sure if it was meant for her.

She shook it, realizing it felt like a book. She walked back into her apartment and carefully opened the package. Her breath caught as she noticed that the book was, in actuality, her notebook filled with all of Blake's notes.

There was a note on top of her notebook that read: "*She took this from you and I wanted to make sure you got it back. I'm so sorry.*"

"Blake," she whispered and then dropped the book as she ran to her door, throwing it open.

And there he was, standing out front of her apartment looking as handsome as ever wearing a grey wool hat, black puffer coat, black joggers, and Nike sneakers.

"She stole it from me when she was here...didn't she? " Charlotte said softly, connecting the dots and knowing how Piper had gotten all of her information for her blog post.

Blake nodded and slowly walked closer to her. "She did," Blake answered. "I'm so sorry, Charlotte. You were right about Piper, about all of it."

"She's not someone who has your best interest at heart," Charlotte answered.

"I know," Blake nodded, locking eyes with Charlotte.

Charlotte stood there, just staring at him, "I didn't think

you wanted to hear from me," she said honestly, gazing at the most handsome man she had ever seen.

"Did you mean everything you wrote in your notebook?" He asked, staring at Charlotte with hopeful eyes.

"In the back of it?" Charlotte asked surprised.

"Yes, everything in the back," he went on. "Did you mean everything you wrote about me?"

Charlotte stared at him with honest eyes, "Every word."

Blake nodded, walking toward Charlotte slowly closing the gap between them. "I'm so sorry I doubted you, and didn't believe you," Blake's voice started to crack, but he went on, "I'm not used to people not having an agenda with me. I'm telling you right now, I'm so sorry. I just hope you believe me."

"I do, and thank you," Charlotte smiled, touched by his sentiment. "I hope you know I would never do that to you, ever. I would never betray you like that."

"I know that," he nodded. "And I need you to know that I didn't mean what you heard me say to Piper on the phone. I swear on my life."

Charlotte smirked, "You mean about dating me?"

"Yes," he smiled. "About dating you. I didn't mean anything you heard, I hope you know that and believe me."

Charlotte nodded, "Yes, I believe you."

Blake looked relieved and closed the gap a little more between the two of them.

"So this notebook," he said, looking at her curiously. "Let's get back to it, that long note in the back that you wrote."

Charlotte smiled, knowing exactly what he was talking about. "Yeah," she smiled. "What about it?"

Blake laughed a little and looked up at the sky and shook his head, "You said you meant every word. It said a lot of nice things about me, but there was one thing that stuck out the most."

"And what was that?" Charlotte asked teasingly, feeling her heart beat faster.

Blake walked directly over to Charlotte this time, completely closing the gap between them, and reached out to grab her hands. "It said something about falling in love with the guy from Rhode Island."

"Did it?" She teased as she blushed in the cold morning air. "I thought I crossed that part out."

"Yeah," he laughed, looking down at her as he pulled her closer, their bodies touching, "But is it true?"

Charlotte looked up into Blake's eyes, feeling nervous, and excited, and vulnerable at the same time. "Before I answer that, I heard you were originally coming over to tell me something last night."

"I was," Blake nodded confidently.

"And what was that?" She asked with a slight shake in her voice, hoping to hear what she wanted to hear.

"I was coming to tell you that I have fallen deeply and madly in love with you," Blake said looking directly into Charlotte's eyes. "And I needed to know if you felt at all the same way about me."

Charlotte's face lit up and she lunged fully into Blake's arms, meeting his lips and kissing him passionately. They fit perfectly together, and as they held onto each other and kissed each other, Charlotte felt her heart beating out of her chest. She knew falling in love came with a risk to her heart, but she was willing to risk it for Blake. This was what she had dreamt about, and she felt as if she was about to explode feeling it come to life.

Blake pulled away from Charlotte. "Wait a second... you

never answered my question," he laughed. "Do you feel the same way?"

"Yes, Blake Manor. I am deeply and madly in love with you, too. What can I say, it's that Blake Manor effect I keep talking about."

Christmas in Barrington had quickly become Charlotte's favorite time of year. She found herself looking forward to her second Christmas in Barrington as soon as the summer ended. In August she had started making plans and lists of everything that she needed to get done before Christmas arrived, but loving every second of it.

"You're sure you're going to make it?" She asked Blake on the phone as she and Mary cross-checked their lists of things to do at the Town Hall.

"Charlotte," Blake responded back with a laugh in his voice, "I'm going to make it, don't worry."

"OK," Charlotte smiled into the phone. "You know you're the guest of honor, so I can't have my leading man miss the festivities."

"Your leading man isn't going to miss a thing," Blake responded back. "I just finished practice and I'm on my way now. I should be there with plenty of time to spare."

"Good," Charlotte smiled back. "Because I also miss you."

"I miss you, too," Blake responded with a smile. "The apartment is way too quiet when you're not home and I hate sleeping without you next to me."

"How pathetic are we? It's only been two days," Charlotte laughed into the phone.

"What can I say, I miss my girl," Blake answered. "Tell my mom I miss her, too. I don't want her to be jealous."

Charlotte smiled, "I will. I'll see you soon. Love you."

"Love you, too."

Charlotte ended her call and looked up to see Mary shaking her head at her with a smile, "You two are pretty darn cute. But tell me, is he on his way yet?"

"Yes, he is," Charlotte replied, walking over to Mary to admire their work at the Town Hall. The tree looked gorgeous in its stature and beauty, a real eye-catcher. "If he's leaving now, it should only be three hours, so that will put him here around 4:00 pm. That's plenty of time."

Mary nodded and smiled at Charlotte, who had become a special part of their family over the last year. It was crazy to think how much had happened in the course of twelve months, but she was grateful for all that had.

Blake and Charlotte had been inseparable since the week before Christmas of last year. Once they had finally been honest with each other about how they felt, all of the puzzle pieces perfectly fit into place for them. It was wonderful seeing her son in love with Charlotte-- who she would have hand-picked herself for him.

Once Blake's suspension had been lifted, he went back to New York City to the Skyscrapers. The four weeks at home were exactly what he had needed to get his head back on straight. But falling in love with Charlotte had sealed the deal. He returned to the field with a refreshed outlook, and without the partying, his game improved even more but, most importantly, management was thrilled to see the new version of Blake.

Life for Blake and Charlotte had really just begun as they were about to celebrate almost a year of being together. Blake woke up every morning thankful for the woman next to him, and couldn't believe how fulfilled his life felt with her part of it. He knew he had hit the jackpot with Charlotte and he would never let her go.

Charlotte had finally fulfilled her lifelong dream about living in New York City. She had originally been hesitant about going with him, worried people would call her a gold digger, but after talking it through with Blake, and even with Mary and Ben, she knew following her heart was the only answer. She had applied for jobs, all while starting a personal blog chronicling her own personal journey about moving to New York City and starting her new life with Blake. What she hadn't banked on was the instant popularity of her blog, and her social media handles. She loved it because she had the ability to write and share anything she wanted without having to run it by an editor, or a staff of people. She was fulfilling her dream of writing, all while living in the city of her dreams with the love of her life.

"I think everything's as set as it's going to be," Mary said, beaming at everything. They had worked tirelessly together creating and prepping for the 2nd Annual Giving Tree Celebration in Barrington. Mary had asked Charlotte to come aboard and be her co-chair, and they had outdone themselves creating a winter wonderland for the townspeople tonight.

"Oh, Mary," Charlotte said with a huge smile. "Everything looks perfect. I think you're right, we're good!"

"Now we just need to go back home, change into our party clothes, and wait for Blake," Mary nodded.

"Let's get moving then," Charlotte answered, locking arms with Mary as they headed to the parking lot.

What Charlotte didn't know was that tonight would be extra special for her. Blake would *definitely* be on time. He had planned this evening down to the last minute. Mary couldn't wait to see the look on Charlotte's face when Blake showed her his own wish for the Giving Tree--a wish with a diamond ring attached to it.

DID YOU LIKE MY BOOK?

Reviews are important for authors (especially new ones). If you liked this book (and any of my others), I would be grateful if you left a short review. They mean so much and go a long way!

~

If you haven't already, make sure you purchase my 4 books in my McKay Sister Series: *Hometown Boy*, *At Last*, *Happily Ever After* and *One and Only*.

JOIN MY NEWSLETTER

There's nothing like a good romance, am I right? There's just something about a happily-ever-after that always gives me goosebumps!

Love for you to join my newsletter to stay in the loop as to what I have coming up. I will also be sharing book giveaways, interviews, special releases, behind the scenes, bonus chapters and so much more.

$\sim$

Join my NEWSLETTER:

www.subscribepage.com/Audrey

ACKNOWLEDGMENTS

Sidelined for the Holidays was a fun one to write and was inspired by the love of football that my husband and sons share. I knew there had to be a way to combine my love for a happily ever afters with the game of football!

Thank you to my husband and sons who were there to answer any (and all) of my football questions that I had as I wrote this book. And special thanks to my husband for coming up with the name!

Thank you to my mom for being an incredible proof-reader and editor throughout the different edits. You mean the world to me.

Thank you to my amazing editor Valerie Gray who goes above and beyond every single time with me. I can't thank you enough!

Thank you to Amanda Griffith for being an awesome friend and an excellent extra set of editing eyes for me. You literally could do this for a living!

And thank you Lisa Costa for the name inspiration. I'll never forget asking about female lead names on Instagram and you messaging me that Blake would be a good name for a character. From that second, my leading man was named.

ABOUT THE AUTHOR

Audrey McClelland, is a digital influencer and the founder of MomGenerations.com, an online destination for mothers. Mom Generations is in its 14th year and is a lifestyle destination for mothers. Audrey is the mother of 5 children.

Audrey was named to "The Power Pack" Moms in Nielson's Online Power Moms list, naming her one of the most influential moms online. Audrey's naturally honest and positive approach to sharing parenting advice has led to features in numerous parenting and lifestyle magazines, TV shows, news segments, radio shows, and popular websites.

She's also the author of the McKay Sister Series: *Hometown Boy, At Last, Happily Ever After*, and *One and Only.*

Audrey has a B.A. in Theatre Arts from Brown University and lives in Providence, RI with her husband and children.

Find me online:

MomGenerations.com

Instagram: @AudreyMcClellan

TikTok: @AuthorAudreyMcClelland and @AudreyMc-Clelland

Made in the USA
Las Vegas, NV
14 December 2021